CHASING WIND

BRANDT LEGG

BOOKS

By Brandt Legg

Chase Malone Thriller

Chasing Rain
Chasing Fire
Chasing Wind
Chasing Dirt
Chasing Life
Chasing Kill
Chasing Risk
Chasing Mind
Chasing Time
Chasing Lies
Chasing Fear
Chasing Lost

*As always, this book is dedicated to
Teakki and Ro*

Vinci Books

vinci-books.com

Published by Vinci Books Ltd in 2025

1

Copyright © Brandt Legg 2019

The author has asserted their moral right to be identified as the author of this work in accordance with the Copyright, Designs and Patents Act 1988.
This work is a work of fiction. Names, characters, places and incidents are the product of the author's imagination or are used fictitiously. Any resemblance to actual persons, living or dead, places and incidents is entirely coincidental.
All rights reserved. No part of this publication may be copied, reproduced, distributed, stored in any retrieval system, or transmitted in any form or by any means, including photocopying, recording, or other electronic or mechanical methods, nor used as a source for any form of machine learning including AI datasets, without the prior written permission of the publisher.
The publisher and the author have made every effort to obtain permissions for any third party material used in this book and to comply with copyright law. Any queries in this respect should be brought to the attention of the publisher and any omissions will be corrected in future editions.
A CIP catalogue record for this book is available from the British Library.
Paperback ISBN: 9781036705220

Printed and bound in Great Britain by Clays Ltd, Elcograf S.p.A.

Chapter One

Chase Malone stood near the center of one of the largest and oldest outdoor markets in South America, lost among thousands of locals and tourists. Hiding in plain sight, where no one would think to look, had become his life. Weeks away from his thirtieth birthday, the billionaire considered himself lucky to be alive.

He paid the old woman three US dollars, Ecuador's official currency, for a basket of fruit, and waved off the sixty cents of change. She smiled a toothless grin. "Gracias."

"De nada," Chase replied, turning to look for his partner, Wen Sung. The two of them had been in Otavalo, Ecuador for twelve days. They would leave tomorrow—always on the run. He spotted her haggling with a man over the price for a loaf of bread. Although Chinese, Wen spoke fluent Spanish, among other languages. The MSS, China's equivalent of the CIA, had trained her to be a lethal spy.

"I told you to pay their asking price," Chase said quietly, self-conscious about his billionaire status. He pulled off his jacket. Even though it was only fifty-three degrees, the sun, at 8,300 feet above sea level, was intense—a good excuse for sunglasses, as they always tried to remain incognito.

"And I told *you* they like to negotiate. Anyway, I always let them win," Wen said, paying the man only a few cents less than his original quote.

The merchant beamed, believing he'd bested the foreigner.

"I love it when clouds ring the top of Imbabura," she said, whirling around and pointing the bread toward the dominant feature shadowing the town, a 15,190 foot, snow-capped volcano. They'd hiked it on their second day in the country, back when they could still semi-relax. Each passing day meant it was more likely someone would find them.

Wen handed him a Morocho, a warm, spiced, corn pudding drink he'd come to love during their short stay.

"I'm going to learn how to make this when we get home," Chase said. They shared a long glance. *Where is home anymore, and when will we ever get there?*

Wen headed to another vendor for vegetables while he sat on a bench and enjoyed his beverage. He thought about the people who were after them. Wen had killed a number of adversaries since they'd gone on the run. Her knowledge of martial arts and weapons scared him sometimes, but those skills—and his smarts—were the only things keeping the two of them alive. They'd used his money and her specialized knowledge of Chinese espionage to vanish as well as anyone could in the modern world. Utilizing an array of sophisticated technological techniques to make sure they were regularly "spotted" in parts of the world where they were not also helped throw off the pursuers.

Wen glanced up and caught Chase looking at her, but could tell immediately that he wasn't thinking about her.

She paid for the vegetables, joined him, and they resumed their stroll.

"You're worrying again," she said, taking his hand.

"Sorry. Sometimes I like to pretend we're a couple of tourists on our honeymoon, but we're not, and we—"

"Is that your way of proposing?" Wen teased.

A woman coming out of a merchant's stall backed into Chase.

"Pardon," Chase said in Spanish.

"Excuse me," the woman said in English.

Chase immediately recognized the voice and turned to find an escape. Wen quickly did a visual search of the area and spotted several CIA agents dressed as locals.

"How'd you find us?" Chase asked, deciding not to run.

"Please, Chase, you're too smart for silly questions."

Tess Federgreen, the director of CISS—Corporate Intelligence Security Section—the CIA's most powerful and secretive division. The fast-growing agency within the agency—a joint operation of the CIA, NSA, and FBI—had almost unlimited power to pursue its mandate of preventing war between corporations and nations.

"Are you going to take me in?"

"Not today," Tess said, waving hello to Wen.

Wen just scowled.

"Then why are you here?"

"I don't often bring good news, do I?" Behind her sunglasses, Tess's green eyes flashed with confidence. Her strawberry blond hair glistened in the Ecuadorian sun, although Chase recalled it had been auburn last time he'd seen her. "I need you to do something for me."

He almost laughed. "Why would I help you, Tess? I don't even *like* you. And I sure don't trust you."

She laughed unpleasantly. "You should never let your personal feelings get in the way of what's good for you."

"What do you know about feelings?" Chase thought, for a quick instant, he detected a hint of pain in her eyes, but it didn't last. They strolled through the crowd, Wen a few steps behind.

"Does the name Curtis Lindbergh mean anything to you?"

Chase stared at her for a moment. "You must know it does."

"I'm afraid your old friend is mixed up in some trouble."

"Doesn't sound like him."

"Yes, well, like you, he is apparently not as smart as his brilliance would suggest."

"If you're done insulting me, I've got—"

"He needs your help." She scraped her gray snakeskin cowboy boots against the curb.

"Lindy can take care of himself," Chase said, thinking of the only person he'd ever known who was miles ahead of him in IQ points.

"I've just given the order to terminate Lindbergh."

"*What?*" Chase said, a little too loudly, knowing Tess was serious. Even if they hadn't been friends, he believed the world needed all the Lindys it could get. "Why?" He fidgeted with the multitool in his pocket. Wen caught up and held his hand, not wanting others to notice his agitation.

"He's made a breakthrough in geoengineering—weather manipulation—and he's planning to sell it to the Chinese and Russians. We obviously can't allow that to happen."

Chase immediately thought of their time together at

MIT and the years since. Lindy was always focused completely on his work. Chase couldn't imagine him blatantly going against the US government. "There must be a mistake."

Tess glared at him. "Yes, the one Lindbergh is making."

"What am *I* supposed to do?"

"Find him. Change his mind."

"You don't know where he is?" Chase scoffed. "Then how are you going to kill him?"

"He'll be found shortly. You have thirty-six hours to work your magic."

"Or?"

"CISS of Death."

Chapter Two

The bustle of the Otavalo market blurred as Chase squeezed Wen's hand, catching his partners look, knowing it meant they could run.

"CISS of Death?" Chase repeated her words, facing the forty-something, fit, youthful looking, master of espionage. "Do you think that's cute? How do you sleep at night?"

"Absolutely horribly," Tess admitted.

"How come you can find me, but you can't find Lindy?"

"Lindbergh disappeared before we knew we wanted to keep track of him," she replied. "But we're getting closer. We may get him before you do."

"Then what?"

"Then you can go back to eating fruit and bread, or whatever it is you fill your time with these days."

"How long have you been looking for him?"

"Ten days."

"But I can find him in thirty-six hours?"

"I have complete faith in you, Chase."

"I'm flattered," he said sarcastically.

"You should be." Removing her sunglasses, Tess gave him a long, almost maternal, stare. "I want updates every step of the way. Let me give you my private number?"

"I've still got it."

She smiled. "It's been changed." She handed him a card. "Then I can count on you?"

"I'll have to think about it."

"Clock's ticking," Tess said, signaling to her agents that they were leaving. "Here's everything we have on Lindbergh." She handed him a flash drive. "Don't forget, I'll need regular reports of your progress."

"Why, so you can kill him?"

"I don't want to kill Lindbergh." She looked at him warmly. "You're just going to have to trust me on that."

Wen closed her eyes.

"Forgive me," Chase said incredulously, "but that's impossible."

She looked sad for a moment. "I've come here and enlisted your help because I want the same thing you do—to save him."

Chase searched her eyes. "I've got thirty-six hours?"

"Maybe less, depending if things change."

Chase moaned, exasperated.

A small, red, beat up ball rolled and hit Chase's feet. He looked down, and then up. A young girl with big brown eyes caught his. She smiled sweetly, he choked up for a second, then picked up the ball and tossed it gently to her.

"*Gracias, hermano*," she exclaimed and ran off.

Tess's expression softened at the little Ecuadorian girl, and then hardened as she turned back to Chase. "If your friend 'Lindy' suddenly turns up in Beijing or Moscow, the timetable will change. That's why you must stay in touch with me, or you may end up just finding a corpse."

Putting on her sunglasses, Tess disappeared into the crowd as easily as she had arrived mere minutes ago

---

Sitting in her private jet, Tess gave final instructions to a CIA agent who would remain in Ecuador. "Make sure we get his plane. I want to know everywhere he goes. If he stops to take a leak, you let me know immediately."

She worried about trusting something so important to a man known as the Buddhist Billionaire and his "killer" girlfriend, but desperate times . . .

Tess also knew that the unlikely duo had defied the odds many times. The fact that Wen had escaped Communist China's Ministry of State Security and remained alive and free was, in itself, an extraordinary accomplishment.

And Chase is a whole other side of extraordinary.

She remembered a promise she'd made long ago, to a man she loved, to help protect the rogue tech genius. It bothered her that Chase despised her, especially since she'd saved his life more than once.

Tess called Dr. J. W. Skyenor, the Director of Defense Advanced Research Projects Agency. DARPA, the Pentagon's emerging technology agency, had been formed in 1958 by President Eisenhower after the Soviet Union's surprise success with launching Sputnik, the first manmade object into space, in 1957. One of the agency's earliest accomplishments was helping to launch the world's first weather satellite.

"Have you found Lindbergh yet?" he said without bothering with a hello.

"Jay, are you okay?" she asked.

"We're being challenged by China every minute of

every day on almost everything we do, and as soon as we get ahead, they steal it."

"I know." That issue was at the heart of the mission of CISS.

"The best chance we have right now is the weather, but I've never seen them so aggressive."

Tess bit into a green apple she'd picked up at the market. "It's the top priority of the MSS right now."

"So, I'll ask again . . . "

"Lindbergh is our biggest priority. We're closing in on him and his stations. Things will look a lot different this time tomorrow."

"I hope so," Skyenor said.

After the call ended Skyenor checked his phone for any updates and, after hearing the voicemail, he did what he always did when frustrated. He went to his office bookcase and stared at the titles for a while until he felt one tug at him. He withdrew *The Elegant Universe*, by Brian Greene, and began reading. J.W. Skyenor believed he alone could keep the world safe by staying at least one step ahead of the Chinese, the Russians, dozens of terrorist groups, and assorted bad actors. It was a near-impossible task—using technology no one had yet seen to develop military applications for preventing or winning wars before the enemy discovered a way to destroy the country he loved. It was also exhausting. In all his years with DARPA, the stakes had never been higher, and counting only on Tess Federgreen to deliver Lindbergh was unacceptable.

Chapter Three

The CIA agent Tess left in Ecuador stayed at a safe distance. His parents had immigrated to the US from Mexico, but he could easily pass for Ecuadorian, particularly in his casual local's wardrobe.

He scanned the information on his phone. Chase Malone, age twenty-nine, held degrees from MIT and Stanford, and had invented multiple artificial intelligence platforms and programs. A net worth in excess of one billion dollars. Studied in China, where he met Wen Sung, a former MSS operative, who has since defected to the United States.

He'd read most of this before, however, Tess had updated the files just before she left and synched his device. Wen Sung's training included weapons, explosives, martial arts, scuba diving, sky diving, piloting, and survival skills. *A highly lethal killer,* he thought, glancing up from his scrolling and looking directly at Wen and Chase as they walked a short distance from him.

Quite an odd couple. He resumed his studying. They'd been

on the run for most of the past year. He clicked to the next screen. Pursuers unknown. He stared at his quarries again, walking slowly through the crowd. *How can we not know who's after them? Must be the MSS.* Then he read that the MSS had no record of Wen Sung. *Somehow Malone and Sung erased her existence from Chinese record. Impressive, very impressive.*

Pursuers unknown, he repeated in his mind. *Do they know who's after them? Could be any number of major companies—domestic or international.* The agent knew of CISS's mission, even though he didn't work that section. Multinational corporations were increasingly conducting sophisticated espionage against competitors in a kind of cold war with each other. The concern of company versus company wars, and even company versus governments, had grown in recent years as technology transformed every aspect of life. *CISS is trying to stop that. It would explain Tess's involvement,* he thought.

He continued reading the file as he began walking to keep them in sight. There was a list of possible corporations that might be interested in eliminating Chase Malone . . . *But why?* He clicked to the next screen, but was dead before he could see it. The CIA agent pursuing Chase and Wen never hit the ground. Two men supported his body until it could be slid quickly into a van behind a nearby stall selling plantains, limes, and other fruit. Chase and Wen never saw him.

"Why do they want Lindbergh so bad?" Wen asked after Tess and her entourage had left the marketplace.

"Lindy is the smartest person I've ever met," Chase said.

"I thought you were the smartest man in the world."

"Well, I'm actually the second smartest." Chase gave a

sheepish smile. "Lindy is so smart, he makes me look like an idiot. He's incredibly brilliant, like a Da Vinci. Lindy isn't just smart in computers, like me, he's smart in computers, lasers, physics, atmospheric science, aerosol and cloud microphysics, molecular biology, chemical engineering, meteorology—"

"I get it."

"No, wait until you meet him," Chase said, shaking his empty Morocho cup. "It's sometimes hard to be around this guy."

"Because he's so pompous?"

"Not at all. He's super nice, but he knows *everything*, and it's as if his mind is always working on six different tracks. It can be difficult to get in, and very challenging to relate to him."

"If he doesn't want to be found and he's that smart, are *we* going to be able to find him?"

"We've got SEER," Chase said referring to a program he'd developed along with his business partner, Dez, called "Search Entire Existence Result." SEER employed advanced photonics, quantum information processors, and utilized deep learning, AI, quantum algorithms, and virtually every data point in digital existence, to predict the future with stunning accuracy.

"And the Astronaut," Wen added, referring to a secret ally who possessed a computer-like intelligence, a man who was, himself, a fugitive.

"But most important," Chase said, "I know where to find the woman Lindy loves."

Chapter Four

Earl Waxxman, a tough looking ex-Army Ranger, glanced at the number on his ringing cell phone, winced as if he'd been punched, then pushed accept. "Yeah?"

"We're overdue for some news," Wiest said. Jeff Wiest, the annoying man who had been paying him for the past six weeks, was one of those nagging clients he couldn't stand.

"It's a big world."

"So you keep saying," Wiest shot back. "Lindbergh leaves a sizable footprint. He shouldn't be this hard to find."

"You didn't have much luck before you brought us in," Waxxman reminded him.

"I haven't had much luck *since* I brought you in either, and you're supposed to be the experts."

"That's right. And you should let the experts handle it."

"Listen, I don't mean to be a jerk. Lindbergh is smart. He obviously doesn't want to be found, I get that. But we're running out of time. I need some results."

"I hear you. Believe me, we're all over it. This is what we do. We'll find your guy."

"And you'll take care of the problem?"

"As agreed," Waxxman assured Wiest again. It wasn't unusual. When Waxxman was hired to kill a person, the client often found the whole process a bit unbelievable, and continually asked if it was really going to happen. The very fact that a person had gotten to the point where they wanted someone dead usually meant they were desperate. Wiest had been extra edgy though.

Waxxman had assembled a strong outfit he called the "Wrestlers" —because they *wrestled* serious problems for their clients. He and his team specialized in removal and rescues, which translated into kill or save. Waxxman and the Wrestlers had earned an impressive reputation with a nearly perfect track record. "We don't miss."

Wiest had found Waxxman through a friend of a friend and didn't generally know about such things as tracking people and ordering hits. Wiest had confidence in Waxxman because he only took a third of his fee up front, the next third was due as soon as they offered proof of Lindbergh's location, and the final payment, plus expenses, would be paid once Lindbergh was dead. "I'm not interested in eventually finding him. We have a time pressure, and it's running out."

"I'm well aware of that."

Waxxman didn't care why they wanted this man dead. His only concerns were money, reputation, and not getting caught. Only four targets had eluded the Wrestlers, and they had all wound up dead anyway—by natural causes, or whatever—just not at the hands of Waxxman's specialists. He hired all men—ex-cops and ex-military, mostly from European countries. Waxxman himself was ex-DIA, but he preferred not to recruit from that pool. He'd found that

Americans generally didn't like to get their hands as dirty as his clients typically required.

"We have three days at the most."

"Didn't you just hear me?" Waxxman had lost patience. This case was not typical. All his clients had unique issues, yet the targets fell into common categories—betrayal, money, revenge. Lindbergh didn't seem to match any of those. That worried him. All the research and information pointed to Curtis Lindbergh breaching some code of ethics or violating an agreement. *Good enough reasons to be offed*, Waxxman had thought. However the client was an amateur, and that could be a problem.

But, more than that, something was *off*. Something that might get him or his men killed instead of the target.

Curtis Lindbergh, a renowned scientist, respected as one of the great minds of his generation, would have been asked for identification if he ever tried to buy beer in Mexico, or just about any place in the world. His underperforming scruff of beard and boyish face made him appear as if he could still be in high school.

"Did you prepare the report drives?" Lindy asked his assistant.

The lab assistant, already with a pepper of gray in his slick black hair, was about the same age as Lindy—both in their early thirties—but he seemed like the older one. Garcia, always meticulous and prideful about completing tasks perfectly, looked at him as if this was a ridiculous question. "I do not understand why you are doing this," Garcia said.

Lindy, who had tried to explain this twice before, tried

again. "Can you imagine if only the Americans, or only the Chinese, or the Russians, possessed this technology?"

"It would be the Cold War all over again," Garcia said.

"A thousand times worse." Lindy looked into the trees on the far side of the biosphere as several birds landed on the upper branches. "These countries do not put men of science, or even of much conscience, into power. The leaders of these nations want nothing but more money, more military, more power. Controlling the weather would give them the opportunity to do great damage, but also give them the chance to cripple their enemies, so of course they will do it."

"And in the process, destroy the planet," Garcia, automatically thinking of his family, finished.

"Without a doubt."

"Then why give it to them?"

"Because one of them will make the discovery before the others, or steal it from me." Lindy looked again at the birds, who had now shifted to another branch. Their coloring, quite saturated, was something one would only see in the tropics—yellows that appeared glowing, blues so bright they seem to radiate. "However, if the three superpowers get the technology at the same time, as well as some of the smaller countries, then we've created the equivalent of the Cold War's MAD."

"Mutually assured destruction." Garcia closed his eyes for a moment, trying to grasp the true reality of those three words. *I just want to love my wife and laugh with my children as I watch them grow into healthy, happy people, and make our village stronger.*

"Yes. They won't be able to surprise one another. Or cripple one country without setting off weather-wars."

"But the risks." *I don't want to hear them or think about them.*

"Considerable. Not just that somebody will make a mistake or mismanage and do serious harm to the environment, but what worries me more is that before we can successfully and simultaneously get the material to each country, one of them will stop us."

"You mean kill you?"

Lindy nodded. "All of us. Any of us."

Garcia thought about his seven-year-old daughter. She'd been practicing so hard for the upcoming dance festival. His son had made a wooden machete and bought used cowboy boots for the same event. *I love my family, Yelapa, and working for this man, but could it all really be lost?*

"We won't let it come to that," Lindy said, seeing the fear in Garcia's eyes.

He nodded. "And what about the light and the slide?"

"No one can know about those. They are more difficult to contain . . . at least until I figure out a way to prevent them from being weaponized."

Chapter Five

Chase, who'd already had to sell two private jets this year in an effort to remain anonymous, had leased another jet through a shell corporation, which always remained on stand-by at the closest airport. The pilot, who had been with him for several years, announced they would be landing in ten minutes.

"How long to the college?" Wen asked, looking at the time on her phone. It was almost four PM. They'd been traveling constantly since Tess had found them that morning.

"About ninety minutes from the airport," Chase replied, checking the route from Houston to College Station, Texas. "I told her we'd be there at five-thirty."

"Drina Snow," Wen began, reading out loud from her computer. "Born in Reykjavík, Iceland. Age thirty-seven. Atmospheric scientist. Very pretty . . . "

"In that Nordic-Icelandic-supermodel way," Chase said with a laugh. "Lindy always fell for the beauty and brains combination."

"In that order?" Wen swiveled her seat to look directly at Chase. "By the way, these seats are *so much* better than the last two planes."

"I thought the same thing. Nice upgrade." He smiled. "Drina was different. I only met her once, but she captivated him like no one else ever had."

"Then why aren't they still together?"

"Lindy stayed with me last year, right after they split. He was in San Francisco for a conference. I asked him that. First he told me that she was distracting him from his work because she was too beautiful, too much fun to be with, too smart, too everything . . ."

"And that's a problem?"

"Apparently it is to a guy like Lindy, who just wants to solve every problem facing humanity and find the answers to all the great scientific questions. But later his story changed a little. Something about a big disagreement over his work."

"The controlling the weather work?"

"He didn't say. Lindy is into so many fields, it could have been anything. She's an atmospheric scientist, so I'd think they'd agree on that topic."

"Manipulating the weather is extremely controversial," Wen said, closing her eyes, as if feeling the weight of always traveling. "Maybe she was on the other side of the issue?"

"I don't know a lot about geoengineering." He scrolled through Internet research.

"The Chinese are farther ahead than any other country," Wen said. "In MSS training, they show us scenarios and tactics for potential weather wars."

"Weather wars?"

"Nothing is more important in the future than clean drinking water and food. Both depend on weather. And to quote your president, Lyndon Baines Johnson, 'He who controls the weather, controls the world.'"

"I've never heard that quote attributed to him."

"I've seen the video, and Johnson's words are inscribed on a large plaque in the MSS Weather Modification Office. The agency works with the China Meteorological Administration and oversees many other Weather Modification Bureaus throughout China."

"I recall reading an article about China using cloud seeding to control the weather for the 2008 Beijing Olympics," Chase said.

"True, but that was nothing. China makes close to seventy-five billion tons of artificial rain a year. The state-owned Aerospace Science and Technology Corporation is setting up tens of thousands of rain-inducing machines across the Tibetan Plateau, but the real action is with the secret MSS division. They're preparing for the weather wars."

"So they need whatever Lindy has created?"

"Absolutely. I wonder what he could have come up with that's so important to bring Tess Federgreen and the CIA down on him."

"With Lindy, it's bound to be something revolutionary. The guy's wanted to change the world since he was born."

Chase knew the history of CISS. The Department of Homeland Security created the sub-agency in reaction to a World Economic Forum report showing that only thirty-one of the top one hundred global economic entities were countries, with the other sixty-nine being corporations. The trend meant that in the next fifteen years, ninety-five conglomerates would dominate the list, with only five countries remaining. A secret government study concluded that a shift from nation states to corporate states made the likelihood of major conflicts, or "wars," erupting between corporations and countries highly probable as the world entered a new phase of decentralized power. CISS had a mandate to keep the peace, which really meant to make sure the "right" side won.

"The US plans to remain the dominant super-power in the world even if all the others are corporations, and there is only one country that can prevent that . . . "

"China," Wen finished.

"Yeah, and if Tess is involved, it's big. Probably China, or one of their big tech firms is in this, too."

The co-pilot interrupted to remind them to fasten their seatbelts. Chase knew aviation rules required him to make the reminder, even though he knew his passengers kept their belts on at all times.

"You can be sure it's the Communist government *and* one of the big companies. They cannot be separate," Wen added.

Chase nodded. He knew all too well about China and its leading companies. The communist nation was, in a way, one huge corporation, with a massive military and the world's largest built-in market of nearly 1.5 billion consumers. "Lindy attracts great minds—both the educated ones and the rogues. His brilliance is like a magnet to characters with sharp intellects."

"Sounds like you," Wen said.

Chase smiled, but then realized that, just like Lindy, people were trying to use his inventions for greed and nefarious purposes instead of their original good intent. And those people, without hesitation, would kill for the power.

Chapter Six

The outside temperature hovered around eight degrees Fahrenheit. Brisk winds clocked at nine miles per hour—a typical night at the remote weather facility in Norway at two AM. Although the conditions were nothing unusual north of the Arctic Circle in January—where during the day the sun never reached above the horizon—the station's equipment had been acting strange.

"Polar night makes me crazy," one of the security guards said in Norwegian, looking out the window.

"What are you complaining about?" the other guard asked, looking up distractedly from his phone. "It would be dark now, even in the summer."

"I know, but it's dark all day. That's my point, I can't tell *when* it is."

"You're never happy." He paused the game he'd been playing on his phone and took another sip of coffee.

"Not true. I'm happy in Spain."

"When were you in Spain?"

"Last night, in my dreams."

"Ahh, last night you were here."

"See? I can't tell when it is or where I am."

Down the hall, two workers, one of whom was a grad student from the nearby University of Tromsø, the northernmost university in the world, barely glanced at the equipment they were supposed to be monitoring. Engrossed in a conversation about a political thriller they had both recently read, they hadn't noticed that the facility had been processing extra data for hours.

"I'm telling you, I believe it. The US elections are rigged. The wealthy elites control the media, the candidates, everything."

"But it's fiction. The book is made up."

"I know, but the Remies are *real*. We're in the middle of a global conspiracy."

"Do you get this way about every book you read? I mean, do you think you're a muggle?"

"No, of course not. I'm a wizard. But I'm telling you there is a CapWar going on!"

Back in the front of the building, the guards, still arguing about the Polar night and happiness, or the lack thereof, didn't notice as the door opened behind them—the lock expertly and silently picked.

Three masked men entered. Both guards jumped up at the same time, but before either could reach his gun, they were efficiently subdued, gagged, and cuffed.

At the same time, three other men entered the main room of the facility and grabbed the grad student and his supervisor. They, too, were bound and gagged.

Outside the building, two massive radar transmitters and receivers stood like alien crafts in silhouette against the snow. The facility, an important outpost to world climate scientists, had just become one of the first battlegrounds in the weather wars.

While the prisoners were being lead outside into the small, snow-packed parking area, two of the intruders remained inside. They methodically removed a specific series of hard drives, replacing them with accurate replica models containing different information. Next they erased and replaced the surveillance video files on the central computer and, finally, one of them installed several listening and monitoring devices and locked the building, leaving it looking as they'd found it. Less than seventeen minutes after they arrived, the team, along with the four prisoners, boarded a helicopter which had only just landed.

Twenty minutes later, the two workers and two guards were placed in weighted perforated bags and dropped from the air into the North Sea. The head of the operation then called in "Mission accomplished."

A world away, on a worse than usual humid day, the CISS IT-Squad drove down a long gravel driveway, winding through dense forest, an hour south of Tallahassee, Florida. At the end of the road they found a cream-colored sheet metal building approximately twenty by thirty feet, with several satellite receivers on the roof and a large radio dish antenna next to it. After parking their two white cargo vans in a small, empty parking area, one of them used bolt cutters on the lock securing a chain-link fence surrounding the structure.

"Team leader, Whiskey-two, we are inside the perimeter."

"Proceed Whiskey-two."

Not expecting any armed resistance inside, they bypassed a keypad security device and forced entry on the building door.

"We are inside the station." They found several small, empty offices and one room locked with another keypad. This one took more time. After a minute, they had wired a loop into an external box. Thirty-seven seconds later, it found the correct code.

"We are in main control room. Five, no, six computer terminals . . . lit displays and sorting. Active streams of data . . ."

Tess, her private plane about to land at Dulles International Airport in Northern Virginia, listened to the audio of the raid and smiled. "We got it," she said to herself.

"Wait, machines are shutting down. Team Leader, did you copy that? All machines are dark. There must've been some sort of fail-safe stop."

Tess closed her eyes and sighed.

"Roger that, Whiskey-two, can you get in and reboot?"

"Negative. I'm locked out."

"Okay, Roger that. Remove all devices and return home. We'll dissect those back here in the lab."

The IT-Squad opened their toolkits to prepare to extract the devices.

"What's that smell?"

"Masks, masks, masks!"

Three of the four agents in the room quickly donned masks, but it didn't take long for them to realize it wasn't a chemical attack.

"Computers are burning!"

"Whiskey-two, repeat status."

"Apparently some sort of kill-code was in place. All the electronics in the room are burning."

Tess shook her head, impressed at the level of sophistication, but frustrated that they were getting nowhere. "I'd been hoping we could locate Lindbergh's entire network from there," Tess said to the analyst sitting across the aisle from her.

"And apparently Lindbergh knew you were hoping that, so he made sure you wouldn't have the opportunity."

She nodded. "Quite an elaborate anti-system he developed . . . but is it *us* he's attempting to thwart," she wondered out loud, "or the Chinese?"

"Or is it both?" the analyst countered as their plane touched the runway much more roughly than usual.

Chapter Seven

Facing each other over a table between their seats, Chase and Wen made several calls during the flight to Houston, contacting the key people who'd helped them disappear ten months earlier.

The first was to the Astronaut, a math savant widely respected and sought out by the world's intelligence agencies—including the CIA, NSA, MSS, Russian SVR, and others—for his uncanny skills at cracking into their systems and detecting patterns and data sets that even machines missed. His unique talents had made him both a highly paid consultant and kept him in hiding. He used his unusual abilities to avoid detection, always staying a step or two ahead of those seeking to control him. The MSS and the CIA had both separately considered eliminating him, and several others like him, to prevent their rivals from being able to utilize his services. However, since they could neither find him, nor resist using him themselves, he continued to live.

Wen had first met him while she was still a rogue MSS agent, and, for an inexplicable reason, even though twice her age, he had fallen in love with her—an innocent, friendship kind of love. It also helped that both he and Wen believed the world was out of whack, its governments screwed up, and the underlying social economic systems unfair.

"I need you to find out two things," Wen said to the Astronaut while she and Chase listened on speaker. "First, where is Curtis Lindbergh?"

"Lindbergh?"

"He's a scientist who has apparently found some new way to control the weather," Chase said. "And is an old friend of mine. Well, he's not *old*. Only a couple of years older than me. Maybe thirty-three."

"Controlling the weather . . . We are an arrogant species, aren't we?"

"Well," Wen began, "it all started when man first cleared forests of trees to plant crops, and then diverted river water into irrigation ditches. In some ways they were controlling nature, and it's just increased ever since. Like when the first of our ancestors threw a rock at an enemy, and now we have nuclear weapons. We're never satisfied . . "

"We need to know what Lindbergh invented or discovered or whatever," Chase said.

"Does anybody, other than him, know what that is?" the Astronaut asked.

"Our old friend, Tess Federgreen, with CISS, must know because she's given us thirty-six hours to locate Lindy or CISS agents will assassinate him."

"Then you think the answer might be in Heaven?"

"Has to be somewhere," Wen said. "And if Tess is worried the Chinese or Russians are going to get their hands on whatever he has done, then they must know, too."

"I'll check Ghost Dragon and Heaven."

Chase remembered Wen first telling him about the incredible intelligence networks—Ghost Dragon, a mass database operated by a 2100-class communications satellite network. Although its software and transmitters were originally developed by the US National Security Agency, the MSS hacked and stole the system. An MSS team then took the program to a higher and more sophisticated level, making it their own. The project had been entrusted to a secret subsidiary of one of China's leading tech companies that worked exclusively for the communist government.

At the same time, the NSA became aware of the breach and modified the original system to create a new database-network called 'Heaven,' because, just like the church's heaven, people believe it's in the cloud, but no one can prove it actually exists.

However, it did exist, and everything one could possibly want was there. Yet, just as with the other heaven, the only way to get there was to die.

The Astronaut promised to get back to them soon.

The next call went to Dez, Chase's business partner. After listening to the full explanation of their latest challenge, Dez gave them bad news.

"SEER is just not working."

"Still haven't been able to correct the eighty-fourth algorithm?" Chase asked, knowing the problem Dez had been grappling with ever since a group trying to stop Chase's work had bombed their company headquarters in San Francisco. The building had been leveled, and although deaths and injuries had not been nearly as bad as they could have been if the attack had happened during the day, they'd both lost people close to them. Chase stared down at the peaceful looking scenery below, urgently wanting answers.

"Yeah, I don't understand what's going on."

The entire SEER system, all its servers and peripherals, had been destroyed in the blast, but the program itself had been backed up off site, and should have been easily restored. Instead, there had been endless bugs and issues. SEER had not functioned normally since prior to the bombing.

"I've looked at all the coding and protocols again. I can't find anything, but maybe it's in the data," Chase said, swiveling in his seat to give Wen a desperate look.

SEER utilized virtually all digital data available, parsing, dissecting, and assimilating in a constant churn of machine learning artificial intelligence. The enhanced process worked in a kind of infinite loop, constantly improving the results, which, in turn, created even better data.

"If it's in the data," Dez said, "we're screwed."

Chapter Eight

Xu Hongbin had made a fortune at the beginning of the Internet boom in China and then moved swiftly into other technologies. At age forty-seven, he was now China's third richest person, with a net worth of more than fifty-three billion dollars. His company, Aznotech, dominated Asia's business world. Hongbin, a member of the Communist Party, wasn't surprised when Minister of State Security Peoples Republic of China, Li Dazhao, showed up unannounced.

The two men had known each other for more than a decade, yet they couldn't be described as friends. Each knew that their respective power was largely dependent on the other. In America, Hongbin would've likely been considered the more powerful of the two. However, in China, Minister Li definitely had the advantage.

Aznotech's headquarters building in Beijing was a glorious skyscraper. Its top three floors, almost entirely glass, housed a small forest growing in a climate controlled bubble. No matter how much smog the city endured or whatever the temperature or weather, everything inside the bubble was perfect. It resembled the biospheres designed by Curtis Lindbergh. That made sense since one of Aznotech's subsidiaries was the world's largest weather manipulation geo-engineering climate control technology companies—its only customer being the Ministry of State Security of the People's Republic of China (the MSS).

As usual, he took the meeting in the "Sky Forest," as the upper three-story bubble was known.

"Have you heard anything yet?" the Minister asked in Mandarin.

"Not a word from Lindbergh for thirty-two days," Hongbin replied as they passed a Gutta-Percha tree, its waxy green and yellow leaves dominating its corner of the Sky Forest.

"What game do you think he's playing?"

"I think the Americans have discovered his plan to sell to us, and either they've arrested him, or he's in hiding."

The Minister took a slim gold case out of his inner jacket pocket, withdrew a cigarette, tapped it on the case, then lit it with a gold push-button lighter. "I have people looking for him," the Minister said.

Hongbin tried not to show his alarm, worried that Lindy would be killed before he could complete the sale of the advanced technology. "Any luck?"

"Not yet, but we have considerable resources devoted to this. I have confidence."

"Good."

"You know the importance," the Minister said, staring at the Aznotech CEO, sensing his reluctance. "If we cannot have this technology," he exhaled a long stream of bluish-gray smoke, "then we must be certain no one does."

"Of course." Implicit in the Minister's statement was the unspoken accusation that Aznotech had not yet been able to match Lindbergh's creation. Hongbin knew, even with his great wealth, letting down the leadership would have dire consequences.

The MSS Minister stopped at the corner, staring out at Beijing. The magnificent view of the 7,750,000 square-foot forbidden city a constant reminder of China's ancient dominance. "We need the technology. We cannot afford to have it lost."

"I understand, but . . . "

Minister Li looked angry at the continued hesitation. "What?"

"We should not let Lindbergh die before we have his secrets."

"The Americans, Russians, Israelis, and Germans are all looking for him. The risks are too great." He took another long drag from his cigarette, blowing the smoke out. The cloud remained for less than a second before the air-filters caught the tiny particles of smoke. "You must be able to replicate what he has done, now that you know it is possible."

"We are working on it, but Curtis Lindbergh is not just an ordinary genius. His brilliance is unique. Many fields come together and overlap in his mind."

"Surely with one and a half-billion to choose from in our country, you can find one hundred scientists smart enough to equal one of him."

"Yes, but you yourself just described our competition and the critical time pressure . . . they could get there first."

"That would be most unfortunate," Minister Li said in his usual understated manner. The message could not have been clearer to Hongbin.

"We will get there first," Hongbin said firmly, but not entirely convincingly.

Li, taking one last look down upon his beloved city, dropped his cigarette onto the smooth limestone trail and crushed it under his foot. "You make sure of it."

Chapter Nine

Chase's final call, prior to landing in Texas, was with his oldest friend—Mars, a forty-three-year-old convict at Lompoc Federal Prison, who had four years remaining on "a dime" sentence. Chase had been waiting for Mars to get back to him.

"Just got your message," Mars said. "Is everything okay?"

"Depends on whether you mean my funeral or yours," Chase said. It was an old joke between them that they used to tell the other when things were bad. Their mutual sense of humor had kept the words alive.

"Firing squad or state-sanctioned-torture?"

"A bit of both, I'm afraid."

"What can I do to help?" Mars asked. He'd gotten his nickname in prison from fellow inmates who often called other cons by the town they were from—Washington, Norfolk, San Diego, whatever. In his case, people thought he was so unusual, that he must be from Mars, and it stuck. Friends would call him eccentric, or unusual, but the simple fact was that Mars believed anything was possible, and he continually tried to test his belief in the most unconventional ways.

Chase never liked to ask Mars for help, thinking he had enough to deal with just being in prison. However, Chase now lived on the run, and no longer always had the luxury of being considerate, and Mars's assistance had proved invaluable in keeping his location secret.

Ever since Chase was a kid, he'd looked up to Mars like an older brother. In fact, Mars had been an honorary member of the family, always very close to his parents and brother, Boone. They'd all been devastated when Mars, a lawyer, had been sent to prison. But Mars had made the best of it. He'd started a mini-empire from inside, actually earning more money than he'd been making while free.

"I need you to lose me," Chase said.

His old friend understood. During his incarceration, Mars had become a powerful and connected person throughout the "underworld." He'd already developed a method to help keep Chase's whereabouts unknown by utilizing a system called decoying. Reports and sightings of Chase would occur at random intervals across the globe. Whoever would be looking for him would get a constant stream of bad information. Through credit card use, surveillance cameras linked to facial recognition data bases, and a number of other related methods, the sightings would flood in and overwhelm those seeking Chase.

"We'll continue to mimic, mirror, and make use of your devices so it will appear you're using them in different locations," Mars said, having set up a network of the IP addresses of computers, tablets, and phones that Chase no longer used or ones that were bogus to begin with. He also had various experts using methods that made surveillance algorithms think they had seen someone they had not. Keeping Chase invisible had kept him alive.

"This one is big," Chase said. "I need you to jam them."

"I'll have you spotted in Manhattan . . . Cleveland, Frankfurt, Stockholm, and how about Monte Carlo? I know you always liked it there."

"Sounds good to me."

"The CIA, or whoever, will get alerts through whatever methods they've set up to monitor that you've been spotted fifteen times every day, and none of them near each other."

"You're beautiful, man."

"It's fun," Mars said. "Anyone after you will have to deploy resources."

"I'll ping you my real locations so you don't accidentally send them to where I really am."

"The real cameras will pick you up soon enough, but they'll have no idea that those aren't more fakes."

"I love it."

"We're keeping the credit cards, computer usage, and phones doing the same thing. Disinformation, dude!"

"Thanks, brother."

"Sure thing. You know I miss you, but I'm not interested in you joining me in here."

"In the morgue would be more like it."

"Don't say that," Mars said gruffly.

"Your funeral or mine?"

"Big party instead . . . one of these days," Mars said, referring to his eventual release. '*No matter how good someone makes their time inside, prison is still prison,*' he'd said many times. He didn't this time, but Chase knew.

"The Astronaut verifies that Aznotech is involved with weather research," Wen said, looking at her special laptop, affectionately known as an Antimatter Machine since it couldn't be seen or traced like normal computers. The custom-made machine also allowed them limited access to the ultra-classified intelligence networks run by the Chinese and Americans. The Astronaut had created the Antimatter Machine specifically for Wen, but even with all its electronic and software wizardry, it couldn't match the Astronaut's own systems, which were much larger, more powerful, and updated hourly. The Astronaut could go far deeper into Heaven and Ghost Dragon. He "lived" in those networks, the darknet and satellite links.

Chase had long been familiar with Aznotech—a giant Chinese firm involved in every aspect of the tech industry. "If Aznotech is developing weather control equipment, then that's the Chinese link to Lindy, and why Tess wants him," Chase said, looking for answers out the plane's window, as he did often, wondering, *Where is Lindy, and what has he created that has so stirred up the world's powers?*

Chapter Ten

"Team leader, team leader, this is Whiskey-seven. Com-stat-nine, we are entering the compound."

Tess walked into the situation room, known as "Mission Control," located underground, beneath the CISS headquarters building in Vienna, Virginia. Several techs and analysts silently acknowledged her as they returned their focus to the large screen displaying a live feed from what appeared to be a futuristic settlement somewhere in northern Mexico. They had good intelligence that Curtis Lindbergh was in Mexico, and this was definitely his facility.

Two IT-Squads, in full-combat mode, breached the outer wall. The CISS IT-Squads were unique among all of the special ops soldiers and intelligence operatives. To make it on the Squad, a candidate must be an expert in weapons, covert tactics, and, more importantly, possess a great depth of knowledge concerning computer and other technologies.

Tess, just back from Ecuador, stood next to her regular station, flanked by control panels that would allow her to manipulate the feeds at any time. Typically during any IT-

Squad raid or action, Tess paced Mission Control, checking on individual analysts screens, absorbing the data. Everyone in the room knew that Tess Federgreen, the ultimate control freak, wanted to be with the IT-Squads wherever they went. She needed the fix of firsthand knowledge, kicking in doors, accessing computers, and questioning suspects.

She studied the geodesic domes on the large monitor, momentarily transfixed by the incredible appearance of the facility. "They fit everything we've learned about Curtis Lindbergh, a man who's earned more degrees than I can recall."

"Six," a technician said.

"It might take a man with six degrees to construct something like this," she said, staring at the green domes, which looked as if they might have just landed from another galaxy. The scruffy, desert-dry landscape of north-central Mexico seemed a strange choice for what could only be called a tech-biosphere.

What would drive such a brilliant man to broker deals with two of our greatest enemies . . .

"Team leader, the grounds appear to be empty. We're going through the gate to the inner courtyard."

"Fire in the hole!" a Squad member shouted as they blew the heavy wooden doors open.

"Go, go, go!"

The screen showed armed agents fanning out inside the courtyard. There was great anticipation in Mission Control that they had finally found Lindbergh. Tess had given the order to take him into custody. Perhaps she was only hours away from a face-to-face conversation with the great scientist.

She watched the monitors as if the fate of the world rested in the outcome. "Damn it," she whispered out loud.

The courtyard appeared empty. She thought someone should have been out there.

The IT-Squad headed to the main entrance that connected all three domes, quickly blowing the lock. Entering the first dome, a different world greeted them—a tropical jungle. Lush vegetation surrounded a small turquoise lagoon fed by a waterfall, a narrow babbling stream trailing off it.

They worked their way through the dense vegetation to hidden doors on the far end. Two Squad members busted in the first door.

"Entering one. Appears to be an office," one of the Squad said. "Office clear."

Tess watched tensely as two members simultaneously barged into the next room.

"Entering two. Appears to be living quarters—some sort of bedroom. Bedroom clear."

Tess sighed, worried it might be a bust.

"Entering three. Storage room clear."

No one is there.

Even the normally stoic professionals inside CISS Mission Control gasped as the camera panned back around the lush and beautiful tropical jungle, filled with colorful flowers and birds. The stream wound its way into the two smaller domes. The smallest was filled with extraordinary large insects—many flying—and beetles of incredible colors and varieties. The final dome housed a swamp, with marshes too damp to easily walk through, and contained snakes, frogs, and lizards of every imaginable variety. A thin trail, barely elevated above the water, let them walk to the other end, but it was already obvious no human resided there.

"Cool place," one of the Squad said as they secured the sides of the jungle.

"Where's he getting the water?" a technician in Mission Control asked.

"That's all the computer hookups here," a Squad member said back in the office. "It appears they took everything except this unit, which, I would guess, is used to control the pumps, temperatures, humidity levels, etcetera."

"Did he know we were coming?" Tess asked.

"No way to tell how long it's been abandoned."

"Why create such an incredible biosphere in the middle of nowhere?" Tess asked.

"And then just leave it?" a technician added.

"I thought we had them," Tess said to one of the subordinates.

"How'd it go in Ecuador with Malone?"

"Better than this."

"You really think he can find Lindbergh?" the subordinate asked, motioning toward one of the most sophisticated tracking and surveillance centers in the world, as if to say, *"If we can't find Lindbergh, how can one guy on the run do it?"*

"Chase has a very special talent," Tess replied. "And his girlfriend has her own unique skill set. They constantly surprise me. And even if they didn't already know Lindbergh, I still think they have a good shot. Chase *reveres* Lindbergh. He wants to save his life."

Tess sent the footage of the raid and related data to J.W. Skyenor at DARPA with a note. *What is Lindbergh doing with this place? And where is he getting his funding?*

She knew Dr. Skyenor would expect her to have the

answers, but the science and technology were much more his expertise.

Skyenor responded immediately that he would send a DARPA team within the hour, declaring, "We have to find Lindbergh before the Chinese get him."

"I know," Tess said.

"No," Skyenor said. "Whatever you think will happen, if they get him first . . . I assure you it will be exactly that—by a magnitude of a thousand."

Chapter Eleven

Garcia, from a prominent family in Yelapa, had been Lindy's assistant since he'd first arrived in the village with an idea of constructing a research biosphere. He'd helped organize local labor and had arranged the land lease that the facility was built upon. Garcia contributed more than just local expertise and contacts, though. He was very smart, and had a degree in earth sciences from a respected Mexican university. He and Lindy had become good friends over the years.

"They hit our sphere in Villa Frontera," Garcia said, running into the office area.

Lindy stepped away from the screen displaying weather satellite data. "How long ago?"

"Hours. Felipe just texted me."

"Who is 'they?' Could Felipe tell what nationality?"

"He heard English."

"Good news, bad news," Lindy said. "Obviously since they hit Villa Frontera, they don't know we're here yet, but we may not have much more time. The backups are even more crucial now than ever before."

"Do you think you'll finish the final Aeolus formulas by tomorrow?" Garcia asked, referring to the last phase of Lindy's secret program.

"I think so. But then I still have to conduct the other four levels, and then make simultaneous connections with the buyers and the recipients—"

"Before the CIA stops us," Garcia finished.

"Exactly. Please re-sync all the modulators and algorithms, in case we get a surprise visit from the Americans . . . or the Chinese." Lindy's shaggy brown hair and deep-set brown eyes were always striking and memorable, even when his mind dipped into the depths of what he knew and how dark the world might become.

"You're still worried about them?"

"They are far ahead of the United States with weather modification. If they are the only ones to get Aeolus, it might mean the US could never catch them, and that would mean they'd do anything to make that happen."

"So even though you've already agreed to sell it to them, they want to make sure no one else gets it."

"Exactly. Same as the Americans," Lindy said, reviewing data from his Alpha Level test.

"And the Russians?"

"I'm sure they'd like it for themselves as well, but the Russians aren't as big a threat as they once were. I just wish these countries could get along instead of looking for better ways to kill each other."

"If you're successful with the formulas, the remaining level test, and can deliver the programs to everyone as planned, maybe that will change all that."

"Sounds like a lot of 'ifs', doesn't it? But you're right. That's what I'm hoping. I better get back to it."

"I'll go re-sync the modulators and algorithms," Garcia said, heading toward the door.

"Keep alert on the monitors."

"The kill switches are active," Garcia reminded Lindy.

"Let's hope it doesn't come to that." The two men exchanged a somber, knowing glance, each understanding their lives were at stake.

Garcia nodded, saying, "*Hasta luego*," as he left the room.

Drina Snow answered the front door of her small, recently restored home, located just off campus. Her face lit up. "Chase!" she said, pulling him into a hug. "It's been too long."

"Yeah," he replied, and once she released him, introduced Wen.

"Hi Wen! You're beautiful," she said sweetly, widening her blue eyes and flashing a perfect, white-teeth-smile.

"Thank you. Likewise."

"Oh, I have nothing to do with it. Just lucky, with good genes," she said, brushing imaginary dust off her old pair of jeans and a faded gray flannel shirt. Chase recalled that she always tried to play down her stunning looks. "Are you two a couple?" Drina asked, smiling.

"Yes," Wen said.

"He's a good catch, this one," Drina said, looking back to Chase. Her laugh was infectious.

"It was the other way around," Chase insisted. "I caught her."

"That's usually how it works." She winked at Wen. "Come in, come in."

Chase tripped over a bicycle as they navigated the narrow foyer.

"Sorry, I like to bike to work. Are you okay?"

"It's fine. I'll live."

Built-in bookshelves overflowed with books, leaving stacks, piles on the floor, and even more volumes on the coffee table. "I have to apologize for the mess. I'm still renovating. Well, not me, but I do supervise occasionally."

Wen, knowing one could tell a lot about a person by what they read, scanned the titles. Most of the books were nonfiction and on a wide range of topics—many on science and nature, plus history, biographies, and travel. She spotted a stack of fiction authors—Ernest Dempsey, Nick Thacker, Mark Dawson, Russell Blake, Hugh Howey, and an obscure vampire thriller by Eric J. Gates.

"The Cosega Sequence," Chase said, picking up a couple of paperbacks. "I loved this series."

"Me too," Drina said. "I want an Eysen."

Chase laughed at the reference to an object from the book. "Who wouldn't?"

"Right?" Drina said. "Now, what's so urgent that you had to come here in person on such short notice?"

"It's about Lindy."

"Oh no, he's okay isn't he?" She absently twirled a lock of her thick blonde hair.

"I think so. I don't *know*. That's why I'm here. We're trying to find him."

Drina looked at Wen. "Why?"

"He might be in some trouble," she told her. "We really need to talk to him."

"Is it about his research? One of his inventions?"

"Something he's working on," Chase said. "I can't really say right now."

"Do you know where he is?" Wen asked.

"I wish I did. I haven't talked to him in eight or nine months." Her face went sad. "You know we broke up, and—"

"I know," Chase said. "I'm sorry."

"Chase, is he okay?"

"I believe he's fine right now. But, like I said, we have to find him as soon as possible."

She looked at both of them with a worried expression.

"Is there anything you can think of that would help us locate him?"

"I'm not sure . . . maybe. Let's go out back. It'll help me think better."

"What exactly do you do?" Wen asked as they walked down a hall.

"I'm a scientist who studies the weather—a meteorologist. But not a weatherman. I research the atmosphere and study the effects of climate."

"Drina Snow is a good name for a climate scientist," Wen said, smiling.

"I do get teased about that quite a bit."

"I'm sure," Wen said. "It's a lovely name."

Drina smiled. "A lot of people think Meteorologists are all weathermen, but it's an important field. And with machine learning and artificial intelligence, it's advancing by the day."

"There has to be enormous data," Chase said as they passed more bookshelves. He noticed books by A.G. Riddle, Matthew Mather, and Marcus Sakey.

"Worldwide, there are more than ten thousand weather stations that provide data multiple times a day, plus there are at least five hundred weather balloons drawing measurements from the upper air. Then there are satellites, aircraft, and radar blanketing the globe. And all this for decades and decades."

"I would think AI would make predicting the weather a lot easier," Chase said.

"Yes, but predicting the changes to the *climate* is more important," Drina replied as she opened the back door. "What Lindy is doing is beyond all of that."

Chapter Twelve

Chase, Wen, and Drina stood before an extraordinary greenhouse that filled most of a half-acre back yard.

"What is all this?" Wen asked

"Lindy built it. He designed it to be a complete biosphere."

"It's so beautiful," Wen said.

"Wow . . . he's a total Renaissance man," Chase said. "What was he working on?"

"So many things," Drina said. "Lindy had all the plants brought in, and he used to do very ambitious climate and weather experiments in there."

She led them to the entrance, a carved glass and wooden door depicting an old man with long hair and a longer beard, blowing full and expanding breaths of wind from his mouth.

"Aeolus," Drina said, pointing to the image, "the keeper of the wind."

"We really need an idea of where Lindy could be," Chase pressed.

"Have you tried . . . I guess, since you're here, you've obviously tried calling him directly, or checking with MIT and the various research centers he was involved with . . ."

"We have."

"Do you think something happened to him?"

Wen could tell Drina still cared for Lindy. She shook her head. They stood in front of a wall of assorted tropical flowers of every color. The fragrance was an incredible mixture that Wen thought smelled like love.

"I have no reason to believe that," Chase said. "I think he just doesn't want to be found right now. He's working on something really important, and you know how he is—no distractions."

"Yes, I do," Drina said, looking sadly into the distance.

"I know it's personal, but it might help me find him if I know what happened with you two. Why you broke up. I mean, it's none of my business, so just tell me to shut up if—"

"No, I don't mind. I know how close you both were. It's what you said—he's consumed by his work, and it was hard for him to find room for me in the middle of all the grand experiments and theories. To Lindy, life is a series of equations and possibilities for what could be discovered. He gets that tunnel vision focus"

Chase nodded, amazed at the different weather in the greenhouse. Outside it was cloudy and cool. In the "biosphere" it was perfect.

"I didn't exactly give him an ultimatum of 'your work or me.' I'm not crazy. I know his career is everything. That's one of the reasons I love him. We had our work in meteorology in common, but, as you know, there's so much more to him than the weather. To hear him speak on any topic he's interested in, it just takes your breath."

"He sounds fascinating," Wen said.

"Yes," Drina agreed, smiling. "But I couldn't keep up, or compete with his work. I think he got bored with me, and once I started to feel that way, I couldn't shake it . . . " Drina wiped away a tear.

"No, I'm sorry, you don't have to say more," Chase said. "I was just thinking if there was some particular project or something that drove him off when you were together, it might be helpful."

"It wasn't one thing."

"It never is," Wen said, touching Drina's shoulder.

"Did he ever talk about a lab project somewhere differently than the rest?" Chase asked.

"He did build a biosphere in Mexico, not far from Villa Frontera. And he was doing experiments down there. But I don't know the exact location. He said he was going to take me there, but it never worked out. I guess that could be a possibility. I'm not sure how you'd find it."

Wen made a mental note of the biosphere and the name of the town. She'd put the Astronaut on it.

"Can you think of anyone else who might know?"

"You know his parents are deceased and he had no siblings. I never even heard him talk about a cousin or anybody other than you and a couple of other people from the MIT days. You know he was always happiest in a classroom . . . Wait a minute . . . there is somebody. Do you remember him talking about his old teacher they called Chips?"

"I actually do," Chase said. "But I never would have recalled that if you hadn't just mentioned him. Back at MIT, Lindy used to tell us stories about this crazy high school teacher. Is that guy still alive?"

"He was last time . . . at least maybe a year ago . . . I remember Lindy talking to him."

"They kept in touch?"

"Lindy loves the guy. Chips would know where he is."

"And you know where Chips is?"

"Yeah, he lives outside Reno, Nevada, but he's totally off the grid. He doesn't even have a phone."

"You just said you remember Lindy talking to him on the phone," Wen said, looking confused.

"Chips would call him from the casinos. That's why his nickname is Chips. He loves to gamble all the time, and he'd often check in with Lindy when he was on one of his poker excursions. Chips played so often that the casinos would give him complementary meals and sometimes rooms. There's a horse rental place outside Reno called Double D or Double A or something like that. The man who runs it is named Bob or Don. He'll know where to find Chips."

"You don't have an address?" Wen asked.

"We used to mail him cards. It's a general delivery mailing address, but I'm sure they can steer you to him at the rental place."

While Drina went inside to get the information she had on Chips, Chase called his pilot and told him they needed to fly to Reno right away.

"I can tell she's in love with him, even though she called it off," Wen whispered, "but she knows something more."

Drina returned a minute later and handed Wen a handwritten sheet. "I'm not even sure of his real name, but I think his last name's Anderson because I remember Chase saying the best teacher he ever had was Mr. Anderson."

Chase repeated his thanks and told her they needed to get going. Drina remained quiet for a few moments.

"Is there something else you can tell us? Chase asked.

She hesitated. "I'm not sure I should."

"It might save his life," Chase pressed.

"He was working on something for the government . . . something huge . . . that could change the world."

Chapter Thirteen

The Chinese agents stationed in a nearby van, who had been eavesdropping on the entire meeting at Drina's, double checked their recording equipment.

"Lindy was involved with HAARP," Drina said, as if the admission had caused her physical pain.

"What's that?" Chase asked.

"The High-frequency Active Auroral Research Program. They created it to oversee a powerful HF transmitter of more than ten megahertz. Actually the world's most powerful, high-frequency transmitter—an IRI, or Ionospheric Research Instrument."

"What is it for?"

"For studying the ionosphere. Scientists who are trying to understand the ionosphere can shoot a massive amount of energy into it, and then see what happens."

"Sounds reckless," Chase said, knowing the ionosphere was part of Earth's atmosphere.

"Much of science is, don't you think? But I do agree

with you that the HAARP program was particularly dangerous."

"Was?"

"There was so much public outcry about it that, *allegedly*, the pentagon shut it down. But it's still going on under another name."

"What did Lindy do with them?"

"Top secret, but afterwards he became obsessed with weather-control."

She offered them tea. Chase, realizing they were onto something, decided to stay longer, and they accepted.

"The climate scientists at HAARP," Drina continued after giving them tea, "utilize a sophisticated suite of scientific and diagnostic instruments to observe the physical and other processes that occur in the excited region of the ionosphere."

"What would have caught Lindy's imagination with all that?" Chase asked, knowing his old friend only worked on areas that he was passionate about.

"Lindy took the IRI observations and applied them to a controlled environment simulation on super computers and found ways to manipulate continuously occurring effects under the natural stimulation from the sun."

"Oh, is that all?" Chase blurted.

Drina smiled, used to people being surprised by her knowledge of complex scientific topics. "I'm trying to keep it simple, but you're a famously brilliant man, so . . . "

"Computer engineering, mainly."

She laughed. "Didn't I mention computers?"

"Please continue," Wen said. "Chase will do his best to keep up."

Drina laughed again. "Generally, Lindy factored in ionospheric characterization data from satellite beacons, telescopic observation of the aurora's fine structure, and long-term variations in the ozone layer."

"But why all the secrecy?" Wen asked, still searching for the missing piece.

Drina sipped her tea and sighed. "Okay, I guess we're going down the rabbit hole. There are those who believe that effects of energy waves directed to the ionosphere—that the rays are reflected back to earth on an extremely low frequency, or 'ELF' waves—have serious impact on Earth's magnetic fields. Others have charged that the HAARP-originating ELF waves can transform human thoughts and emotions, are mood-altering, and can perhaps brainwash specific populations."

"Do they?"

"I don't know, but Lindy probably does."

"Didn't he talk to you about it?"

"Only about certain parts of it."

"Because it's classified?"

"That, and because he didn't want to get me involved. And I guess I never pressed him on it because once he started, he never stopped. For *days*. He'd talk of nothing else, and he worried about . . . "

"You mean he didn't want to endanger you?"

She sighed heavily. "Yes."

"Where is the danger coming from?"

"Some experts have warned that the ELF waves can be used to cause a rapid heating of the earth's atmosphere, change wind patterns."

"That was Lindy's interest?"

"Partially. You have to understand that the waves could be strong enough to affect the tectonic plate movements."

"Is that possible?"

"The moon affects the tide. The plates are essentially

just floating on a different kind of liquid. Research suggests it could be. The pentagon denies all of this, but conspiracy theorists have blamed HAARP for earthquakes, floods, super storms, even air crashes. Whether any of that is true or not, there is no denying it is an insanely powerful tool."

"How would they affect human emotion?" Wen asked, recalling MSS experiments in that field.

"Someone involved with HAARP identified emotion signature clusters in EEG signals and frequencies. The theory is that they stored the information on large computers, and then they could be paired onto silent sound carrier frequencies. Those would trigger the emotion carried in that frequency in another human being. And they could do it to people anywhere else in the world."

"Yikes," Chase said, looking at Wen, as if to say things just went to a whole different level.

"That's all I know," Drina said. "I hope it helps you find him."

"Drina, you've been a big help. If you think of anything else, please call me. You've got my number from when I called you earlier."

"It's in my phone. You'll let me know when . . . ?"

Chase nodded. "You bet."

"I miss him." Her eyes teared again, but she fought them off as Wen gave her a hug.

Chase hugged her next.

"Can you give him this letter if you find him?" Drina asked, taking a copy of *A Hole in the Wind*, by David Goodrich, off a shelf, pulling out a sealed envelope from between the pages, and handing it to Chase.

"Sure," he said, looking at the envelope curiously.

"It's personal," she said, smiling self-consciously as she saw his expression.

"Don't worry, I won't read it."

Tess Federgreen digested a report that the CIA agent she'd left in Ecuador had turned up dead.

"They found his body near the Peruvian border," the analyst told her as she read more details from her private screen in Mission Control. "A small coastal town, Huaguillas," he continued. "It's about an eleven hour drive from Otavalo, Ecuador."

Tess knew that ruled out any involvement from Chase and Wen. She didn't think they would have killed a surveillance agent anyway.

"Someone else was in that market," the analyst said. "Who?"

Tess shook her head. She understood that Chase and Wen were in the middle of more than they were aware—the danger could not be greater.

"The truth is," Tess admitted, "we will probably never know who killed him."

Chapter Fourteen

On the way to the airport, Chase and Wen checked in with the Astronaut for more information on HAARP.

"The program started in 1993, during the Clinton administration. US government officials claimed it was a research program on radio waves operated by the US Air Force, US Navy and the University of Alaska," the Astronaut explained. "The initial phase involved the study of the ionosphere."

"Exactly what is that?" Wen asked, looking out at the open fields stretching to forever.

"It's part of the upper atmosphere that is ionized by solar radiation. Relevant to HAARP, the ionosphere influences radio waves propagation across the planet."

A light mist began to fall. "But the government lied?" Wen asked.

"As they often do," the Astronaut replied in monotone. "Many scientists and others have suggested that HAARP was designed to develop an array of weapons using amplified radio waves—a kind of death ray."

"Nice," Chase said sardonically, turning on the windshield wipers.

"The main HAARP facility is in a remote region of Alaska. Thirteen hectares filled with high-frequency antennas."

"That's a lot of antennas," Wen said, thinking of the capabilities. "How much power?"

"Officially, three point six megawatts, but it could be substantially higher."

"Into the ionosphere?" Chase asked. "What does that do?"

"Causes a mighty disturbance. It's all recorded and analyzed."

"Why?" he asked, still not sure how the atmosphere could be used to make "super weapons."

"Some experts have charged that this is a weather controlling operation. Foreign leaders, the European Union, and others, have complained to the US government, and even passed measures to investigate."

The rain grew heavier. "What did HAARP do?"

"In 2013, at the height of the controversies and conspiracy theories that the US was trying to weaponize weather, they shut it down temporarily, and in 2015 ended HAARP. What was left of the program was turned over to the University of Alaska."

"But they didn't really stop, did they?" Wen asked as the wind blew stronger, pelting the rain against their rental car.

"No. They renamed the program and moved parts of it."

"What's it called now?"

"Weather Ionosphere National Defense. Although it doesn't *officially* exist. It's buried in DARPA."

"Defense Advanced Research Projects Agency," Chase said. "I sure know them."

Minister Li's office contained a wall of large color photographs of some of China's greatest accomplishments and engineering feats, including the Great Wall, Three Gorges Dam, the Qinghai-Tibet Railway, Shanghai Tower, the world's longest High-Speed Railway, and fastest bullet trains.

Li pushed a concealed button in his desk, causing the picture wall to slide away. An adjoining room opened, revealing a space almost entirely filled with a futuristic command console that allowed him to view live feed satellite footage, China's facial recognition system, data feeds, computer networks, and access to Ghost Dragon and other important points from around the world without having to go to the MSS situation center.

The Minister sometimes went a week or two without going through the wall. However, recently, it had been opened on a daily basis, and sometimes remained that way for eighteen hours at a time while he managed multiple crises, as well as the typical problems and projects mandated by his charge to advance the People's Republic of China's influence, power, and control in the world. Yet mostly it was the Curtis Lindbergh issue which had become his top priority, garnering more frequent phone calls with China's leader than was normal.

Li watched on one of the monitors as an MSS field unit from San Francisco landed in Reno.

He opened up encrypted communication with the officer in charge. "I want you to be prepared when Chase

Malone lands at the airport. We should be able to provide identification assistance via satellite," the Minister said. "We need you to physically tag his plane, once we've identified it, for satellite tracking."

"I understand," the officer said. "But will he be boarding that plane again?"

The Minister knew the officer wasn't wondering if Chase would be taking a different plane, but rather would he still be alive. Once the tag was in place, the MSS would have the ability to track the plane's flight paths, destinations, and location at any time across the globe.

"That is yet to be determined," the Minister replied. "We need Malone to lead us to Lindbergh. However, we do not want him, nor can he be allowed, to *reach* Lindbergh."

"Understood."

"We have intercepted information from another source. We know where Malone is going in the morning. He'll be on horseback. The operation will require the utilization of long-range surveillance mics to eavesdrop and record the conversation he has at his destination."

"I just received the file," the operative said, looking at a computer tablet. "I see his meeting will take place at a remote cabin."

"Once you relay the recordings of the conversations to us via Ghost Dragon, you are to keep the subject under surveillance, awaiting my orders," Li said. "At that time, you will either terminate Chase Malone, or continue to trail him until he gets on that plane."

"Understood. To confirm, aside from ancillary intelligence, the key information we are seeking is the location of Lindbergh."

"Correct, and your secondary assignment is to prevent Malone from conveying that information to anyone else."

"Understood."

"Therefore, if you are certain Malone is going to convey that information to another party, and he is about to take such action, you are authorized to use any means necessary to prevent that from happening. You *must* prevent that from happening."

"Understood."

Chapter Fifteen

The Astronaut sent Chase and Wen an encrypted text message on the Antimatter Machine as they arrived at George Bush Intercontinental Airport in Houston.

"It's the instructions," Wen said.

"Tess might be expecting this," Chase replied as they entered a parking garage. A car and driver were waiting for them, arranged by the Astronaut. Half an hour later, they arrived at William P. Hobby Airport, where the Astronaut had a chartered plane waiting to take them to Reno, Nevada. By then, Chase's plane had taken off from Houston on its way to San Diego with only the pilots on board.

Waxxman and several Wrestlers waited at the Reno-Tahoe International Airport in his Cessna.

"Why aren't we going to follow them?" one of the men

asked Waxxman, ready to get off the plane and see some action.

"No need to risk blowing cover out in the open range when we know they'll be coming back to the plane." Nothing was more important to Waxxman than appearing tough in any and every situation. He had no patience for others, and that conflicted with how he pictured himself: always the hero, always in control.

"But what if Lindbergh is meeting them out there?"

"We know he's not in the Reno area," Waxxman said, squinting his obsidian eyes. "And we've already been where he's going."

"Yeah, there's some crazy old man who lives up in the mountains," another one of the wrestlers said. "They call him Chips, because he comes into the casinos and gambles a whole bunch, but other than that, he lives out there like a hermit. No phone, no television. Weird."

"We set up listening devices out there one time when the old guy was on one of his gambling binges," Waxxman said. "So if he gives them any kind of actionable information, we'll know even before they get back to their plane."

"Cool," the man said. "What about food?"

Waxxman laughed. "It's always about food with you guys, isn't it?"

Several of them nodded and answered at the same time.

"Fine, we've got time. Two of you go into the airport and pick up some pizzas or whatever." Sending them off like that made him feel like a great leader of some sort, dealing kindly with the peasants.

Tess and Dr. Skyenor had a brief phone conversation while the DARPA Director wandered around a simulation center, where technicians were attempting to dissect data that was coming in from the Mexico and Florida raids.

"The HAARP station in Tromsø was hit," Tess said.

"By the Chinese?" Skyenor asked, alarmed. He crossed his arms and relaxed his gaze out the window to a fleet of weather drones being prepared for flight.

"We can't confirm that, but it's almost certainly an MSS job."

"What did they get?" he asked, walking past a large wave machine producing humid air, which illuminated a series of colored LED lights.

"It appears they just took the personnel—two experts, two security."

"No. They don't need people."

"What did the experts know?"

"Nothing more than thousands of others." A grid of purple lasers appeared above his head, then converted into mist. "The Chinese took data, or put something in place. Have we had a team in there?"

"Not yet, we just got word."

"This is no ordinary site, Tess. Send an IT-Squad. If the Chinese have decided to start going after HAARP installations, then they're close."

"And the only way to stop them . . ."

"Curtis Lindbergh," Skyenor said.

"Dead or alive?"

"Yes, depending on the circumstances."

One of the DARPA technicians called him over, pointing to a screen.

"Tess, hold on a minute." Skyenor asked several questions, and the technician entered more information into the computer. "I think we might have gotten something from the Mexico drives."

"Something I can use?"

"Is that it?" he asked the technician. "Excellent work, Mike. Please send that over to CISS right away. Here we are. Tess, I'm back with you. I just sent you coordinates to a Lindbergh facility in Montana. We need to get there fast."

Chase and Wen had arrived in Reno aboard an "anonymously" chartered plane mid-evening. Wen slept during the flight, but Chase wasn't good at sleeping on planes, boats, trains, or cars—he often said that beds, beaches, and hammocks were more his style. They took an Uber straight to a chain hotel, unaware that the Chinese and Waxxman's group had noted Chase and Wen's arrival and were monitoring their every move.

"We could have stayed at one of those fancy casino hotels. Gotten a romantic suite," Wen teased.

"I don't consider casinos very romantic," Chase said, slowly undressing her. "Especially after what happened in Vegas."

"What happens in Vegas, stays in Vegas."

"Reno has a slogan, too," Chase said in between kisses. "Everything's better in Reno."

"Is that true?"

"Let's find out," Chase said as they fell naked onto the bed.

"Are we staying on the plane all night?" one of Waxxman's men asked him, alarmed after Chase and Wen departed the airport.

"No, just until we know for sure they aren't coming back until the morning. Joe's tailing them, and once we hear back, we'll head over to the hotel. I've already booked a few rooms at the same place where they're staying."

A short while after the pizza was inhaled, the tail reported that it appeared Chase and Wen were all tucked in for the night. They'd asked the front desk man about renting horses. He'd recommended Double R Horse Adventures.

Waxxman waited until they were all settled in at the hotel before he called Wiest to give him a report. "Hopefully we'll have an idea where Lindbergh is by this time tomorrow."

"And then you'll take care of it?" Wiest asked.

"Asked and answered," Waxxman said impatiently. "Talk to you tomorrow."

I might decide to kill Wiest instead of Lindbergh if this guy keeps pushing me, Waxxman thought as he texted his assistant to check to see if Jeff Wiest was even his real name.

Chapter Sixteen

Aznotech chairman, Xu Hongbin, leaned forward and asked his driver if he thought they were being followed. He pressed his hands against each other, cracking every knuckle.

"Which one?" the driver replied, checking the rear view mirror and trying to determine which one of the vehicles his boss was worried about. Being worth an excess of sixty-two billion dollars meant a lot of things, one of which was enemies.

"That black Mercedes," Hongbin said. "I noticed it a few kilometers back. It's still with us."

"Should I take the next exit?" His eyes were cunning and sharp in the rear view. Although quite short in stature, he made up for it with insane diligence to detail.

"Yes," he said as his phone buzzed. It was Minister Li's number.

"We may have our first break," Li began. "One of our agents in Texas has had some success."

"Have you located Lindbergh?" Hongbin asked, checking the cars behind him again.

"Not yet. We have had a man shadowing Lindbergh's former girlfriend for several weeks. He planted listening devices in her home and office. Fairly boring dead-end stuff up until now." Li's secretary came into his office and placed a stack of documents requiring his signature on the desk. Li nodded and mouthed a thank you. "Today she had a surprise visitor. Two, actually. Quite interesting, I think you'll agree."

The driver veered off onto the exit. Hongbin watched out the back window as the black Mercedes did the same.

"Does the name Chase Malone mean anything to you?"

"*The* Chase Malone? Of course it does. Why, was he there? What's his involvement with Lindbergh?"

"We checked, and it seems they were at MIT at the same time. Apparently they have remained friends."

"Is Malone involved in the weather project?"

"We don't know yet."

"Something else to worry about," Hongbin said.

"What else has you worried?"

Hongbin hesitated as he motioned for his driver to speed up. "Uh, whether or not we'll beat Lindbergh, or find him in time."

"There are plenty of other things that should concern you," Li said in a tone that made Hongbin nervous.

"Yes, there are . . . You said *two* visitors."

"A Chinese woman accompanied Malone."

"Really? Who is she?"

"Facial recognition so far yielded no results."

"Then she is not a Chinese national."

"It would appear not, but we're still digging. A Chinese woman in the mix seems odd."

"Maybe it's just a coincidence."

"I do not like coincidences. I learned long ago that a simple coincidence is rarely either, and instead, is usually a door to danger."

The black Mercedes was maintaining the same distance to Hongbin's car, no matter what speed the driver kept.

"What did Malone discuss with Lindbergh's girlfriend?" Hongbin asked, loosening the necktie that suddenly felt like it was strangling him.

"Drina Snow, Lindbergh's ex-girlfriend, is also a climate scientist. She used to work with him."

"It does keep getting more interesting."

"She claims not to know where Lindbergh is, but she gave Malone a good lead. He's off to Nevada to visit an old teacher."

"Of Lindbergh's?"

"Yes. She thinks the old man knows where Lindbergh is hiding."

"Excellent," Hongbin said, motioning the driver to take another road.

"I've got a unit flying in from San Francisco. They will arrive in Reno before Malone."

"And then what?"

"One way or another, Mr. Malone is going to lead us to Mr. Lindbergh."

"I hope it is that easy."

"Nothing ever is, that's why the MSS employs the resources it does. We never leave anything to chance. There are always one hundred ways to do one thing."

"Good. I look forward to the next update. Thank you for keeping me informed."

"Of course," Li said. "Enjoy your evening."

Hongbin realized he was sweating as the call ended.

"Sir, the Mercedes has just turned off," the driver reported.

Hongbin spun around in his seat to check, and sure enough, the car was gone.

"That's a coincidence," the driver said.

"What?"

"That they followed us from the time you got that call until you finished it."

"Yes," Hongbin said quietly, while shifting in his seat. "It was definitely a simple coincidence."

Chapter Seventeen

Tess received a call from Mission Control as she headed home.

"Ma'am, his plane landed in San Diego," a CISS Analyst said as she answered her phone.

"Do we have him?" she asked, referring to live satellite coverage of his movements.

"Yes. We'll know all his movement while he's there."

"Good. Let me know right away if anything unusual happens. That would include losing him."

"Yes, Ma'am."

That evening, Drina's current boyfriend, who liked to be called Tab, made her a late dinner. As they ate the vegetable stir-fry, he asked her about her meeting with Chase Malone.

"What's he like?" Tab's short-cropped brown hair and matching beard framed a square, handsome face.

"He's like a billionaire. Drove up in a gold-plated Rolls-

Royce, came in here and offered to buy my house, then lit his expensive Cuban cigar with a hundred dollar bill." She winked, swished her silky blonde hair, and batted her eyes expressively.

"Funny. I didn't mean that. I've met billionaires before."

"You have not."

"Well, I know Bill Watkins on the alumni Association."

"He's not a billionaire," Drina said teasingly.

"He's worth a hundred and twenty million. That's pretty damn close, at least from where I'm sitting."

Drina laughed. "Anyway, I told you I met Chase before. He's really nice, and his girlfriend, Wen, is a total sweetheart."

"Great, we'll put them on the Christmas card list. But do you think he's going to be able to find Lindy?"

"I have a good feeling about it." She stopped talking and put her fork down. "Did you hear that?"

"Neighbor's dog."

"I didn't think they had one."

"And what's Chase's interest in Lindy again?"

"He said he's trying to protect him." She sipped her wine, seemingly lost in thoughts.

"Then he knows about Aeolus?" Tab continued, referring to Lindy's secret project. His raised eyebrows relaxed as he leaned back in the chair.

"He doesn't know specifics." She got up and walked to the window. "Why is that dog barking so much?"

He followed her with his eyes. "And you didn't tell him?"

She pulled back the curtain and looked out, but couldn't see the dog. "Of course not. I don't know his real motives, or if he's involved with the government."

"A guy like Chase Malone could be involved with any

government in the world, including China. I mean, you said his girlfriend was Chinese?"

"She is, but a sweetie," she said, returning to the table. "Either way, I was careful. I didn't tell him anything he didn't already know except how he might be able to track Lindy down."

"I sure hope he finds Lindy. I'm afraid something might happen if he doesn't get to him soon."

"I wish that dog would shut up, he's driving me crazy."

"You want me to go take a look?"

She shook her head. "I wonder where Lindy is?"

"Brazil?" Tab said taking a bite of stir-fry.

"Maybe . . . Could you imagine if Lindy was still doing the research here? We'd all be in danger."

"We might all be dead," Tab said, thinking back on the excitement when the three of them were working on the project together. "Still, those were awesome times."

"Except I was with Lindy then." She blew him a kiss.

"I can't blame you. I was in love with him, too."

"Tab!" She shooed him.

"Not in that way, of course, but man, watching his brain unravel any problem that got in his path . . . You know how it is when he's in that zone and it's like he's twenty years ahead of the rest of the field."

A sad expression washed over her face. "I do, but that's what got him in trouble. He goes so darn fast."

Tab, forking several green beans and putting them in his mouth, nodded. "It was his decision to share it that really got him in trouble, not the breakthrough itself."

"I know, but it's hard to separate the two. That kind of discovery, what's possible. Climate control on a scale you never thought possible. Once that genie's out of the bottle . . ."

"Yeah, well. Lindy trusted the wrong people. He thought his magnanimous gesture would ensure peace and tranquility. That was pretty naïve thinking for such a genius."

"As it turned out. But Lindy meant well." She turned her head again toward the barking.

"The road to hell is paved with good intentions."

"Tab, why would you say that?"

"I don't know. I'm just sorry it all went this way."

She nodded. "You said it yourself. He goes so fast."

"I didn't say that, you did."

"Did I?"

"Yeah, but you're right."

"Lindy should have concentrated on cloud seeding and using the fifteen to twenty percent results. What if we doubled that? Wouldn't that be a game-changer."

"Boring," Tab said, abandoning his meal and walking toward the front door.

"Not to the people who need rain. Where are you going?"

"But boring to a great mind like Lindy." He opened the front door. "I want to see why this dog is so irked up."

She swirled her wine glass. "I hope I did the right thing telling Chase about Chips."

"You did. Chase is in a whole different league than us."

"Gold plated Rolls Royce and all."

Tab laughed.

"Do you see anything?" Drina asked.

"No . . . I think those dogs are barking just to annoy me. There's nothing out there."

Chapter Eighteen

The following morning, while it was still dark, an Uber driver picked Chase and Wen up at their motel and dropped them off at Double R Horse Adventures. They quickly made their way into the office, a room of knotty pine and leather that smelled like coffee and newsprint. A tall, lanky man with a handle-bar mustache greeted them with a smile.

"Y'all're getting an early start this morning," he said in a full country accent. "Care for a cup of Joe?"

They both accepted, needing the wake-up, but Chase secretly would've poured some alcohol into his if he'd had it. Horses made him nervous.

The gray hair peeking out of the man's white cowboy hat almost reached the collar of his worn denim shirt. He looked as if he'd been riding horses longer than either one of them had been alive.

"I'm Rod, by the way."

"One of the Rs in Double R?" Chase asked.

"Both, actually." He grinned. "Full name's Rod Richmond." He pulled up their reservations. "Where y'all headin' today?"

"Seeing an old friend."

He gave them a funny look. "Do you know where you're going?"

"We were hoping you could tell us that," Wen said, smiling.

"Well, I can make some good suggestions, if your friend's got a name."

"Do you know a man that goes by Chips?" Chase asked.

"Sure, I know ol' Chips. I suspect everybody 'round here's got a Chips story or two. He's a friend of yours?"

"He is. A friend of a friend actually, said we should look him up."

Rod chuckled and mumbled something to himself. "You watch out, Ol' Chips might try to get you into a card game."

Chase was about to say they didn't have time for cards or games or anything else, not even this conversation. Rod, Nevada's slow-west pace, the idea of having to ride a horse because there was no other way to get out to see this crazy old kook—it was all beginning to wear on his patience. He wanted to get out of there, but instead he just smiled. "Thanks for the tip."

"I thought y'all might be here for the wild mustangs," Rod said. "That's ninety percent of our rentals."

"Wild mustangs?" Chase echoed, as if it might be something he should be afraid of.

"Sure. We got more than thirty-thousand wild horses in the Virginia Range. Beauties. Herds of them running the way God intended. Something magnificent to see."

"Maybe next time," Chase said, thinking all he needed was *more* horses.

Rod nodded, as if he knew that would never happen. "I got two horses, a palomino and a real pretty paint. Are you both experienced riders?"

"I've been on horses all my life," Wen said.

Rod smiled. "Good girl. I knew I liked you."

Chase shot Wen a 'teacher's pet' look. "I guess this will be my second time on a horse," Chase admitted. "That was probably twenty years ago."

"Son, you don't look like you're much more than twenty. Did you ride your way out of the womb?"

Chase forced a laugh. "Not a big fan of horses. And I'm thirty."

"Not a fan of horses?" Rod looked at Chase as if he'd just said he barbecued kittens. "Well that'll change today. Ol' Hellfire is a good horse. She'll get you out there fast as lightning."

"*Hellfire?*"

Rod laughed. "Nah, I'm just messing with you, city boy. All our horses are as gentle as the morning dew. You'll be on Gumdrop. She'll show you what a good horse is all about."

Chase took a deep breath.

"Don't worry," Rod said. "There's not much to it once you're up there. Gumdrop knows the trails, and it's an easy way out to Chips' place."

They both signed the release forms and agreements stating they'd pay for the horses and tack should anything happen.

"I'll take good care of them," Wen said.

"The horses, or this one here?" he said, pointing to Chase and taking another sip of his coffee just as a teenage boy walked in. "Jimmy'll get them saddled up for you and help y'all get on your way. Hey, tell Chips ol' Rod said hello, and that I'm still itching to get my sixty dollars back."

Wen smiled. "We'll do that."

"Make sure you don't stay out there too long. We might have some weather coming in later today."

"Thanks kindly," Chase said, trying to sound like a cowboy.

Jimmy helped Wen get up on her horse, and was about to walk away, assuming Chase didn't need a hand. Then he saw Chase wasn't sure of himself and came back. "Mister, you ever been on a horse before?"

"It's been a long time." Chase had told Wen about his only other horse experience, as a ten-year-old kid, when a group vacation horse ride with his family had not gone well. He'd been last, and his horse wouldn't listen. Soon "the beast" took him away from the others and he wound up lost in the desert for forty long, scary minutes, before they found him. "I'd appreciate a hand up," he said, trying not to think about it.

"Sure."

Once Chase was in the saddle, he asked where the clutch and brake pedals were.

Wen laughed, but Jimmy didn't see the humor.

"Oh, almost forgot. Here's a map of the area. It shows you where the water is and all the trails."

"Rod was going to show us where Chips lives."

"Sure," Jimmy said, and marked it for them. "It's a straight shot out there, but don't let him hustle you into a card game. Damn lost my whole paycheck to him once."

"Thanks for the warning."

"Have a good time. There is, believe it or not, some cell coverage out there, so if anything comes up, you might be able to get us. The spots are noted on the map where you don't get reception, but otherwise it should be good."

"Thanks," Wen said, pulling the reins to turn the horse. "See you later." But she had a sudden strange feeling that she'd never see him again.

Chapter Nineteen

Waxxman and the Wrestlers were back on board their plane before Chase and Wen even arrived at Chips' ranch. They played cards and complained while they waited. These were the type of guys who would rather be hunting or tracking, fighting or shooting. Sitting around waiting made them feel like caged animals, and the Curtis Lindbergh case had been strangely boring for weeks.

"Don't worry, soon enough we'll be in the game."

Tess, still angry that Chase's plane had flown to San Diego as a decoy, would rather be at Mission Control searching for her rogue "friend." Instead, she had a meeting with DARPA. Tess had left her best people in charge of finding Chase so, through him, she could find Lindbergh and learn what he was doing before the Chinese, or someone else, found him.

No wonder Tess had a headache when she arrived at

one of DARPA's classified facilities. She cleared through four different security zones before she was greeted by Dr. J. W. Skyenor, a tall, skinny man in his late-fifties. Even to someone as powerful and "battle-hardened" as Tess, Skyenor's distinguished and intelligent persona was somehow intimidating.

"Tess, thanks for coming," the director of the Defense Advanced Research Projects Agency said, extending his hand.

"Jay, good to see you again. How's Jennifer?"

"Doing well, thanks."

"Is she still at NIH?"

"Yes, working more than ever, now that the kids are both out of college."

Tess out-ranked Skyenor in the elite hierarchy of the US Government intelligence communities, and they'd been friendly colleagues for years, yet he had an air about him that always made her uneasy. They walked down a wide hallway, passing a brass plaque engraved with the words: *Formulating and executing research and development projects that expand the frontiers of technology and science.*

Dr. Skyenor and Tess continued their small talk until reaching a secure door at the end of the corridor. Skyenor looked into a retina scanner and the door slid open. They entered a long conference room, the walls on the left and the right covered with gauges and monitors. An all-glass wall opposite the entrance overlooked a classified DARPA testing area filled with dozens of soldiers wearing exoskeletons—suits made mostly of flexible textiles with embedded sensors, robots, and micro drones, all involved in simulated war games.

"Battlefield of the future," Tess said, impressed by the display.

Chasing Wind

"The future is now," Skyenor replied.

The "proving ground" space was as big as two football fields. Half of it replicated desert terrain, the other half was landscape-accurate forested and open fields, complete with a winding stream.

"I'd like to borrow this for IT-Squad training," Tess said.

"We do this phase of testing indoors so it can't be monitored."

Tess knew the Chinese were always watching, just as the US was always watching the Chinese. She stared down at the battlefield of the future and wondered how soon the first war between robots and drones would occur.

"It's not too far off," Skyenor said, noting her delayed interest, as well as a hidden pained expression.

"Can something in here read my mind?" Tess asked, only half joking.

"That's not too far off either."

She'd been briefed on several projects in that realm, and knew he was quite serious.

"How's the weather?" he asked.

"We're still looking. Do you have any idea how he's doing it?" Tess asked.

"As you know, he consulted briefly on HAARP."

"You mean WIND," Tess corrected. HAARP had been shut down, but the defense portion of the program had moved to DARPA and been renamed Weather Ionosphere National Defense.

"Of course." Skyenor smiled, a serious kind of smile. "I would assume he started with the concept that we've had success with by shooting an IRI into the ionosphere."

"But you've got hundreds of scientists working on it, and they haven't been able to take it to the next level?"

He shook his head. "That's why we need Lindbergh."

She looked at him hard for a moment. "I've never met the man, only read the files, but you worked with him quite a bit, right?"

"Yes."

"Then do you have any idea why he would be cutting a deal with the Chinese and the Russians?"

"Lindy is a very unusual man."

"Obviously."

"He isn't particularly loyal to the idea of any one nation. He considers himself more of a citizen of Earth, his allegiance strictly to science. I believe when he saw the potential to control the weather and what we were doing here at DARPA, he realized that it was just the next phase in modern warfare, and I think that scared him. Not that I saw this coming, but when it happened, I wasn't actually surprised."

Tess thought of Chase and his undeclared mission to make sure technology was used for the good of all instead of only the elites, powerful countries, or trillion dollar companies at the exclusion of the general population. "What you're saying," Tess began, "is Lindbergh thought he could prevent the weaponization of weather by making sure everyone had it?"

"That's my guess."

A projectile disc hit the thick glass window. Sparks flew.

"That may be true," she said, taking in the light show.

Skyenor shook his head. "If it is, his efforts will only delay the inevitable. One side will get an advantage eventually, even if we all start at Lindy's level."

"Secrets don't stay secret for too long," Tess said. "He hasn't proven his claims yet, has he?"

"We don't think so, but we can't be sure."

This surprised her. "I don't understand."

"There are constantly major weather events across the globe. Approximately one hundred lightning bolts strike the Earth's surface every second. More than eight million every single day. Thousands of storms. We have no way of knowing he's testing for sure unless something truly out of the ordinary occurs. But if Lindbergh is smart—and I don't mean in the form of his brilliance, I mean smart about how he approaches this, which is a different thing altogether . . . he'll keep it in one of his biospheres."

"Will he?"

"I doubt it. Although Lindbergh is the smartest man I've ever met in the sciences and the disciplines he pursues, what he's doing now requires a street smart strategist to pull off. He can easily make a miscalculation about how to deploy what he's created."

"You think he'll test in the open and screw up?"

"That's what I'm counting on."

Tess could feel her entire body go tense. "I hope you're counting on more than that, because he could, just as easily, get it right. He understands the stakes, and I'm sure he knows we're looking for him. I don't expect him to make a mistake."

"Then start brushing up on your Mandarin."

Chapter Twenty

Chase and Wen reached Chips' hobbit-like house, wedged in between trees as if it had grown there naturally a century before. Even before seeing his spread, they expected Chips to be an odd character, based on all they'd heard.

"Anyone who lives this far out, this much off the grid, is bound to be a little strange," Chase said as they trotted up to the property.

Several outbuildings, no less unusual than the main structure, greeted them. Everything had round windows and door handles of smooth, curving wood. Strange metal sculptures five to seven feet tall were planted among the trees, catching the breeze, silently twisting and spinning into new shapes and designs. Behind the main house, the land fell away. Above it, multilevel decks, looking like something out of Robinson Crusoe, followed the contours down. More wooden platforms covered the ground, weaving in and out of boulders.

Wen and Chase dismounted the horses and tied them to an old hitching post. The whole place, and the fact that they had ridden across the wilderness to reach it, made Chase feel like he was in an old western movie. He actually looked around for gunfighters that he worried might be real.

"I hope he's here," Wen said, walking on a stone path leading toward the main house.

"Yeah, this already feels like a wild goose chase. Hope we didn't come all this way for nothing," he said, noticing his rear was sore from the ride.

The scent of cedar wood smoke caught the crisp air. Wen zipped up her jacket. "It's cold. I thought it would get warmer once the sun came out, but it really hasn't."

Chase knocked on the door and waited. No answer. Wen knocked again, louder. After a couple of minutes, they walked around back, past a freshly built shed and a couple of aged chicken coops that were surrounded by their occupants. An old golden retriever gave them an unconcerned look before resuming his nap.

Finally they ventured down one of the tiered decks. Wen touched Chase's shoulder and pointed to an old man in blue jeans and a faded green flannel shirt. He lay motionless on a lower deck.

"You think he's dead?" Chase whispered.

Wen pulled a pistol from her pack and began scanning the area. The body was down three levels. Wen took one side of the steps, Chase took the other, each facing a different direction. By the time they finally reached the platform where he lay, it seemed clear no one else was around.

"Chips?" Chase said loudly, looking at the man, whose face was wrinkled and leathery, and might've easily been a hundred years old. They couldn't tell if he was breathing. Chase knelt down a little closer and was about to say his name again when he thought he detected a rising in the old man's chest.

"Hey!" the old man yelled, springing to his feet like a teenager. Chase rolled backward, landing on his side, heart racing. Chips spun, as if ready to fight. "Who the hell are you crustliders?"

Wen had slipped the gun under her coat, but was still braced for the man to attack her.

"You stealing my peace?" Chips yelled.

"We're friends of Lindy's," Chase said, getting to his feet.

"Lindy? How do you know Lindy?" the man asked, looking unsure.

Chase held out his hand. "I'm Chase Malone. I've known Lindy since MIT."

"Well I've known him since high school," Chips said. "Not from back when *I* was in high school, of course. I taught him in high school."

"I know," Chase said.

"Chase Malone . . . I recall Lindy mentioning you a few times," Chips said. "What the hell did you scare me for like that?"

"We thought you were . . . "

"Dead?" Chips laughed. "I'm never going to die. I was meditating. Sun warm in my bones. Out here in the peace. You came and took my peace."

"Sorry about that," Chase said. "I yelled your name and you didn't move. We would've called first, but—"

"Oh, phones aren't worth a damn," Chips said. "You yelled my name? Hmmm . . . I guess I was far out!"

"Why did you move way out here?" Wen asked. "Don't you like people?"

"Not most of them."

Wen nodded. "I can't disagree with you."

"And what brings *you* all the way out here?" Chips asked, eyeing them suspiciously.

"We're trying to find Lindy," Chase said. "Do you know where he is?"

"Lindy? Don't know any Lindy . . ."

"Curtis Lindbergh. You used to be his teacher. You just told us—"

"Yeah, I remember him," Chips said, looking angry. "But I can't help you none."

"Why? I'm a friend of his."

"Because Curtis Lindbergh is dead."

Chapter Twenty-One

Chase looked at the old man for a moment, panicked, believing him. "I hope that's not true."

"Sorry to break it to you. But Lindbergh died in a lab accident last week."

"No he didn't," Chase said. "I know you're trying to protect him, but I really am his friend."

"Do you know where we can find him?" Wen asked, staring into Chips' weathered face. His bright blue eyes seemed younger than his age. "Please?"

Chips looked up into the white sky, as if wondering what happened to the sun. "That depends on what you need him for."

"So you *do* know where he is?" Chase asked.

"Now I didn't say that."

"You do know."

"Maybe, maybe not. But since you *don't* know where he is, there's a right possibility that he doesn't *want* you to know where he is."

"Because he doesn't know we're looking for him."

"If he wanted you to know, wouldn't you know?"

"Chips, please," Wen said. "It's vital that we find Lindy. Today, if possible. He's in some danger."

"Is that so?" Chips stared at Chase for a moment, then looked at Wen, as if seeking some sort of confirmation. "What if he's in danger from the likes of you?"

"I love Lindy," Chase said. "All I want to do is help him, but that means I've got to talk to him."

"You play cards?"

"We don't have . . . " Chase began before Wen touched his arm. "Yeah. I play some."

"Good. Let's have a game then." Chips led them to the upper deck. "You came here, took my peace, and now the sun's disappeared, too," Chips mumbled as they entered the back door to the cabin. A spiral staircase led upstairs to a circular loft. The structure was much bigger inside than it appeared from the deck. A series of circular rooms connected by spoke-like walkways were drenched in defused light from a number of skylights.

"I like cards," Chips said as they entered a room with large windows. In the center of the small space, a round table, covered with green felt, was stacked with poker chips and several decks of cards "Five card draw?"

Chase nodded.

"Let's say ten dollars minimum, jacks or better to open. What do you want, three hundred dollars to start?"

Wen encouraged Chase with her eyes.

"Sure." Chase opened his wallet, took three hundred dollar bills and handed them to Chips. Half an hour later, Chase bought in another three hundred. It took him only another twenty minutes to lose that.

"Not that good at cards, are you, Chase?"

"Not today."

Wen smiled, knowing Chase had long been known as a card shark among his friends, with the ability to count cards and calculate all the odds in his head. She was impressed he was using his talents to make his losses look legitimate.

"I wish we could play longer, but I'm out of cash, and, more importantly, out of time."

"Hmm," Chips grunted, stacking his chips.

"I've enjoyed the game. You're a damn fine player, but we've got to keep going and try to find Lindy." Chase raked his hair with his hands, then patted his stomach.

"Are you heading to Mexico?" Chips asked, shuffling the cards.

"Is that where he is?" Chase asked.

"It was, last time I saw him."

"How long ago was that?" Wen asked.

"Two or three months ago. You hungry?"

"Where?" Chase asked.

"I tell you what, Chase. I'll whip us up some eggs and bacon, then decide whether I can trust you or not. Of course, I'm not sure Lindy would even want to see you, but guess I don't really have to make that decision."

"We need your help," Wen said. "And thanks, but we're not hungry."

"And I'm gonna give it," Chips said, pulling out a pipe and slowly packing a tobacco blend into it. "You go to Puerto Vallarta, find a man named Ash, and he'll make the decision."

"Ash?"

"That's right."

"You want us to go to a large Mexican city and find a guy name Ash?"

"He's a good listener," Chips said to Wen as he lit his pipe.

"Can you give me a little more to go on?"

"I think his real name is Ashton Stewart, or Stewart Ashton . . ."

Chase looked at Wen for help. "*Where* in Puerto Vallarta do we find him?"

"Go to a bar called el Naufragio."

"The Shipwreck?" Wen asked.

"Yeah, do you know it?"

"No. Never been to Puerto Vallarta, but I speak Spanish."

"Me too," Chips said. "Buenos días. ¿Has visto mi paz?"

Wen laughed. "He wants to know if I've seen his peace."

Chase smiled.

"Does Ash work at el Naufragio?" Wen asked.

"Nah. Ash kinda works everywhere, but he shows up at el Naufragio whenever he's in town."

"Wait, so he might not even *be* in Puerto Vallarta?" Chase, so frustrated he could barely handle it, paced the cabin, looking at pictures and trinkets while trying to figure out how to get through to the 'old kook.'

"He'll get there eventually."

"We don't have *eventually*," Chase implored, picking up a rusty metal box.

"Please, Chips," Wen said. "For the last hour you've been telling us stories about Lindy. Clearly you love the guy, too."

"Like a son. He was my best student ever. Course he ended up teaching me maybe a lot more than I taught him. That ol' container was buried on this land when I purchased it, filled with cigars!"

"There are people who want to kill Lindy," Chase said,

putting the rusty box down again, his voice emotional. "We're trying to save him."

"I'm an old man. Helped you all I can. Go find Ash. He's much younger than me, older than you, but he'll know what to do."

Chase was about to say something else, but Wen shook her head. "We should go," she said.

"Puerto Vallarta," Waxxman said to the pilot after finally hearing from the man monitoring the bug inside Chips' cabin. "Davidson heard enough and says it's definitive. Malone will be heading back here soon."

"What's he waiting for?" one of them asked.

"Apparently the old man is making them play another round of poker."

They laughed.

"Are we going to wait for Malone to come back to the airport?" one of the men asked.

"No. We're going to get a head start on him," Waxxman said. "Joe will hang around and make sure they get on their flight to Mexico. Take us up."

Chapter Twenty-Two

"I've interrogated enough people to know," Wen said while they mounted their horses, "he's not going to tell us more. At least not unless we torture him."

"Maybe we should," Chase muttered as snow began to fall. "He's our only hope of saving Lindy."

"He gave us Ash. Let's go find him."

"Assuming he's even real, and that el Naufragio actually exists. What if Ash doesn't show up until next week? We've only got twelve hours left."

"Ask Tess for more time."

"She won't give it."

"She will if she hasn't already found Lindy. Tess can't kill Lindy unless she finds him."

Chase nodded. "Good point. Still, it's been two or three months since Chips saw him. What if Lindy isn't even in Mexico anymore?"

They rode fast.

The snow grew heavier, making the landscape appear entirely different than when they rode in several hours earlier, when the sun had just cleared the peaks of the Virginia range. The rugged, rocky, scruffy landscape of sagebrush and wild grasses absorbed the snow like a desperate, thirsty animal.

"What do we do if we get to Puerto Vallarta and we can't find the Ash guy?" Chase asked as they slowed to let the horses drink from a shallow watering hole.

"We'll find him," Wen said.

Chase adjusted himself in the saddle. "We may have to consider calling Tess to use her resources to locate him in the surrounding area."

Wen took a sip from her water bottle while she thought about that. They'd been keeping up a pretty good pace, following the trail back to town. Wen scoured the area with her binoculars. They hadn't seen anyone other than Chips all day, but she felt too exposed out in the open.

"You're thinking Tess will still give you the chance to talk with Lindy before she kills him?"

"It would be part of my condition to telling her."

"You trust a lot more than I do."

"I don't trust Tess at all." Chase brushed snow off his jacket. "We'd better keep moving or we might get buried out here."

"Don't worry, I won't let you get lost in the desert."

They rode on, but ten minutes later, were having trouble seeing the trail. "The horses know the way back," Wen said as Chase stopped to get his bearings.

"They may also know the way to lots of other places, too."

Wen glanced over her shoulder and saw four horses riding up fast. "Trouble headed our way in a hurry," she said, pulling a set of digital binoculars out of her pack.

Chase spun around. "They're riding hard, no doubt after us," he said.

"Oh no," she said, staring into the binoculars. "They're Chinese."

"Haw, giddy-up." Chase kicked the horse into a gallop. "I guess I picked the wrong day to learn how to ride a horse."

"Just hang on!" Wen said as she passed, kicking up clumps of snow.

"I assume they're armed?" he yelled as he caught up to her.

"Machine guns. Looks like JH16-1s, China's new 9×19 submachine gun."

"Great, they'll shoot our horses out from under us."

"They've got to catch us first. There's no reason to believe their horses are any faster than ours. They probably came from the same place."

"Maybe they can ride better than me, and shoot better, too."

Even at a full gallop, Wen managed to pull the gun strap around her shoulder.

"What do we do when we get to the stables?" Chase yelled.

"Those four will be dead by then," Wen yelled back.

Chase marveled that she was already planning and looking for a way to get the upper hand. A few hundred yards later, Wen apparently saw what she was looking for and veered off the trail. "Follow me!"

"I wouldn't dream of doing anything else," Chase shouted as the storm worsened. "If my horse can keep up."

"It's not the horse, it's the rider," she yelled back. "Don't worry, yours will follow my horse."

"Why would I worry? I'm on a horse, in the middle of

nowhere, a big snowstorm's bearing down, with four assassins following me!"

But Wen couldn't hear him.

The men began shooting at them.

Chase got his horse next to Wen's as the snow whipped all around.

"They're still not close enough to hit us," she yelled.

"Then why are they shooting?"

"They're taking a chance, before we get away, because they're seeing the same thing I am."

Chase looked ahead and saw some rocky outcroppings—an entrance to what appeared to be a pass between two small ridges. Even without her saying anything, he understood her plan. He'd seen enough Western movies. They were going use their lead, then find a place to dismount the horses and get cover. He recalled in those same movies there was always a gunfight. Chase knew he'd be the worst shooter in the bunch, but they would still win because of Wen.

Suddenly the canyon narrowed. Wen was looking for a spot, an angle, *anything*, as they raced through what might've been a dry creek bed. Chase worried they had boxed themselves in. He yelled to her, wondering if they should make their stand sooner rather than later. She didn't answer.

The snow became blinding. Chase's hands were freezing, making it painful to hold the reins. The canyon abruptly opened into a field and suddenly hundreds of wild Mustangs appeared, sweeping them into the herd. Chase's horse completely stopped responding to his commands. Instead, it followed the herd.

Chase fought to hang on as the horses went faster and faster, sweeping them up over rocky slopes, down through a gully of deeper snow, and into trees. He bounced into the

Chasing Wind

air and barely stayed on the horse. For almost fifteen minutes, they were carried along.

The herd of mustangs must've been well over a hundred head strong. Chase was relieved that for the moment they seemed to have lost the four Chinese agents, but they'd traded that trouble for this new one that he wasn't sure was going to end well. He tried yelling to Wen again, but she was almost twenty feet away from him, caught up in a different part of the herd. Even if she'd been on the same horse with him, she wouldn't be able to hear him above the sounds of thundering hoofbeats.

The stampede and blowing snow created a blinding blizzard. As its intensity increased, so did the speed of the horses. He lost sight of Wen, and wasn't sure he could grip the reins much longer.

Chapter Twenty-Three

A few miles from the Canadian border, just outside Tinker, Montana, two IT-Squads disembarked from a pair of UH-60 Black Hawk helicopters. Their target was a quarter-mile away; however, this was as close as they could land in the thickly forested area.

"Team leader, team leader, this is whiskey-nine. We have target in sight."

Tess paced Mission control, hoping they'd finally caught a break. The site had only been discovered twelve hours earlier. "Due to the sophistication of the construction, I believe there is a decent chance that Lindbergh could be present," Tess said to Dr. Skyenor, who had come to CISS HQ to watch the raid live. "In either case, there is no doubt he was involved in this facility, so at the very least, we're going to gain valuable intel."

"Unless this is another unmanned operation," Skyenor said, wanting nothing less than to watch them take Lindbergh into custody.

"I don't want another Tallahassee," Tess said to the team leader.

"We are prepared for a go-slow, and will be able to loop and bypass any self-destruct systems we encounter."

Tess had already been assured that anything could be disabled. "Let's be sure. This may be our only shot at it."

"Team leader, we are under the canopy. Are you seeing this?"

Tess and Skyenor marveled at the facility. A section of forest had been cleared to accommodate a giant array, which had not been visible via satellite or drone surveillance. A lightweight, camouflaged, high-tech fabric had been hung in the trees to completely conceal the facility and yet allow transmissions to proceed.

"This is definitely Lindbergh," Tess said. "Jay, do you believe this?"

"Lindbergh is apparently quite serious. I would suspect he's got security at that site. But I'd be surprised if he's there."

"Why?"

"Because you found it," Skyenor said, looking at her like *'you're too smart to ask why.'* "If he thinks you can find it, he won't be there."

"But that doesn't mean it's not important."

"Absolutely," Skyenor said, smiling wryly. "If there's personnel inside, we may just have our best chance of finding him yet."

"Team leader, we have detected perimeter security electronic surveillance."

"Circumvent," Team leader said.

"Roger that." The IT-Squad utilized specialized equipment to locate the power feeding surveillance grid and cut it. "We are inside perimeter."

Tess and Skyenor watched as four armed security personnel emerged from one of the buildings.

"They obviously know you've breached the perimeter and shut off their surveillance system," Tess said. "Show them there is no point."

IT-Squads emerged, dressed as FBI agents, wearing Kevlar vests and bulletproof face shields. "FBI, FBI, put down your weapons! We are serving a federal warrant!"

The security guards complied. Tess breathed easier, always happy to avoid killing innocent Americans whenever possible. Two more security people were found inside.

"It's going well," Skyenor said, placing his hands in his pockets and leaning against a wall.

"Take us to the control room," the IT-Squad leader told the security guards. "We're heading to the control room." At the same time they reached the door, another Squad member cut power to the entire facility. "Blow the door!"

"Do not touch a single button!" a Squad member yelled to the personnel at the controls. "Not one more keystroke!"

Both of the people on staff in the control room put their hands on their heads and complied.

"Damn it, we got smoke, we got smoke. They have battery backups in here powering some sort of self-destruct system. *Damn it.*"

The IT-Squads quickly removed panels and drives. Others pulled lines to disconnect power supplies. After a tense few minutes of watching with no updates, one of the IT-Squads leader reported.

"Looks like considerable loss of data. However, there is salvageable data that can be retrieved."

"Well, let's see what we get," Skyenor said. "How long until we can see it?"

"They can link what's left to us now," Tess said.

"Really?" Skyenor started pacing

"Portable hook up to Heaven," Tess said. "Bring those workers back to DC for full interrogation. We want to know everything they know by the end of the day."

A short time later, the transmission came through. "Not bad," a technician in Mission Control announced. "Sixty percent recoverable data."

Skyenor began looking at some of the reports on a smaller monitor at a private workstation. "Wow," he said as Tess joined him. "Lindbergh is even farther ahead than I thought."

"What's he working on?" Tess asked, pulling her hair into a ponytail.

Skyenor reached over and pushed one of her earrings that was halfway out back in her ear. "Changing the future of life on this planet."

Chapter Twenty-Four

The deafening sound of more than a hundred wild horses pounded on until, for no apparent reason, the horses suddenly slowed and split into two groups, as if parted by some invisible force. Chase, looking ahead through the heavy snow, saw what had caused their diversion and was stunned. A man in a leather jacket stood in the middle of the herd, calling out what sounded like Indian war cries, whooping. Several mustangs walked to the him. He stoked their necks until the wild animals became as docile as house cats.

Chase's horse also stopped, and he stared disbelievingly at the man. With brown skin, long black hair blowing in the wind and snow, Chase guessed he belonged to a nearby tribe. The man began petting and talking softly to the horses as more came to him.

For a moment, Chase wondered if he'd drifted into a dream—the canyon, the horses, no sign of the modern world, and a Native American man standing in the middle of a snowy western meadow calling out to the great spirit . .

The entire herd was almost instantly calm, gentle and relaxed.

Wen coaxed her horse back over to Chase and the two of them rode directly to the Native American. "How did you do that?" Chase asked.

At the same time, Wen said, "Thank you."

"I've known these horses a long time," the man said, smiling. "Are you okay?"

Chase nodded.

"Yes," Wen said.

"You might be lost, though?"

Chase, still in his saddle, turned around to figure out where they'd come from and how far it'd been "There's a pretty good chance of that."

"Some men are after us," Wen said, to Chase's surprise. "They have guns and mean to kill us."

The man looked bewildered for a moment, then deep concern overtook his face. "Why would they do this?"

"That's a long story," Chase said.

"We are trying to help a friend. They are trying to stop us." Wen explained simply.

"Are they the law?" the man asked.

Wen looked into the man's eyes. His weathered face made him appear older, but he was probably only in his thirties. "They are Chinese agents. They'll be here soon, and will shoot us."

"How can we get back to town without going back the way we came?" Chase asked.

The man, still staring at Wen, replied, "I might be able to help you. There is a shortcut. My brother and I can take you on our ATVs."

"What about the horses?" Wen asked.

"Did you rent them from Double R?"

"Yes."

"I will get them back for you."

Chase looked out at all the mustangs running free. "Won't that be a lot of trouble?"

"No trouble."

"Let's set them free," Wen said, stroking her horse's head. The man looked bewildered again.

"Rod won't like that that. He'll charge a lot to your credit card to pay for these horses."

Chase looked at Wen. "I don't care," he said. He got down and started trying to take the saddle and bridal off. The man came over and had them removed in seconds. Wen got hers done at the same time.

She said something to the horses in Mandarin and gave them each a swat.

"What about their shoes?" Chase asked watching the Double R horses disappear into the herd, which was now moving away.

"I'll get them off later," the man said.

Chase tried to warm his hands and stomped his feet in what was now four inches of snow. "You think you'll see them again?"

The man smiled. "The horses run through me."

"Can you use the saddles? Chase asked.

"They're not your saddles."

"I'm sure Rod will also charge me for those. They're yours, if you want them."

"All right, I'll pick them up later. We better get going before the danger arrives."

They followed the man at a brisk pace, continually looking over their shoulders.

"My name's Blair, by the way. Blair Grayfeather."

Chase and Wen introduced themselves as they followed Blair through the trees. The snow was falling so hard, their tracks wouldn't last long. A few minutes later, they reached a small cabin. Two ATVs were parked under a crude shelter of long, thin, bark-covered poles and tarps.

A man came out of the wooden front door.

"That's my brother, Tomas."

Blair gave Tomas a very quick explanation of the situation and introduced them.

Tomas took Chase, and Wen got on the back of Blair's ATV, but even before they could start up, Wen spotted the agents through the trees, still a few hundred yards away.

Blair looked over, followed Wen with his eyes, saw the Chinese, their guns, and could tell that they hadn't seen them yet. "We should wait a minute so they don't hear our engines."

"They'll double back as soon as they see our saddles laying in the field," Wen said.

"Can you outrun their horses?" Chase asked.

"Where we're going, no problem."

Chapter Twenty-Five

"Any sign of Chase?" Tess asked one of the techs in Mission Control who'd been working non-stop, reviewing satellite, surveillance, and drone feeds, looking for him.

"Nothing, other than the normal forty or fifty false sightings of him all over the world."

"He's a clever boy, I'll give him that."

"We'll find him sooner or later. It's impossible to stay invisible outside a cave."

Tess nodded while checking one of the screens displaying AI-reviewed communication and data waves across Heaven. "And the Astronaut? Have you traced any of his footprints?"

"Sorry."

"And what's that?" she asked, pointing to another screen.

"Activity around the ex-girlfriend's house about the time he was there."

"Zoom in."

He brought the street closer.

"And move that way . . . Look at who we have there. Is there enough on the driver of the van for facial recognition?"

"Maybe."

"And that blue car was in the feed a few weeks ago, remember? Someone was watching the place?"

"ID on the van's driver is coming back. He's Chinese, but no match yet."

"I'm certain that will be MSS. Damn, Chase doesn't know how much danger he's in."

"I can't even see anyone in the blue car, but I can bring back the prior feed when we had a better view. Caucasian, but we ran him before and it wasn't good enough for a match. Russian?"

"I don't know."

"Where did that car go?"

He keyed in a rapid strings of text and commands until one of the bigger screens clipped through a series of images and video of the car. "Bush Airport, Houston."

"Cross check times, departures, inside surveillance cameras, and tell me who that driver is and where he went."

"Think he's following Chase?"

"I'd bet on it," Tess said, looking again at the Heaven screen. "How many analysts are on the search for Chase?"

The tech looked around the room. "Four, counting me."

"We're going to get you some help." She made a short call. "I've just put eighteen agents from IT-Squads on this. They'll be working on it upstairs, but link into a joint-com with them. We need to know where Chase is right now," she said, still staring at the monitor displaying the blue car. "Who are you blue car man? And why are you following Chase?"

Garcia's sister brought Lindy and Garcia chile rellenos for dinner. It was Lindy's favorite meal. He thanked her and asked her to stay, but she couldn't. They were working late, about to conduct the critical Beta level test that would prove his theories, and, if it went well, his work would be ready for a controlled-environment simulation.

Just as they were finishing their meal, one of the network computers issued a warning.

"Looks like they hit Montana," Garcia said after checking it out. "Tinker Center is offline."

"Damn it!" Lindy said. "Anybody responding?"

"I can try to bring up the last surveillance video," he said, typing. "There. Looks like Americans."

"Same get-ups as hit Tallahassee," Lindy said. "What did they get?

"I don't know."

"Why don't we know?"

"Because it looks like they got everything, including the entire staff."

"Where did they take them?" Lindy asked, typing into his own laptop.

"We may never know."

Lindy pulled up another feed showing two UH-60 Black Hawk helicopters landing in a clearing.

"What's that?" Garcia asked.

"That is a team of US Special Ops soldiers landing to make the raid at Tinker," Lindy said. "Now all we have to do is identify what dark corner of the US intelligence community they work for. Why am I being persecuted for trying to make the world a better place?"

"That's how they always treat geniuses," Garcia said in an affectionate tone, hoping to appease Lindy's stress.

"If I'd started a company and gone public on Wall Street, they'd love me. Instead, there's probably a price on my head."

"Tinker was a critical site. Are you still going to be able to do the Delta and Epsilon tests?"

"I think there's still a way," Lindy said, watching the helicopters take off with his employees. "Unless they come here next."

Garcia smiled, handing Lindy a plate. "Better finish these rellenos before they get us then."

Chapter Twenty-Six

Chase and Wen watched through the trees until they could no longer see the Chinese agents in the distance, then gave the go-ahead. Blair and Tomas started the engines. An instant later, they raced out of the enclosure and were tearing through the woods. As they shot up a steep hill, they caught a glimpse of the Chinese agents turning the horses toward Blair and Tomas's cabin.

"Don't worry," Tomas said. "We've got enough of a lead. They won't catch us."

But Chase knew they were back there, and that there may be more waiting at the airport.

The roar of the ATVs' engines made it difficult to hear, but that didn't stop Tomas from talking.

"What do you do for a living? When you aren't running from foreign spies?" Tomas asked.

"I'm an engineer."

"Cool, you drive a train?"

"Not that kind of engineer."

"I didn't think so," he said, laughing. "Are you a computer engineer?"

"Yes," Chase replied, noticing his voice was getting hoarse from trying to yell above the horses and now the ATVs.

"I code a little myself," the man said. "Hold on!"

The ATV caught air as they sailed over an icy ditch.

"Really, you're a coder?"

"Yeah. I write apps. I'm no Mark Zuckerberg, you know, but I make enough to help pay the bills."

"What kind of apps?" Chase's head was pounding as the loud engine and freezing, bumpy ride took its toll.

"Gambling techniques, discussed as mathematics aids."

A dump of snow fell on them as they brushed too close to a big evergreen tree, its branches heavy with white powder. "I could have used that earlier today."

"Were you at the casinos?"

"No, I got caught up in a poker game with an old man."

"Were you out at Chips' place?"

"Yeah." The ATV slid around a big tree as if a hidden trail required the turn.

Tomas laughed loudly. "Did he at least leave you some gas money?"

"Barely."

"He's a good card player. That's why they call him Chips, you know. I would have guessed you were smart enough to *not* play poker with a guy named 'Chips.'" He laughed again.

"I am now." Chase could barely move his frozen hands. Snow continually pelted his face.

"You like this snow?"

"It's pretty out here, but I prefer summer and a deserted beach."

"Me too. I also did an app on weather."

Chase thought he might fall off the ATV. He wondered if it was just a coincidence. "Really? What kind of app?"

"It's for ranchers and farmers. Predicts the weather and updates in real time based on the current radar, temps, and the like."

"Sounds complicated."

"Nah, I ain't smart enough for complicated. I piggyback data from NOAA and the National weather service and aggregate it for the forecast specifically tailored to ranchers and farmers. Precip and temperatures for the next hour, and twelve hours. Pretty precise."

"Is it accurate?"

"Can predicting the weather ever be accurate?" He laughed. "But, yeah, I get good results. My customers are happy."

"Nice." Chase said, looking back into what now looked like a winter wonderland, with still no sign of the Chinese.

"What do those men want to be killing you for?" Blair shouted to Wen.

"They really want to kill our friend," Wen answered. "We're just in their way."

The ATV bounced over a rut hidden in the snow. "Why do they want to kill your friend?"

"He's a scientist. He invented something. The Chinese are trying to steal it."

"What did he invent?"

"I don't really know. It's classified. Something to do with the environment."

A couple of the ATV's wheels lifted off the ground as he

took a turn too tight. "Your friend, is he trying to help nature, or hurt her?"

Wen looked behind them. It had become more difficult to see as the snow grew heavier, and it would be impossible to hear another approaching ATV over the noise of hers and the one that Chase was riding on just ahead.

"He's trying very hard to help. It's his life's work."

"Duck!" Blair yelled as he swerved the ATV, driving under a large branch weighted down by the heavy wet snow. Wen barely managed to get her head out of the way in time. "You okay?"

"Yeah, thanks."

"Is this invention worth killing your friend, the scientist?"

"They think so." She looked ahead at Chase, barely hanging on to the other ATV.

"And what do you think?"

"Is anything worth killing for?" she asked, avoiding the question.

"I don't know, but there's plenty worth dying for."

"True."

"Are you two willing to die to save your scientist friend?"

"It's beginning to look that way."

"It is a good day to die."

Chapter Twenty-Seven

The ATVs carrying Chase and Wen rolled through the snowy back country, still with no sign of the Chinese agents. The two Native American drivers continued making endless conversation with them. Fifteen minutes later, they suddenly emerged from the woods and parked behind an old grocery store.

"Walk through the parking lot and you'll find a vegetarian diner called Becky's Place. An old hippy runs the joint. He'll let you use the phone, if you need it, to get a car to take you back to the airport. While you're waiting, try the Reshi Mushroom Tonic. Really nice."

"Thanks for everything," Chase said.

"You saved our lives," Wen added.

"Let me pay you something." Chase held out four one-hundred dollar bills.

"No thanks," Blair said. "The saddles are enough. "You'll need that money to pay for Rod's horses. He's not going to be happy about losing them, but he's a good man. He'll respect what you did."

Chase smiled. He believed all living creatures deserved to be free and able to live without suffering.

"But Rod's a businessman. Respect or not, that cowboy will ding your credit card for two or three grand for each horse."

"I know. It's okay. It was worth it to see them go free," Chase said. "Please, take it." He pushed the money toward the men.

"No, we're good. If we take your cash, we lose the power. Understand?"

Wen put her hands together and bowed.

Later, Wen told Chase that Blair had told her they were going to take the saddles back to the rental place because they belonged to Rod and it would save Chase from being charged even more money on his card.

"Why did he tell me the saddles were his payment?" Chase asked.

"He told me that if you thought they weren't going to keep the saddles, you would have insisted on paying them something."

"I would have."

"I know . . . Blair knew, too. Good man."

Chase and Wen were surprised to make it back to the airport without incident. Their plane was the last flight out before the airport closed due to the snowstorm.

As promised, Chase phoned Drina once they were in the air.

"Thanks for calling," Drina said. "Did you find Chips?"

"We did. He's quite a character."

"Isn't he though?" She laughed. "Did he make you play cards?"

"Oh, yeah. Took quite a bit of my money."

"I'll bet! Oh, sorry, poor choice of words." She laughed again.

Chase also laughed. "Yeah."

"But was he helpful?"

"I think so. We'll find out later today. Chips told us that there's a man in Puerto Vallarta who may know where Lindy is."

"Is it starting to feel like a wild goose chase?"

"Definitely," he said, not wanting to worry her with the details of the horse chase and narrow escape.

"That's Lindy. He's always keeping everyone guessing."

"I'll have a talk with him about that once we find him."

After the call with Drina, Chase and Wen ate sushi and tried to relax for a few minutes until Chase announced it was time to check in with Tess.

"Do we have to?" Wen asked, steadying a cup of green tea as a long patch of turbulence jostled the plane.

He took her hand. "Did you think this is what our lives would be? Always on the run?"

"Not sure I know any other way to live." She kissed him. Their eyes locked, both in their silent thoughts—*Kids? House? Normalcy . . . ?*

They smiled at the same time. She eyed him a beat longer.

"What?" Chase asked.

"The MSS is after us again."

"But we survived." The MSS was Wen's biggest fear.

They had made her, and she knew they could destroy her. "They won't get us."

She nodded. "Are you sure you want to call Tess?"

"I never ever want to call her, but we should keep the channel of communications open. We may need her to call off the dogs if we don't find Lindy in time."

"Or even if we *do* find him," Wen said. "I think she plans to kill him, no matter what."

The Astronaut patched Chase's call through to Tess without a trace.

"Well, if it isn't the invisible man," Tess said. "I was beginning to think you'd already found Lindy and had decided to join his band of merry men in Sherwood Forest."

"Nothing yet. But we're on the trail."

Tess wanted to say that he damn sure wasn't in San Diego, but she didn't want to give them the satisfaction. She was certain that Chase knew of her attempts to track him. However, with all the false sightings of the elusive billionaire around the world, he knew how to vanish.

"Where are you?"

"That's not part of the deal. I check in, and I let you know once I've found him. We don't need you and your agents clouding the skies."

"Interesting choice of words. Do you understand this isn't one of your causes, and it's not about your friendship with Lindy?"

"No, I don't understand that. Maybe *you* understand that, but for me, it's about those things."

"That's only because you don't realize what Lindy's messing with."

"You know what I do get? Generally speaking, if the

CIA is trying to do something, more times than not, I won't agree with it."

"Don't you love your country?"

"Whoa! Hold on . . . " Chase blurted as his phone flew off the table from a jolt of turbulence. "I feel like we're in a fighter jet with all this turbulence."

"Sorry about that," the pilot announced over the speaker. "We should be out of the storm soon."

"You still there?" Chase asked Tess, after picking up the phone.

"Weather can be a dangerous thing," she said.

"Touché. And back to your question, I do love this country. I think the United States of America is a great experiment. I'm glad I was born here. I also love the earth, and all the people on it."

"Well, aren't you the great Gandhi of tech," Tess countered, acidic and impatient.

"The problem with you, Tess, is that you think the world is a chessboard for you to play with."

"What are you, thirty now? Because it's hard to tell when you act all naïve and idealistic. Judge me all you want. The fact is, I go to work every day and try to hold the world together. You and I aren't that different, except you want everything fair and equal, everything to balance—and I know it never will." Tess turned to the closest technician in mission control and mouthed, "*Anything?*"

He shook his head. "His signal is all just bouncing and pinging across Heaven."

Damn the Astronaut! she thought.

"Why don't you tell me everything you know about Lindy," Chase said to Tess and winked at Wen. "It may help us find him faster, and might just make me see things from your point of view."

"I'll think about it. In the meantime, try to keep an open mind."

"About what?"

"That your friend might just screw up the world so badly that they won't be able to fix it."

"They? Who's they, Tess?"

"Just find him before it's too late."

Chapter Twenty-Eight

Waxxman had his team of Wrestlers stationed throughout the Puerto Vallarta airport, and two more down by the Los Muertos Pier, an elegant curved structure, shaped like a sail, where most boats to other destinations in Banderas Bay were moored.

He expected to see Chase and Wen arrive at the airport, but in case he missed them, he didn't want to take a chance that they could catch a boat and be gone forever. He suspected Lindbergh was hiding on an island, or at a secluded part of the coast.

"Got him," one of the Wrestlers reported to Waxxman. He sent a photo from his phone. Waxxman checked it against what he had, and noted the large black duffel bags the couple carried. "That's them," he said, "And they're carrying enough weapons to start a small war . . . "

"Worried?" the Wrestler asked.

"Always."

They followed Chase and Wen's taxi to historic old town

Puerto Vallarta. Eventually, they were dropped at el Naufragio, a bar near Los Muertos beach.

Chase checked the street for agents before they entered the funky, authentic, homey bar.

"This is a local's joint," Wen said as they walked through the long, narrow, dimly-lit room, acting as if their black canvass cases containing their weapons were regular tourist luggage. "Better let me do the talking?"

"Why? Because you're so much prettier than me?"

"No, because I speak Spanish and you don't."

Chase nodded, smiling, putting his arm around her as he removed her pack containing the Antimatter Machine and the various guns.

The place was filled with artifacts—some real, some not—from shipwrecks. Not in a pirate loving motif, either. These were serious items—old anchors, brass diving helmets, chests, barnacle covered masts and beams, pulls and rigs, medallions, and even a large locked case that appeared to be full of gold and jewels—the not real part. Mexican rock blasted out on good speakers.

"Do you know a guy named Ash?" Wen asked the bartender in Spanish.

"He keeps a table in the back," the man mumbled, looking at them as if they were cops.

Chase glanced toward the dark end of the room.

"Is he back there now?" Wen asked.

"Hey honey, I don't keep track."

She thanked him, ordered two Negra Modelo beers and a side of fries, and headed to the back.

As they reached the last table, a man working a new Mac laptop under the red glow of a table lamp looked up.

"American?" Chase asked, guessing the man to be in his mid-forties—handsome, tanned, short gray hair.

"Not anymore."

"Are you Ash?" Chase asked.

"Do I know you?"

"Chips sent us."

Ash looked at him, then at Wen. "Really? When did you see that old cuss?"

"This morning."

"This morning? Where was he?"

"At his place outside Reno."

"And how did you get there?"

"We rode . . . horses. Do you mind?" Chase motioned to the other side of the booth for himself and Wen.

Waxxman and one of the Wrestlers went into the bar a few minutes after Chase and Wen. With her back to the door, a position she loathed, Wen couldn't see the men. Ash glanced up, but didn't seem bothered.

Ash smiled. "How is old Chips?"

"He took me for six hundred bucks at poker."

The bartender brought over the drinks and fries as Ash laughed. "So why did he send you here—*this* morning?" he repeated. "Y'all got here pretty fast."

"Salud," Chase said raising his beer. "We're looking for Lindy."

"Lindy?" Ash shook his head and shrugged. He closed his computer and slipped it into a bag on the booth-seat next to him.

"Look, man, let me start over. I'm Chase Malone, and I'm one of Lindy's oldest friends. It's urgent that I see him immediately." Chase reached for the salt shaker.

Ash rubbed the gray stubble on his chin. "He ain't here."

"So you *do* know him?" Wen asked.

"Maybe."

"Can you call him?" Chase asked, shaking salt on his fries, then eating one. "Tell him I'm here. He'll want to see me."

"Come back in five minutes," Ash said.

"Wait, you want us to *leave?*"

"Beat it."

"Come on," Wen said, pulling Chase back toward the front of the bar. She smiled at the bartender as they went by and handed him a twenty. He gave her an indifferent look. They barely noticed the two men drinking Pacificos in a shadowed booth near the entrance.

"How do we know there isn't a back door?" Chase asked. "I think you should just pull your gun and make him take us to Lindy."

Wen smiled. "That's not really how this works. He's calling Lindy now and he just didn't want us to see. He's afraid we might grab his phone."

"That's a good idea. Let's get his phone when we go back in."

Wen chuckled. "Yeah, then we'll drug him with the knock-out gas I have in my fountain pen that isn't really a pen at all, and we'll break into the vault by going through the ventilation ducts. Don't worry, he's going to take us."

"How do you know?"

"I think he works for Lindy. And as soon as Lindy hears you're in Puerto Vallarta, he's going to want to see you."

"Do you really have a pen like that?"

She shot him a goofy look.

Chase laughed, then checked the time. Three more

minutes. He paced nervously and wondered if he should call Tess, wondered if she was watching him right now via satellite or drone.

Chapter Twenty-Nine

Chase and Wen strolled back through el Naufragio bar, nodding to the bartender as if they were regulars. He squinted and scowled like he'd never seen them before.

"You ready to go?" Ash asked as they approached.

"Where?" Chase asked.

"To see Lindy. Isn't that why you're here?"

"Yeah, but where is he?"

"Can't say, but I'll take you there. Five thousand pesos."

"Five thousand pesos?"

"Each."

"Ten thousand pesos for a ride? Where are we going, Guatemala?"

"It's five hundred bucks," Ash said casually. "That's less than you lost to Chips."

Chase opened his wallet and pulled out five hundred American and handed it to Ash, a man who gave the impression of being their old college buddy. "Why so much?"

"It's a long way."

"How far?" Chase asked, afraid their final hours would be spent driving into the Mexican countryside.

"Not that far. An hour by boat."

"Boat?"

"Why is he repeating everything I say?" Ash asked Wen.

"He's stressed," she replied.

"That's obvious," Ash said, handing him a Negra Modelo. "Relax man, you're in Mexico. Nothing here is urgent . . . get it? Mañana."

"Mañana?" Chase asked, and then laughed.

Ash laughed, too.

Wen smiled. "I'm Wen, by the way."

Waxxman and the other man, sitting in a booth closest to the front door, used a specialized piece of surveillance equipment—a digital zoom mic, which would have worked as well if the place had been much more crowded—to listen in on the conversation. Even with the relatively quiet conditions, it only picked up about forty percent of Chase's conversation, but it was enough to know that the man they were talking to worked with Lindbergh, and was going to take them to him via boat.

Waxxman began texting wildly to make arrangements for three boats. He sent a couple of his men south and a few others north so that they would already be out on the water, hoping to avoid any suspicion when they went in the same direction as the boat Chase and Wen were on. He planned to stay back on the third boat and follow at a wide, safe distance. It wasn't a plan he felt that good about, but he could not come up with any alternatives on such short notice. He would've preferred to have some helicopters, satellite reconnaissance, more men, and more boats, but he wasn't with the government anymore. He was also working with a fairly small budget.

Still, he was encouraged. This was as close as he'd come to Lindbergh since the job had begun.

Ash wanted to finish his beer, and the one that Chase didn't drink. Almost fifteen minutes later, he led them toward the beach with Wen and Chase each lugging their black duffel bags. They walked down a crowded street in the warm afternoon sun, the sparkly Pacific Ocean just up ahead.

"Wen . . . that's a pretty name. Fits a beautiful woman like you," Ash said. "You may not be as stressed as stiff-Chase here, but your vibe is also pretty intense. Both of you need lots of Negra Modelo—maybe something stronger."

At the southern end of the Malecon boardwalk, they went onto a concrete walkway, then up to the sail-shaped Los Muertos Pier. Once they reached the end of the pier, Ash spoke to a local man in Spanish. The man called for someone to get Ash's rig, a small covered fishing boat with twin outboards. A few minutes later, another man pulled the craft up to the pier and tied it off. Ash slipped the man some pesos and stepped on board.

"Let's go, mister, I'm in a hurry," Ash said to Chase, laughing.

Chase and Wen climbed on board, maneuvering their gun-filled duffels. As the man on the pier untied it, Ash pulled away. A minute later, they were bouncing over the choppy waters of the bay, heading south along the coast.

"What's your story?" Chase asked Ash. "How long have you been in Mexico?"

"I don't know . . . twenty years? Maybe more. I took a year off from college and I never went back."

Apparently you like it," Wen said.

"I can't imagine me anywhere other than down here. It's a different time in Mexico, a different way of everything."

Chase looked out over the water, wondering if he could figure out a way to save Lindy if they didn't get to him in time.

Chapter Thirty

Waxxman's plan actually worked out fairly well—except for one small glitch.

"I've been out of it for a couple of years," one of the Wrestlers said, "but those dudes over there sure look like Chinese agents to me."

Waxxman took a look, and again would've liked to have had some facial recognition, but he no longer had access. If he wasn't out in the remote wilds of Mexico, he might've been able to call in a favor and get some information, but that wasn't an option either. "Guess we'll have to improvise," he said.

"If they're following Malone, then they're looking for the same guy we are," the man said. "Lindbergh."

"It's not a good development," one of the other men added. "Taking out an unarmed scientist is one thing, but getting caught up in the middle of an MSS operation is another thing altogether."

"I don't have a death wish, Waxxman. If that's MSS,

then we can take them—but *only* if we get some additional coverage."

"I'm going to call Wiest and find out what's going on, what we're missing, what the hell the scientist is working on . . ."

But there was no coverage.

Aznotech chairman Xu Hongbin and MSS Minister Li Dazhao watched as more than a hundred MSS trainees navigated a rigorous obstacle course. "A dozen agents are in Puerto Vallarta, Mexico," Li said as the two men walked along the perimeter of a paved trail, bordered by a mile-long elevated balance beam that circled the course.

"So Lindbergh is in Puerto Vallarta?" Hongbin asked.

"Chase Malone is there, probably on behalf of the CIA," Li said, taking a cigarette from his gold case. "But we don't believe Lindbergh is in that city. It's just the closest major airport to him."

"Then where?"

"Just before I came out here to speak with you, I received a report from the field. Malone and a Chinese woman just boarded a boat heading south along the Mexican west coast."

"A Chinese woman? One of ours?"

"We don't know who she is yet," Li said, lighting the cigarette. "But we're working on it."

"Interesting. And Malone went to MIT at the same time as Lindbergh, so that's their connection."

A cadet ran past them on the three-inch wide beam at full stride, as if he were in a track meet.

"I thought we could have stopped this in America." His

eyes darted back and forth, watching three female trainees leaping over moving laser fences. "The surveillance in Texas told us that Malone was going to Nevada. There we learned they were going to Mexico, but then, unfortunately, they lost him in the mountains."

"How?"

"Bad weather."

Hongbin couldn't help but laugh.

"Irony is amusing," Li said, "if it wasn't so important to the state." He inhaled deeply, letting the smoke fill his lungs. "Just remember, irony can also be cruel."

Two fit young men scaled a narrow tower and then engaged in hand-to-hand combat at the top.

"Why do we think the CIA is involved?" Hongbin asked, trying to shift the conversation.

"Our agents monitoring Malone's conversation at Lindbergh's ex-girlfriend's house picked up a mention of Tess Federgreen."

"Of course. It makes sense that she is involved," Hongbin said, knowing Tess by more than just reputation. He had clashed with her in the past. "Tess is a dangerous woman."

"One of the most dangerous," Li said, looking into Hongbin's eyes briefly, pointedly. The Minister and the tycoon's relationship, mirrored by the two men battling on top of the tower, was clear to both of them.

China was at the forefront of CISS and Tess's initiatives. The communist country's state owned corporations, massive economy, and growing military were the greatest threats to the US government and its multinational companies. No one could deny that, primarily, the US and Chinese corporations posed the strongest chance of igniting corporate wars. The MSS, like CISS, understood that the issue of geoengineering and climate control were among the likeliest flash-points.

"She could easily bring us to open war with the United States," Li said, turning back to the cadets as one of them shoved the other off the tower. The loser fell into a hard net.

Chapter Thirty-One

In the absence of another call from Chase, Tess boarded her private plane, always on standby at Dulles International Airport in Northern Virginia.

"Where are we going?" the pilot asked.

"South," she replied, handing him the itinerary. Then she placed a call to the DARPA Director.

"The Montana results show Lindbergh was setting up for a Delta level test," Dr. Skyenor said.

"Is that a real world—"

"Yes. He'll unleash a storm out in the atmosphere somewhere."

"Storm?"

"A significant storm, to avoid any anomalies of chance."

"Where?"

"We're trying to triangulate based on what we have, but our data is incomplete. However, with the data our intercepts have collected, and by applying simple logic, we can ascertain somewhere in the central United States."

"Can we stop it?"

"Do we want to?" he said in a bedroom voice.

"No," Tess said. "Just find out where so we can be there."

Chase was happy to be in the warm Mexican sun instead of the snowy back country of Nevada—and especially happy to be on a boat instead of a horse.

"Where are we actually headed?" Chase asked, wiping the spray from his arms.

"Tiny little village called Yelapa. No cars, not many tourists, only accessible by boat."

"Why did Lindy choose Yelapa?"

"No cars, not many tourists, only accessible by boat," Ash repeated.

"Makes sense."

"While you're here, I could take you on a sea safari out to the Marietas," Ash said. "It's a really beautiful National Park covering a group of uninhabited islands—pristine beaches, serene. It's the real deal, man. UNESCO protected reserve. Seriously, you might get to see a Blue-footed Bobby. Other than the Marietas, the only place you'll find them is the Galápagos Islands." He winked at Wen.

"I don't think so," Chase said.

"It's a magical journey. Only five hundred to get out there for the day. Then you can relax and unwind, get over some of your uptight gringo world. Oh, and there's this big opening, and—"

His words were interrupted by the sound of gunfire.

"Chase!" Wen shouted, tossing him a submachine gun.

"These guys friends of yours?" Ash yelled, opening the throttle full.

Chase fell backward with the thrust, but recovered quickly and crawled to the stern, joining Wen in returning fire. "Who are they?" Chase asked.

"Wen, here." Ash slid a set of binoculars to her. She scooped them up while staying low, then trained the glasses on their pursuers.

Wen let out a stream of expletives in Mandarin before saying in English, "They're Chinese. Most likely MSS." She looked at Chase for a quick moment, their eyes filled with unspoken grief, wondering if the MSS were after Lindy, or her. Either way, their situation had just grown exponentially more dire and complex.

The Chinese were closing the distance between the two boats. Wen continued to return fire.

"Can we go any faster?" Chase yelled.

"I've got it full open," Ash shouted back. "They've got quite a bit more horsepower than us."

"There must be something we can do."

"I'll see if I can slow them down in the wake." Ash steered the boat sharply back and forth. The swerving motion left a high trailing wake, impossible for the pursuers to avoid. Their boat bounced in the deep wake, slowing them down and making it much more difficult for the Chinese to shoot with any accuracy.

"Nice!" Chase yelled.

"How much farther?" Wen asked while changing ammo clips.

"Maybe seven or eight more minutes at this speed, but we'll sort of be cornered once we get there. It's a small bay."

"Isn't there somebody there who can help us?" Wen asked.

"Can you call ahead?" Chase added.

"It's not like America, okay?" Ash said. "This little village is run by four or five families. They aren't going to like *you* any more than the guys shooting at you."

"Is there somewhere else we can go? Someplace you can lose them?"

"Sure, I can probably get rid of them in the Louisiana bayou, maybe slip on into the Everglades. There's all sorts of backwater channels and places we could disappear to there, but we're here on the seventh largest bay in the world, and there's nothing but a few small coves and the wide open waters of the Pacific beyond."

"What about the national park you were telling us about?"

"That's too far. We don't have enough fuel, and anyway, they'd catch us before we even got halfway there. Yelapa is our only hope."

"Sooner or later, they're going to hit us," Wen said, taking a break from shooting.

"Can't you hit them first?" Ash asked.

"If you can hold the boat steady," Wen said, flashing a smile.

Suddenly, the front of the boat burst into flames.

"What the hell!" Ash yelled.

"That was some sort of projectile," Chase yelled. "They're trying to sink us?"

"RPP-99," Wen said. "Chinese made Rocket Propelled Pyro-99, kind of like a super-Molotov cocktail. If it was an RPG, *then* they'd be trying to sink us."

"There's an extinguisher in the front compartment!" Ash yelled as Chase jumped to the bow to try to put out the flames.

"If they don't want to sink us . . . ?" Chase yelled.

"Damn them," Ash moaned, flipping the bird at the

Chinese. "Shooting at us is one thing, now they're setting my boat on fire!"

"They want to board us," Wen replied.

"Which compartment?" Chase yelled.

Ash peered around the front of the cabin. "The one that's on fire."

"Fantastic." Chase grabbed the cushion from the bench across from the fire and began beating out the flames.

The swerving routine was keeping the Chinese at a reasonable distance, but it was also slowing Ash down. "The next inlet is ours," Ash yelled. "I want to take a wide sweeping turn to try to throw them, but they'll be close enough for those bullets to hit, so . . ."

The cushion Chase was using to extinguish the flames caught fire.

Chapter Thirty-Two

As Ash steered the still burning boat into a long, arching turn, the Chinese continued their straight forward course, bringing them closer than ever. Wen, now shooting out the port side, kept a continual stream of bullets going at them.

"I don't know how long I can keep them pinned down," Wen yelled.

"The fire is totally out of control," Chase shouted.

"Can you drive a boat?" Ash asked Chase above the roar of the motor, the shooting, and raging flames.

"Yeah, but can you put out a fire?"

"Come take the wheel!"

Some of the bullets had penetrated the hull. The awning above the captain's seat was in flames. Ash opened the compartment near Wen and got out some tools, then crawled to the bow and quickly took off some of the rails, which he used to pry open the melting and smoldering compartment. With a pair of gloves he'd gotten out of the toolkit, he reached through the flames and pulled out the extinguisher.

The other boat sped ever closer.

Chase could now see Yelapa, with its traditional, bright, multi-colored buildings climbing the hillsides from the water's edge. "Where are we going?" he shouted.

"Head for the river."

"I don't see a river."

"That stretch of sandy beach over on the left, head for that," Ash yelled while spraying the fire.

"Port side! They're going to ram us!" Wen yelled as the Chinese boat barreled down straight for them.

"I can't go any faster!" Chase yelled.

Ash looked up and checked the oncoming boat, only twenty feet from them. "They'll miss us." A burning chunk of cushion suddenly blew into his stomach. He turned the extinguisher onto himself.

"I don't think they're going to miss," Wen shouted, continuing to fire upon the other boat, now with two machine guns.

"They'll miss!" Ash yelled as the Chinese boat blew by, missing them by mere inches.

Wen had timed her shots perfectly, killing the boat's captain as they passed. "That should slow them down for a few minutes."

"What?" Chase asked, now soaring toward the beach.

"I hit their captain."

"Good work!" Chase yelled.

"Don't celebrate yet," Ash said after the fire extinguisher ran out of propellant. "I'm sure one of those other bastards knows how to drive a boat."

"Here they come," Wen said as she finished reloading. "They'll have to catch us first. Not as easy in the tangle of all this traffic."

Yelapa's small bay was cluttered with fishing boats,

water taxis, luxury yachts, and tourists. There were even a few kayaks and personal watercrafts.

"Careful," Ash warned. "We don't need a collision. The water is almost a kilometer deep here—I don't want to lose what's left of my boat to the bottom."

"Forget a collision," Wen said. "A few more bullet holes and we'll sink on our own, and that fire is *not* helping."

The flames reached around and burned out one of the fuel lines. The boat stalled.

"No!" Ash yelled as he leaped to the stern. It took only a few seconds to get the motor going again, but by then the Chinese were within striking distance.

"You should take over!" Chase yelled, weaving in and out of bigger boats in an effort to elude the pursuers.

"I can't leave the engine," Ash shouted back. "Besides, you're doing fine. Just get to the river."

"*What* river? There *is* no river!"

"Trust me, it's there."

The Chinese, although close enough to fire, appeared reticent. Either they didn't want the attention of a gun battle in the middle of a crowded cove, or they were content in the knowledge that they had Chase and Wen trapped. After all, where were they going to go with such low fuel remaining, a damaged engine, and their boat on fire?

Chapter Thirty-Three

The Chinese, only twenty-feet behind them, were still holding their fire.

Wen had moved to the bow to work on extinguishing the flames.

"That's the river?" Chase yelled. "On the other side of that beach?"

"That's it," Ash called back, still manually holding the line to keep the steering working.

"How do we get to the river?" Chase asked, not seeing where the mouth of it was.

"Listen to me carefully," Ash began. "An extremely shallow channel separates the river from the bay—"

"*How* shallow?"

"Damned shallow. Little kids walk across it."

"The extinguisher is empty," Wen announced.

"Are you kidding? Where is the damned channel?"

"To the left of that open spot of beach."

"That's not a channel!" Chase cried, steering toward it anyway, unsure how the boat would make it across. His only other option was to swing wide around the bay, and that would only take him farther from where he needed to be, and there was no fuel and nowhere to go. He pushed the throttle wide open.

"Go right in the middle or you won't make it," Ash yelled.

Chase had to build up speed while navigating through many more small boats by the shore. "There's a water taxi already stuck in the channel," he shouted. "And the channel isn't even straight. It's a dammed S shape . . . is it even a channel?" He watched a couple of tourists walk across it. "The water is only up to their knees!"

"Avoid that beached water taxi," Ash yelled.

"Thanks for the tip."

"And keep the boat right in the center of the channel."

"Stop calling it a channel!"

"Just stay in the middle or it won't be deep enough. And try to time the waves, we need the extra lift to make it through."

"If you're so good at it, maybe *you* should drive," Chase suggested loudly.

"No, I've only watched the bad ass captains do it. I don't even know how."

"*Great!*"

Chase revved the engine one last time, steered clear of a final sailboat, and raced into the channel.

"Did you catch the wave?"

"No idea! It happened too fast."

They missed the stuck water taxi by inches. A split second later, Chase cut the wheel hard to make the turn into the S curve and caught some sand, but not enough to stop them. After that, he realized the next problem.

Ash was seeing the same thing. "Throttle down!

Chasing Wind

Throttle down fast!" Otherwise they'd never make the turn into the river, and instead would sail across it into the other bank. The boat swayed dangerously as they took the turn, scraping a layer of river rocks in the shallows as they came close to side-swiping the bank, but they made it.

"Nice driving, Captain!" Ash yelled.

As they headed upriver, Chase realized it was too shallow to make it very far. "How is this going to be any better?" he shouted. "We're heading right into a trap."

"Trust me."

"They didn't make it through the channel," Wen announced. "Their boat slammed into the water taxi."

Chase stole a quick glance back and saw that, indeed, the Chinese boat had hit the water taxi and beached. "They took the wrong angle and sped into the channel," Chase affirmed, like a seasoned expert, as they rounded a bend in the river. Suddenly he hollered, "We're out of water!"

"The keel's in the muck and rocks," Ash answered loudly. "Time to bail."

"To where?" Chase asked. "All the Chinese agents have to do is jump out of their boat and run along the sides of the river to catch us."

"Not even," Wen said. "The river is shallow enough to walk in."

"We'll get away," Ash said.

"We're going to have to shoot them," Wen said, pulling out a gun she had just stowed in one of their weapons bags.

"No guns, *no* guns!" Ash yelled. "Chinese are one thing. We don't want the locals after us. We'll make it."

Grabbing a duffel, Chase dropped into the murky water and sank several inches into the silt, but it was only twelve feet to the shore.

"The boat is still on fire. Is it okay to leave it?" Chase shouted.

"Is there a choice?" Ash yelled back.

"No," Wen said.

"Come on," Ash said, running up a steep, narrow path.

Chase and Wen, each carrying half of their precious weapons, looked back, but could no longer see the channel.

"I hope you have a jeep hidden up in those hills," Chase yelled. "I'm not interested in a foot race against guys with machine guns."

"No cars here, but don't worry. I've got horses."

"*Horses?*" Chase yelled.

In spite of the danger, Wen couldn't help but laugh.

Chapter Thirty-Four

Hongbin was in a meeting when he received a call from Minister Li. He quickly excused himself and took the call in the long, wide, carpeted hall outside the conference room.

"Our agents in Mexico have reported in," Li began. "We've got a good lead on Lindbergh's whereabouts."

"Excellent."

"Yes. Unfortunately, they lost them temporarily, but it is a small mountain village on the coast of Mexico. Less than two thousand people, counting tourists. Not many places to hide. We should have him soon."

"Excellent," Hongbin repeated, not sure why he was being given this update.

"How is your progress?"

"Good." He had paced to the far end of the hall and felt oddly cornered.

"Not excellent?"

"We will be ready for the test," Hongbin said, waving off his assistant, who had come looking for him.

"I'm glad to hear that, because we can't count on taking Lindbergh alive. Even if we do, he may not cooperate."

"Hopefully, it won't matter. The test will succeed."

"Excellent," the MSS Minister said.

In Yelapa, the path up from the river met another, wider trail. Wen quickly scanned every direction. Knowing MSS tactics, she expected an ambush. "Clear," she said to herself, momentarily relieved. "Caballos!" Wen said the Spanish word for horses to Chase.

"You really weren't kidding?" Chase said as they reached three mares tied to a fallen tree. "No other way to get there?" He looked around for a vehicle of any kind. "Even a trail bike?"

"You don't like horses?" Ash asked.

"No, it's just . . . " Chase looked at Wen. "I had a bad experience once."

"Ohhh. Well, these are Mexican horses. They don't do bad experiences."

"Then I like Mexican horses," Chase said. "How far is it to the biosphere?"

"About three miles on horseback. Much farther on foot." Ash laughed.

"Don't listen to him, Yegua," Wen said to her horse.

"Whose Yegua?" Chase asked.

"It's Spanish for mare," Wen said, petting her horse on the side of its neck.

Chase shook his head. "You think those guys back there will give up?" he asked rhetorically.

"No way," Wen said.

"They might run into trouble with the locals," Ash said. "Especially if they wave their machine guns around."

"They'll just kill the locals," Wen told him.

"You don't know these locals. They're serious. Those guys flash their guns, and they're done."

"Whoever sent them will send more," Wen said. "I'm sure they're already on the way."

BOOM! BOOM!

"What the hell was that?" Chase yelled, thinking they were under attack again.

"That was my boat," Ash said. "The fire must have reached the fuel tank."

"Sorry," Chase said. "We'll replace it."

"Kind of irreplaceable with the modifications and memories I put into her, but I guess I can make do with a new one . . . A little bigger and with more horsepower."

"You got it," Chase said.

"Thanks, I appreciate that. Guess I have to keep you alive then . . . at least until you get me that new boat."

Ash was about to help Wen onto her horse, but before he could get into position, she was already in the saddle with her duffel. He smacked her leg affectionately. "You're something, now, aren't you!" Ash pulled himself easily up on his horse.

Chase would've like help, but managed.

"You *really* don't like horses?" Ash asked Chase.

"I don't *dislike* them, I'm just much more comfortable on something with a motor."

"Let's not wait around for your friends back there," Ash said.

"Won't they just follow us?"

"Not unless they know where we're going. The jungle is full of long trails. If we get a good lead, we'll be okay."

They were quickly up to a full gallop until they reached a steep grade. Ash, in the lead, set a fast pace. Wen, in the middle, kept looking back to check on Chase and look for agents. Chase, on the third horse, had flashbacks of that time as a kid when he'd ended up lost in the desert. He kept checking behind him for any agents and was relieved, once they got up on the first high point in the trail, that he could see no signs of trouble.

Soon they were completely enveloped by jungle. The trail climbed and twisted, crossing many other trails and forks along the way.

"It's another twenty-five minute ride from here," Ash yelled back.

Both Chase and Wen had their guns strapped across their chests, the rest of the weapons still in duffels tied on the horses. Chase was remembering Nevada, and knew this time there wouldn't be any wild mustangs to save them.

Chapter Thirty-Five

Waxxman and the Wrestlers chose not to follow the Chinese and Chase to the channel. Instead, they pulled their boat up to a small pier in the middle of the cove. The two other boats he'd sent ahead caught up and docked just afterwards.

"What is this little town?" one of the Wrestlers asked as they walked off the pier and past a waterside restaurant.

"You speak Spanish," Waxxman said. "Go see if you can find a taxi driver. They always know what's going on. Two of you stay down here. See what you can find out. The rest of us will go into the jungle and see if we can pick up Malone's trail."

"Aren't we going to track down the scientist?"

"That's the only reason Malone is here. If we catch up to him, we'll have the scientist."

A few minutes later, one of the men jogged back as the group of Wrestlers were walking up a winding cobblestone slope. "No taxis," he said. "Turns out there are no cars in the whole town."

"What? Who ever heard of such a thing?"

"I guess that explains why the roads are so narrow."

"Fan out. Find a bar, or tourist information. Someone around here will know where a gringo scientist is living. There can't be more than one of them in this backwater town."

Chase took another look back, anxious to put distance between them and the MSS.

"When I first came to Yelapa, there was no electricity. It was like another era," Ash said as they slowed the horses to cross a dry creek bed. "Now it's a center of international intrigue—a crazy scientist, Chinese spies—"

"Lindy's not crazy," Chase yelled back as Ash pushed his horse to a gallop and theirs followed. Lindbergh had been a couple of years ahead of Chase at MIT, and although Lindy was only thirty-three, he looked as if he were still eighteen. However, when he spoke on scientific topics, he left no doubt that he possessed endless energy and depth of knowledge, exceeding that of his peers. Chase recalled their good times in college. They had shared a house with seven others. Although they'd stayed friends since those days, as each rose to the top of their respective industries, they'd had less contact with each other. In recent years, Lindbergh had sought so much isolation, he could never easily be found.

Darkness came faster in the jungle. The horses only slowed at switchbacks and the steeper climbs. Ash had explained that Lindy's "office" was located on the other side of the ridge line.

They stopped at a high point and Ash called a friend

who worked at a bar on the beach next to the channel. "My amigo tells me the Chinese dudes were detained!"

"They'll send more," Wen said.

"Maybe, but we're safe for now."

Wen looked down the twisting trail and thought, *What is safe?*

Lindy watched them approach on the cameras that monitored the trail leading to his biosphere complex. By then it was dark enough that their images on the monitors were lit with the ghostly green hue of the night vision filter. He knew the timing of the visit could not be coincidental. Trouble had been closing in on him for months. Each day brought him closer to the end. Lindy just didn't know if it was the end of his life's work, or the end of his life.

Chapter Thirty-Six

Chase and Wen both marveled at the series of futuristic glowing dome structures—one large enough to contain a cruise ship, and three others, each about a third as big. Small amber lights illuminated the area.

"How'd you find me?" Lindy asked, greeting them as they dismounted.

Chase flashed back to having said those exact same words when they'd encountered Tess in Ecuador the day before. "That's a long story, Lindy. So long, I could write a book."

"About our college days, for sure," Lindy said, smiling. "Ash already told me you found Chips, who sent you to el Naufragio. How is the old swindler?"

"Took me for six hundred bucks."

Lindy laughed. "He's quite a card player, but, as I recall, so are you."

"Chase played soft," Wen said. "I'm Wen."

"Oh, sorry," Chase said. "I'm a little out of it."

"Wen, a pleasure. I'm Curtis Lindbergh. My old friends call me Lindy."

"What do your new friends call you?" she asked.

"I'm not sure. I really don't make too many new ones anymore." He looked sad for a moment, and then smiled before grabbing Chase into a hug. "How've you been, Chase? I always knew one of us would get rich, I just hoped it would have been me. Ash, did he tell you he's a billionaire?"

"Nah, he was complaining about my prices . . ."

Chase shook his head and held up his hands defensively.

"But all joking aside," Ash said, "a group of Chinese agents blew up my boat."

Lindy looked at Chase.

"They were waiting for us," Chase said.

"I'm not surprised," Lindy replied. "I'm caught up in the middle of it myself."

"Dealing with the Chinese, the Russians?"

"Maybe I'm looking for something I can't have."

"What's that?"

"World peace . . . I can't help myself. You know, it's attainable."

"Is it?" Chase asked. "Show me the way, brother!"

"I don't know how much time we have until they find this place," Wen said. "We really should leave."

"I can't. We still need to do a Gamma level test."

"What's that?" Chase asked.

"Come in and I'll explain."

Inside the largest geodesic dome, a flourishing pine forest filled the space, as if Lindy had transported it from northern Canada. As they pushed through to another dome, suddenly they were in an Arizona desert, complete with saguaro cactus, rocky ledges filled with barrel cacti and spiny plants, and a stream-fed "lake" about the size of an olympic swimming pool.

"How did you build all this?" Chase asked. "And how did you get all the materials way up here?"

"Burros. The locals are incredibly hard workers. They can seemingly move anything on a donkey, or their own backs. It's no accident that I built here. It's constructed of steel tubing and high-performance glass, steel frames . . . parts of the design go back to Buckminster Fuller."

"I can't believe you created this," Wen breathed.

"Thanks," Lindy said, flipping a switch. "You'll have to wait to see the rest of it in the morning. The area is covered with an anti-surveillance camouflage high tech fabric that we can see out of, but they can't see through."

"Meaning from the air, they see only jungle?" Wen asked.

"Right."

"So maybe the MSS won't find us so quickly."

"Let's hope not," Lindy said, leading them to one of the smaller domes. They entered a room containing an unbelievable rig of computers. "A Gamma level test," Lindy began, "to answer your earlier question, is a controlled environment event that verifies a computer simulation."

"Event?" Chase echoed.

"Weather event."

"So that's what you're doing? Making weather?" Chase asked. "That's what everyone is after?"

"The holy grail, baby!"

"You can actually *do* it?"

Lindy nodded while he typed. A monitor display came to life and showed a swirling storm. "I made that—at least inside the computer."

"And you can do it for real?" Chase asked, staring at what was way beyond simple cloud seeding.

"We'll see in the morning. But, yes. And I plan to make sure it doesn't wind up in the hands of just the United States or China."

"Why?" Chase asked.

"If *one* of them has it, they'll dominate everyone else. Aren't you tired of technology being weaponized or used only for the benefit to the few?"

"Absolutely," Chase said.

Lindy noticed Wen trying to see out of the dome. "Don't worry, I've installed infra-red, night-vision cameras and sensors all along the trail and at key points in the surrounding forest. If we're going to have visitors, we'll know long before they arrive."

Wen smiled.

"Why did you all come looking for me, anyway?" Lindy asked.

"I know a woman who runs a powerful division within the CIA," Chase said.

"The hell with the CIA!"

"You say the hell with the CIA," Wen said. "But what about the MSS, or the Russian SVR RF?"

"The hell with them *all*. That's why I came to Yelapa, so I could do this research without anybody stealing it for their weather wars. *I'm* attempting to solve global warming. *They're* just trying to kill each other, dominate the world, and make more money for their greedy billionaires—no offense, Chase."

"None taken."

"Well, I'm all for your ideas," Wen said. "We work with people trying to do similar things. But, Chase, you should tell him."

"Tell me what?"

Chase hesitated before finally saying, "The CIA's going to kill you tomorrow."

Chapter Thirty-Seven

Chase, Wen, and Ash, had slept in a barracks room inside one of the smaller domes, originally built to house workers during the around-the-clock construction. At around 4:30 in the morning, Lindy woke them. They stumbled into another room of the same dome, where they met Garcia and his sister, who had brought breakfast.

"We're going to do the Gamma test in about thirty minutes," Lindy said. "If all goes well, we can get the data backed up and delivered to the light house by nine AM, and then we can catch the next boat out of here before the CIA-MSS-SVR-RF-MI6-MOSSAD show up." He said all the names of the intelligence services as if they were one long, sinister word.

The night before, Lindy had explained his elaborate backup system.

"I can't back up the traditional way over the Internet—because the data will be hacked—so I created a special method using light technology. I developed a way to make light transmit high volumes of data in several short blinks to a receiver on the other end." Lindy's small, pale fingers tapped the keys as if they had a life of their own. His lips flattened into a grimace of concentration.

"We have that already," Chase said. "It's called fiber-optics."

"No, I'm talking about *photonics*, wirelessly sending data across real distances—miles." He looked at them with a conceited, boyish grin.

"Miles?"

"Yes. LiFi is how I back up my research."

"Light?" Chase asked. "Can't that be detected?"

"My signal looks the same as normal light, and so it attracts no notice. But even if it did, it's impossible to unencrypt without a wavelength key."

"I could see the CIA killing for just that technology," Chase said.

"Light is the fastest and most energy-efficient way to transfer data."

"But don't the rapid attenuation of light signals in microchips prevent it from being used to transmit data?"

"I created a nanosized amplifier to get around that. Signal attenuation is all but eliminated when data is transferred inside the chip." He held a small, glassy marble between his fingers and twirled it in their faces, catching the light.

"From one processor to another?" Chase asked, taking the marble.

"Yes. I used the atomic layer deposition method, a thin film built upon a gas phased chemical process."

"You boggle my mind," Chase said, tossing the marble up in the air.

Lindy snatched the marble in mid-air, and spun it on the desk. "It's a subclass of chemical vapor deposition."

"If that's just how you back up data," Wen said, "I can't begin to imagine how you control weather."

"It's all about the wind," Lindy said, watching the marble spin until it stopped. "Moving the jet stream."

"Chase, did you remember the letter?" Wen asked suddenly, as hearing 'jet stream' had jogged her memory.

"Oh, no, I forgot," Chase said, digging out the letter. "This is from Drina."

Lindy looked puzzled.

"She's how we found Chips."

He nodded, as if that made sense. "How is she?"

"Good," Wen said. "I think she misses you."

Lindy read the letter quickly, then folded it and stuffed it in his pocket without comment.

Wen walked outside to check on the beefed up security Garcia had brought with him—eight locals with AK-47s. She wasn't impressed.

Two MSS agents could easily take them out, she thought. *And even his cameras and sensors can be detected and avoided.*

Wen continued to formulate the plan she'd been working on since they'd arrived at the biospheres.

"Why don't you have more security?" she asked after finding Lindy back inside.

"If someone gets this far, how am I going to defend against them? We have to be gone before they come."

"MSS is not going to be slowed by your sensors, and these men are all going to die," she said, pointing outside the sphere. "We should go *now*."

"They shut down three of my stations in the past two

days," Lindy said. "I can't go until I complete the Gamma test."

"Stations?"

"After Gamma, I do a Delta level test. That's a real-world storm. That requires a network of weather stations and transmission sites."

"Can you still do it?"

"Only if I complete this Gamma test first. Otherwise, it's too risky. Originally we planned it for yesterday, but some of our data went off-line when your friends at the CIA raided our facilities."

"Not *our* friends," Chase reminded.

"I know."

"Wait," Chase said. "When you say Delta is real-world, you mean *out there* . . . "

"In the real world," Lindy repeated.

"You're actually going to *make* a storm in some unsuspecting area?"

"I'm not gonna put it in the city or anything."

"Still, isn't it dangerous?"

"That's why we need to do Gamma in here first."

"About ready," Garcia called.

"Anyway, we shouldn't do too much other than rip up some open areas during a Delta test. Might lose a tree or two."

"Is it really possible to control it that specifically?" Chase asked.

"Absolutely. At least that's what we're going to find out —as long as they don't get too many more of my stations."

"How many do you have?"

Lindy clicked a few keys, then pointed to the largest monitor, displaying a world map featuring blue, green, and yellow dots.

"Dozens," Chase said.

"Sixty-six still operational." Lindy looked proud for a moment. "Anyway, let me review the process for you. Alpha level is the formulas working that prove the theory is sound. Beta is a computer simulation that proves the formulas. Gamma is a controlled environment test that verifies the simulation. Delta is a real world test that confirms the controlled environment."

"And then we're done, you can distribute the data?" Chase asked, referring to Lindy's plan to make the weather control and creation tools available to a number of countries so that weather could not be used as a weapon.

"There's one more. Epsilon is a real world test that repeats the results of the Delta test."

"I don't think we can stay alive that long," Wen said.

"We have to make it to Zeta," Lindy said. "Zeta is a whole new world where, potentially, weather modification is in use every day."

Chapter Thirty-Eight

Dawn's pre-sunrise light had barely illuminated her front porch when Drina answered the door, surprised to see a woman, with an air of some authority, standing in front of what were obviously two federal agents or police of some kind.

"Yes, can I help you?" Drina asked, somewhat hesitantly.

"Miss Snow, my name is Tess Federgreen," the woman said, then introduced the other two agents as her Associates. "I work for a secret task force of the Federal Bureau of Investigation." She opened her identification, showing she was with the FBI. "We're looking for information on a former colleague of yours, Dr. Curtis Lindbergh."

"I'm sorry, I don't know where he is."

Tess studied Drina for a moment as if trying to determine if she were telling the truth. "Be that as it may, I'm certain you will be able to provide us with some help in this matter. May we come in, please?"

Drina stammered for a moment before agreeing, unsure what else to do.

"Thank you," Tess said, nodding to one of the other agents to remain outside, which seemed odd to Drina.

"You say you're looking for Lindy. Why?"

"I'm not really at liberty to discuss the specifics of the case," Tess said, looking around at all the books. "It's a matter of national security. I'm sure you understand."

"But then how can *I* help?"

"May I call you Drina?"

She nodded.

"Drina, based on everything I've read about you, you're a scientist, a very intelligent woman. I may not be a scientist, but I assure you I am also a highly intelligent woman. There's no need for you to insult me or your own intelligence by pretending you don't know why we need to find Lindy." She emphasized Lindy's name as if it were a quaint item, like a child's lost teddy bear.

Drina stared at Tess self-consciously, unsure how to respond.

"Where do you think Lindy would go?" Tess asked, sitting leisurely on Drina's couch, pressing her slacks smooth, one of her cowboy boots resting on the very edge of the coffee table. She looked up slowly, catching Drina's worried expression.

"I really don't know," she replied, as if trying to sell her honesty.

"But that's not true," Tess said, staring like a cat who'd trapped a mouse. "You *do* know, don't you?"

"Yes," Drina admitted.

"Good, so all the games are out of the way. Why don't you tell me what you told Chase Malone."

Drina shifted uncomfortably, clearly surprised that Tess knew she'd met with Chase. "I, I am not, I mean…"

"Remember, Drina. We're done with games, right?"

Drina nodded. "Chase Malone? I don't . . . how do you . . ."

"Drina, please, you're trying my patience, and wasting my time. Chase Malone was here, and you told him to go see someone in Nevada. Don't embarrass yourself anymore, and don't make me have to issue threats. Instead, simply fill in the blanks for me. *Who* was he seeing? *Where* in Nevada? And *why*?" She glared at Drina while at the same time smiling—an unusual trait that Tess had mastered to insidious perfection.

"There's a man named Chips. His real name is something Anderson. Chips is an old friend of Lindy's. Chase came here looking for Lindy, and like I told you, I really don't know where he is, but I thought that Chips might, so I suggested he go and see him. He lives in the Virginia Mountains outside of Reno, Nevada."

"And did Chase find this Chips fellow?"

"I don't know."

"Drina, you're not playing by the rules we agreed upon. I'm a few seconds away from asking Agent Keswick here to read you your rights and handcuff you. Is that what I have to do?"

Drina fidgeted with the collar of her turtleneck, glanced at Keswick, sighed, and then looked down at the worn wooden floor. "Chase found Chips, yes."

"And?" Tess said, trying not to sound too exasperated. "What did Chips tell him?"

"He didn't . . ."

"Careful, Drina, because the fact that you're taking so long to answer, that you are hesitating, that you are not looking at me, are all signs that you're foolishly attempting to conceal the truth."

"No—"

"Watch it!" Tess' words were harsh. "Chips told Chase where Lindy was, so don't lie and say that he didn't. Tell me what Chips told Chase, right now."

"He told him that Lindy is in Mexico, that . . . " She began fidgeting with her shirt again. "In Puerto Vallarta."

"Good. Now, that wasn't so hard, was it? *Where* in Puerto Vallarta?"

Drina shook her head. "Chips doesn't know. He really *doesn't* know."

Tess regarded her subject for a brief moment. "Okay, you're telling the truth. But surely Chase isn't going to go into a city the size Puerto Vallarta and just start hollering out Lindy's name hoping that Dr. Lindbergh will hear him."

"I told you what I know," Drina said angrily. "Maybe you should ask Chase, or take agent Keswick and go down to Puerto Vallarta yourself and see if you can find Lindy or Chase or whoever . . . I hear Mexico is beautiful this time of year."

"A little spunk. I like that," Tess said. "However, your suggestion is a trifle inefficient. Although I must say I could do with a little beach time, I'm a bit busy at the moment. So I wonder if you would do me a favor and give Chase a call and ask him if he found Lindy and where he is right now." Tess looked at the coffee table where Drina's phone happened to be sitting on top of a copy of a Clive Cussler book.

"Call him right now?" Drina asked.

"Yes," Tess said, widening her eyes and smiling. "You have his number."

Drina stared at the phone for several seconds, then

shook her head. "No, I think I'd like to call my attorney instead."

Tess frowned. "Oh, would you? If you'd really like to call your attorney, I can help with that. Agent Keswick, please handcuff Miss Snow and read her her rights. We'll take her to the airport. She'll fly to Washington DC with us, where she can be officially charged."

"Charged with what?" Drina asked in a shaking voice.

"Oh, it'll be a long list," Tess said. "I'll tell you on the flight. And that'll just be until we can convene a grand jury. They'll indict you for dozens more crimes. Don't worry, as soon as we get to DC and you're officially fingerprinted and charged, you can call your attorney . . . *or*, we could forget about all that, and instead you could just call Chase right now."

While shivering and sweating at the same time, Drina reached for her phone with trembling hands.

"You make sure to *only* call Chase, understand? Or there'll be no more deals, only more charges."

Drina nodded, found Chase's number, and tapped the screen to connect the call. As the phone began ringing, Drina had a sick feeling that this might be the last call she'd ever make.

Chapter Thirty-Nine

Just before the Gamma level test was to begin, Wen went back outside to give the eight local men with AK-47s some basic anti-MSS training. At first, they weren't sure what to make of the skinny Chinese woman, but her challenge, given in fluent Spanish, to have all of them take her down intrigued them.

Thirty-seven seconds later, all eight were on the ground and ready to listen.

She spent almost twenty-five minutes giving them pointers of what to look for, how to defend, and when to retreat into the jungle they knew so well. They thanked her, and she could see they appreciated her lesson. Wen went sadly back in to watch the demo, knowing that if the MSS found the biosphere, even after her lesson, each of those men was going to die.

Lindy was in the middle of telling Chase about the history of weather control. "Most climate scientists know about Project Cirrus, an operation to artificially modify a hurricane, started in 1947. Project BATON, Project StormFury, kept pushing the limits. But there were dozens of other highly classified programs that are still kept secret to this day."

"People don't want the government playing God," Chase said.

Lindy scoffed. "The government does it anyway. From 1967 to 1972, the US government spent *millions* on a program run by the CIA to make monsoons stronger and last longer in Vietnam to hamper the Viet Cong and damage enemy supply routes. Weather as a tactical weapon is real."

"Why don't we hear about it?" Chase asked while Lindy made the final preparations for the test.

"In 1978, the United Nations banned weather warfare."

"Because it can be used to incite uprisings, civil wars," Wen said, "based on damaging food supplies and disease based on floods. It's a dangerous thing to mess with nature."

"Yes," Lindy agreed. "However, it can be used to reverse global warming by keeping it cold over the ice caps, we can grow crops where they couldn't grow before. Imagine ending drought and floods."

Wen looked doubtful. "The biggest militaries in the world will always turn something good into something evil."

"I've created the biospheres to study the effects of weather manipulation," Lindy said. "As you can see, outside is a jungle, yet inside the biosphere, we have duplicated the environment and temperatures of an arid desert climate. The other spaces include a northern pine forest, and one of a fertile area similar to the great plains in the United States."

Chase pointed to the large monitor displaying Lindy's stations around the world. "That one just blinked to red and then went dark."

"It appears somebody, most likely the CIA, has located another one of my stations. All my facilities have fail-safes, meaning when security is breached, it will shut itself down and destroy data so they won't be able to find the links to the other sites."

"Will that lead them here?"

"No, you're the blame for that," Lindy said.

"*I'm* not the one building a doomsday weather bomb. Anyway, they were already coming for you."

"Not this soon," Lindy said. "None of my stations link here. The only way in was through Ash."

"You underestimate the CIA," Chase said. "Especially Tess Federgreen and CISS. Apparently she has quite the crush on you."

"Maybe. It doesn't matter now. We're where we are. But I need to complete this test so I can do a Delta level before they shut down any more of my stations."

Drina had been relieved when Chase didn't answer his call because he was out of range. Tess had already tried to track his phone, and hadn't been surprised at the lack of success. She knew Chase and Wen had become experts at staying invisible. A CISS agent remained to keep Drina's house under surveillance, but otherwise left her alone.

Tess considered staying in Texas to be closer to where

Chase and Lindy were, somewhere in Mexico. The CIA had several facilities in the state where she could "set-up shop." However, she decided that the situation was too critical, and it would be best to command from Mission Control.

On the plane, she reviewed the latest ninety-eight sightings of Chase—none of them real. She vowed to find out how he was doing it. Then she read the latest report from Skyenor. After digesting the troubling conclusions from the DARPA director, Tess poured herself a scotch and stared out the window at the layers of clouds, wondering if she was seeing the start of war.

Tab arrived at Drina's home not long after Tess left. Drina, still shaken, told him about the encounter with Tess.

"So why is the FBI after Lindy?" Tab asked.

"She didn't say, but you know why? He's trying to sell his invention to the Russians and Chinese."

"Lindy is crazy. Did he think the government wouldn't find out about that?"

"Do you think they'll find him before . . . "

"I wonder if he's done the test yet. He can't sell it if he hasn't proven it."

"I called Chase again after the FBI was gone, but he must still not have service because it went straight to voicemail. I left a message and told him that an FBI agent named Tess Federgreen was here looking for Lindy."

"Why?"

"If they know, they can warn Lindy."

Tab looked at her.

"Lindy will run, and if he hasn't done the test . . . "

"I'm surprised you don't know him any better," Tab said. "Lindy will never run unless he's completed Gamma and Delta level tests."

"You're right."

"Don't worry. They'll find him in time."

Drina's eyes teared. "I hope you're right."

Chapter Forty

Chase checked his voicemail through the Astronaut's encrypted system. "Drina called. Tess just paid her a disturbing visit. Claimed to be FBI."

"Looking for Lindy?" Wen asked.

"Yeah. Tess threatened Drina. Scared her enough that she told her about Chips and Puerto Vallarta."

"Great," Wen said, checking her watch. "How much time do we have?"

Chase shook his head. "Not enough."

"Hey, I'm heading out," Ash said while drinking one of Lindy's Mexican Cokes.

"Where're you going?" Chase asked.

"I've got some business in town to take care of."

"Business?" Chase echoed. "This early?"

"You can bet it's nothing legitimate, or useful for the public good," Lindy said, walking in from his office.

"What you talking about?" Ash protested. "I keep this town running."

"I'm surprised it's just the town," Lindy said, laughing.

"Actually, it's quite difficult to imagine Mexico getting along without me," Ash said with a smile.

Chase and Wen, in the very short time they had known Ash, had grown quite fond of him. "You'll let us know if the Chinese agents are prowling around town," Wen said.

"Of course," he promised, giving her a hug.

"And watch yourself," Chase said. "They may well be able to identify you as the man on the boat with us."

"My poor boat."

"I told you, a new one's waiting for you in Puerto Vallarta," Chase said, having already called his financial representative, Adya, to make the arrangements. Without telling Ash, he'd purchased a much nicer boat as a replacement.

"I know," Ash said, patting Chase on the shoulder. "I really appreciate it, man. And that's one of the things I'm going to do in town—arrange transportation for us back to PV."

"Just remember what happens when you leave Shangri-La," Lindy said, referring to the nickname he'd given the biospheres after the fictional and legendary village in James Hilton's 1933 novel, *Lost Horizon*. Shangri-La was a mythical utopia in the Himalayas. Its inhabitants, whose lifetimes spanned hundreds of years, showed no outward signs of aging.

"Paradise is a state of mind," Ash said. "Shangri-La isn't a place that I visit, it's who I am." He winked.

"I believe you might be a mystic after all," Lindy said, laughing. "Just don't forget to replenish the coke when you come back."

"*Au revoir*," Ash said with a final wave.

"Dude," Garcia yelled after him, "we're in Mexico, it's *adios*!"

"We may be in Mexico," Lindy said, "but Ash is in Shangri-La."

They headed back into the control room, happier than they should have been.

"Gamma level countdown," Garcia said.

"I still don't know how you're going to do this," Chase said. "I mean, I *get* cloud seeding, but . . . "

"Cloud seeding is nothing compared to altering temperature. I've devised a way to precisely control temperatures at all levels in the atmosphere, which means we can manipulate the jet stream, the winds, move clouds, and produce storms in blue skies."

"My God," Chase said. "The weather wars *are* real."

Waxxman had grown frustrated with Yelapa, calling it the most backwards place on earth. "Who wouldn't want cars?" he said. They'd spent the night in some drab, open-air, concrete home upriver since "anything decent was long-ago booked."

"This isn't the same river as the one Malone blew up that boat on?" one of the men asked, confused.

"No," Waxxman said. "Different river."

"Because, apparently, the scientist lives up in the jungle somewhere, in a big dome or something, but no one can tell us exactly how to get there. Just that it's beyond the waterfall."

"This river has a waterfall," Waxxman said.

"Different waterfall," another Wrestler said. "Each river

has at least one. I talked to some people." He showed them a map, which showed both rivers.

"Let's head that way," Waxxman said. "And find someone to pay. Throw some American dollars at them. We need to find Lindbergh before those Chinese agents do."

"Why not just let *them* kill him?"

"Because I suspect they didn't come to kill him. They're here to grab the scientist and take him back to China."

Chapter Forty-One

Lindy turned to Garcia and tossed him a flash drive. "Ready?" he asked Chase and Wen as Garcia jogged to the other end of the biosphere.

"So you're really going to make it snow in the desert?" Chase asked.

"Not just snow," Lindy said, smiling. "It's going to be a blizzard."

"All set!" Garcia yelled.

"How is this going to work?" Wen asked. "I understand cloud seeding, when they shoot silver iodide into existing clouds or drop it in from planes."

"Right, the moisture already present is attracted to the seeding agent—dry ice or silver iodide. It acts as a nuclei, causing the water vapors to condense, thereby increasing precipitation. Simple," he said, moving his hands across a large touch pad.

"I get it, you can make snow or rain, but how are you going to create a *blizzard*?" Chase asked

"If we move the vertical air currents, additional

moisture will move into the clouds, and by adding heat, the upward drift of the thermals will bring about further increase to the available water vapors, which will cool and crystallize into ice. The entire micro physical process occurs at the cloud interior." Lindy keyed in long strings of code he had apparently memorized.

Garcia ran along the side wall until he came to a rock formation. After manipulating some kind of switch, a panel was revealed, full of gauges and buttons. After pushing several to set up a sequence, he jogged back and joined the others.

"You're right to ask though, because conventional cloud seeding will only increase precipitation by around twenty percent, and that's *if* the clouds were already present. In a blue sky, the traditional methods are ineffective—can't get blood from a stone."

"Then what do you do that's different?" Chase asked, looking at the thermometer—thirty-seven degrees Celsius, which he didn't need to be told was around a hundred Fahrenheit.

"Storms in the colder months are a little different than in the summer. They derive their energy when air masses of differing temperatures and moisture content clash. Imagine cold dry air hitting a warm air mass—that's how a front is created. Typically, in the United States, it's generally a Canadian cold air mass colliding with Gulf moisture. Cold surface air combining with warm moisture-filled air from the Gulf gets lift and rises . . . then boom, down comes precip!"

Lindy continued typing commands while he spoke.

Wen checked the bank of monitors.

"Still clear," Chase said, noticing her looking at them.

"But for how long? It's amazing they haven't found this yet."

"They will," Lindy said." However, I chose this location carefully. I'm sure you noticed on the way that it isn't easy to find without a guide."

"Can't be too hard from the air," Wen said.

"That's what the canopy is for. It completely conceals the entire campus."

Wen didn't want to get into a debate with a technology genius about all the ways the Chinese MSS could see through his special fabric.

"Back to the lesson?" Chase asked.

"Cloud seeding isn't controlling the weather, it's simply manipulating the weather, making clouds produce a little more than they were already going to do," Lindy said, pushing a button, which closed off the space they were in with what was essentially a gigantic sliding glass door. "To actually *control* the weather, you must control the wind."

"How do you do that?"

"Airflows from high pressure to low pressure," Lindy said. "And that is simply what causes wind. The Earth's rotation is obviously a factor, but if you can change air temperatures, it's really not that difficult to create the desired weather."

"It can't be *that* easy to change the temperature of such huge volumes of open air," Chase said. "And even if you could, I can't imagine that it would be possible to do it by any significant amount."

"That's because you are not a climate scientist," Lindy said. "And it doesn't just require a brilliant mind like yours, but also a great imagination. Watch."

Lindy pushed a final button on the keyboard and, almost instantly, the temperature began to plummet. First it was just flurries. However, within a few minutes, Chase was shivering, and the snow was pounding.

Chase, although impressed, wondered if it was all just computer manipulation of the self-contained environment. "Are you just adjusting the air masses temperatures with the computer?"

"Where would the fun be in that?" Lindy mused. "Besides, couldn't very well get away with doing that out in the real world, could I?" He pointed to the far back corner of the biosphere. "That's what's doing it."

Chase and Wen noticed, for the first time, some kind of radio antenna dish. "Where did that come from?" Chase asked.

"Normally I keep it covered," Lindy responded. "It's an IRI."

"A what?"

"Ionospheric Research Instrument. It's a high-powered radio frequency transmitter operating in the HF band. It excites small areas in the ionosphere—but don't worry, it's only temporary."

"In English?"

"Were heating the atmosphere, changing temperatures," Lindy said proudly. "But if that's all we were doing, it wouldn't be anything new." He hit a few more buttons. "Pay close attention to this now."

A series of almost invisible laser beams, coming from different angles around the biosphere, climbed into the internal "sky," resulting in an immediate change. The winds exploded into hurricane force, and there was so much snow they could no longer see inside.

"There's someone in there!" Wen suddenly shouted, pointing inside. She grabbed her gun and ran to the sliding door connecting the domes. "Stay out here and cover. There are probably more."

Lindy checked the camera monitors and sensors.

The large sliding glass partition couldn't be opened in the middle of the blizzard, so Wen went around to a side door.

"The indicators all read clear," he shouted.

"I saw someone!" she yelled back as she slipped into the sphere.

"Be careful, that's a real storm!"

Chapter Forty-Two

Even though the sensor showed no one approaching the biosphere, and neither he nor Lindy had seen anyone inside, Chase ran outside to warn the guards.

Wen, armed with her Glock 19 and HK MP5N 9mm submachine gun, had to fight her way in through the turmoil of winds and blinding snow. She only had a light jacket on, and could not believe the drastic change in temperature. The interior temperature had gone from a hundred to below freezing in less than ten minutes. Although she'd seen on the gauges that six inches of snow was already on the ground, stepping through it was an entirely different sensation.

"There are drifts in here that have to be two feet deep," Wen shouted, even though they couldn't hear her. The shocking realization hit her as the force of bitter cold air blasted icy pellets of snow onto her face.

Lindy had done all this. He had used technology to create a real and brutal storm out of nothing.

"The world will never be the same again," she whispered, her words lost in the wind. "He is just a man, a man who has become a God—a weather God."

Unable to see Chase and Lindy, Wen trudged through the snow, searching for the man. As she walked, a cactus fell in front of her, unable to withstand the blizzard. Wen recalled the world before, the hot, arid desert they had been standing in fifteen minutes earlier—now transformed into an Arctic wasteland. She was having a tough time keeping her footing now, with no sign of the intruder.

This is a deadly storm, she thought, *an actual weapon. No wonder the MSS and CIA are willing to kill for this technology. Does Lindy even realize what he's done?*

The rawness of the storm, tasting the authenticity of a manufactured blizzard that felt as real as any weather she'd ever encountered, scared her more than she'd ever been in her life—not of the swirling blinding snow, rather the potential of what man-made weather would do to civilization. She was freezing, and thought that if there was anyone else in there, they must be frozen by now.

What if they've gone out and attacked Chase and Lindy? I've got to go back.

Suddenly, Wen realized she didn't know which way was back. All she could see was white. Her hands felt like ice, her feet were numb, her face hot with wind burn.

There's no direction to get my bearings. Wen took her best guess and moved as fast as she could. *Why doesn't he shut down the damned storm? There has to be nine inches of snow now.* The drifts were everywhere, towering walls of snow up to four feet high. "Hey!" she yelled. "Hey, can you hear me?"

If I go far enough, it won't take long before I hit a wall, then I can follow that back. But even then, I don't know what direction to go. She laughed a worried laugh as she wondered if, after all she'd been through, she might actually freeze to death; dying here while Chase was in the next room.

Chase found Wen feeling her way against the outer wall. He had fought through the white-out after arguing with Lindy to shut it down. The scientist had insisted she was still okay, that it was too soon for frostbite. He had to finish the full run of the storm to be certain everything worked as designed. It could not be stopped.

"You're okay," Chase said, warming her with his body while rubbing her back.

"Where . . . are . . . we?" she asked through chattering teeth. "How?"

"The biosphere, Mexico. The storm isn't real."

Wen looked at him as if he'd told her he'd traveled in time from the future. "Not *real*?" she said in angry disbelief, shivering uncontrollably.

Chase got Wen back into the warmth of the control room. "Look at her," he yelled at Lindy. "You should have shut down the damn storm!"

"Look, I'm sorry that happened to her," Lindy said. "But every minute counts. We may not have another chance to repeat this simulation. Those agents you led here are in Yelapa. They are going to find us, and when they do, this place will be destroyed, and there'll be no other opportunity to test the system."

"It's okay," Wen said, coming back to herself. "No one else came out?"

"No."

"Then he's dead," she said flatly.

"I didn't see anyone," Chase said.

"But you were in there, and you saw something more frightening than an agent. Didn't it scare the hell out of you? That a man could create *that*!"

"I was just trying to rescue you," Chase said softly.

"Up until half an hour ago, what just happened and is happening inside there," Wen said, pointing to the storm, "was just the purview of nature. But now he's made himself a weather God."

"Aeolus, keeper of the winds," Lindy said while checking readouts. "Greek mythology."

"But this isn't a *myth*," Wen said, much stronger now. "Remember Lyndon Baines Johnson, 'He who controls the weather controls the world.' He's done it. Lindy has conquered nature. Everything in nature—the entire ecosystem, Earth's environment, the planet itself—is dependent on the weather. And now, all of that is dependent on him."

"Thank you," Lindy said, taking a bow.

"You may be a good man, but it won't take long before someone gets a hold of this with ideas that are different than yours or mine, and then what? How long before lives are destroyed, whole regions are wiped out, death tolls in the hundreds of thousands, probably millions—how long? And if we start playing God with the weather . . . you think we're going to do it right? Because we're not a perfect God, we'll screw it up. In what? In a year, five, a decade? Will it take a century before we destroy the environment and make life on this planet impossible?"

Chapter Forty-Three

Through the glass top of the biosphere between the spaceframe, Chase saw a helicopter approaching in the distance. "That looks like trouble," he said, pointing it out to Wen.

Lindy pulled out a tablet computer and began tapping away. "I'm assuming we're going to be outnumbered, and that you won't be able to fight them off," Lindy said, still not looking up from his work.

Garcia burst into the room. "The sensors picked up an incoming helicopter!"

"Do you know how to use one of these?" Wen asked him, showing him a MP5N submachine gun.

"How hard can it be?" he asked in accented English. "Just point and shoot."

"Something like that," Wen said, handing him the gun and an extra magazine. "You can't really go wrong with this." She showed him how to reload. "Just make sure you aren't shooting anywhere near the general direction of the good guys."

"Got it." Before turning away, Garcia met Lindy's eyes and saluted him.

"What about you, Lindy?" Chase asked.

"Yeah, if you've got an extra one, I'd love a gun."

"Sure," Wen said, laying one next to him. "Do you know how—"

"I'm a Sig Sauer man, but I don't mind using Heckler and Koch. However, I prefer the MP7."

Wen nodded, impressed, as she switched his gun out for an MP7.

"Thanks," he said. "We've got to get the backup with the Gamma test results to the lighthouse, so we can't be fighting to the death here."

"Is there some other place you'd like to fight to the death?" Chase asked.

"Actually, none come to mind."

"Good, because I generally try to avoid fighting to the death. I like pizza too much."

"You could have said you like Wen too much," she said, hitting Chase playfully.

Lindy pulled out a large flash drive and handed it to Wen. "I believe you're the most likely to survive." He looked at Chase. "Sorry, old friend."

"No offense taken. You're probably right,"

"Especially since he'll be eating a pizza," Wen said.

"Head up to the lighthouse," Lindy said to Wen. "Once you get to the top, you'll see an old rusty green metal panel. Reach under that and you'll find a very small lever about the size of a paperclip. Pull it down. A compartment with just enough room to insert the drive will slide out."

"Looks like ten agents have dropped out of the helicopter," Garcia interrupted. "I'd say we've got about two minutes before they get here."

Lindy gave Wen the remaining instructions for how to position the light to transmit the data to Puerto Vallarta.

Wen quickly gave instructions on the best way to defend the facility, and ran out to check on the eight guards.

"What are you doing?" Chase asked Lindy, who was back on the computer.

"I'm making final preparations to destroy all the data."

"So all we have is what's left on the drive?"

"That's about it," Lindy said. "It'll be on the timer, so even if we die, the data will be destroyed."

"And if we live?" Chase asked, readying his weapon.

"Then I'll have time to stop it. There are some other parameters at play, too."

"I'm sure there are."

"Nice gun," Lindy said, picking up the MP7.

"What if they get the drive that Wen has?" Chase asked, a pained expression on his face, knowing the only way anyone could obtain it would be to kill her.

"The encryption is impenetrable. The key is hidden in PV."

Even before the agents reached the biosphere, the cameras installed along the trail had confirmed they were Chinese. Wen shuddered, knowing the skill level of the ten MSS agents.

She told the eight guards that they should leave, but they refused, even when she told them that the men coming were like killing machines.

Once the agents get past them, then it will essentially be eight against one, Wen thought. *Or worse, because I have to keep Chase and Lindy alive instead of just worrying about saving myself.*

But the mission, from her own training, was simple. Kill ten people. That's what she had to do. If she was lucky, Chase, who had been improving in his weapons handling, might prove more of an asset than a liability. The other two, however, she had less hope for. Only the fact that they were now armed with submachine guns and could hardly miss gave her a glimmer that they might prove effective.

Her big advantage was knowing MSS tactics. She knew they would enter in pairs, in intervals of approximately ten seconds. The first ones would disperse smoke, the second would bring fire, the third would pick targets based on the cameras worn by the first two teams. The fourth and fifth groups would react to what had happened in the prior thirty seconds—more difficult for her to predict.

Wen had her people stationed as best she could. She watched the monitors. It took less than nine seconds for the eight local guards to die.

The MSS suffered no losses outside. The first two agents burst into the biosphere under a shroud of smoke and machine gun fire, knowing they would not have the element of surprise. Wen hoped the controlled environment, its terrain unlike that of the Mexico coast, would throw them off. The agents entered through the desert, which afforded them little cover. The sandy ground, still soggy from the Gamma level test, bogged them down. As the smoke cleared, Chase was able to pick one off, but that immediately drew the fire of the other one. Wen waited, thinking Lindy would be able to get the other one before he got to Chase. Lindy came out from under the bridge where she'd positioned him and took out the MSS agent with one impressive burst.

He's had training, Wen thought. *That was not a lucky shot. Maybe we have a chance.*

She had given them each second and third positions to go to whenever they blew cover because the agents wore body cams—which meant even if they were shot, their comrades would know exactly where the attack had come from, and possibly even still be able to view the area.

Wen expected the next two in three seconds, but ten seconds came and went with nothing. She looked around, worried the agents were deviating from standard procedures, and then she realized what was about to happen.

"They're coming through the walls!" she yelled loudly, unfortunately knowing the agents would also hear. An instant later, the shattering sound of exploding glass and steel echoed throughout the enclosed space. MSS agents poured in from three other points. They blasted, bombed, and shot their way through the walls in a hellfire attack.

Chapter Forty-Four

Garcia's hiding place, exposed to the exterior wall, left him simply in the wrong place at the wrong time. He took a shot in the back and never knew he'd been fatally wounded.

Wen's position, still hidden in the upper catwalks, gave her an advantage by design. She took out two agents at once by utilizing her training and knowledge of their tactics, shooting out their legs first and, as an expert marksman, while they went down, put bullets in their exposed necks.

"Six remaining," Wen whispered to herself.

Two agents that had taken shelter behind some cactus and large boulders began shooting up at the catwalk, but Wen was already gone. She'd slid down one of the supporting poles and landed, still above the ground, wedged between part of the exterior wall and an air exchange system. She had a clear shot at one of the agents, but then no escape. She had a rope, but would have to wait before shooting or descending further.

Lindy suddenly appeared from behind a small prickly pear and viney, cacti covered sand dune. At almost point-blank range, Lindy executed one of the agents. At the same moment, Wen shot the other one, and then swung down on the rope.

The man she'd shot didn't die. Although injured, he rolled over and shot Lindy. Chase, appeared from behind some rocks and finished off Lindy's shooter.

The remaining two MSS sprayed machine gun fire toward Chase, but Wen returned fire as she dove for cover behind the sand dune. Chase went down. She couldn't tell if he'd been hit, or was just trying to conceal himself. Chase crawled toward Lindy's body and pulled him behind a boulder.

"Where were you hit?" Chase whispered as he got Lindy onto his side.

"Where wasn't I hit?" Lindy asked in a hoarse whisper, color draining from his face. "My leg, my side, my arm . . . "

His breaths were labored. Chase tried to look at the injuries, but Lindy winced.

"Forget it!" He pulled out a phone and began punching in a code.

"What are you doing?" Chase asked, thinking Lindy might be trying to call for help.

"I've initiated the self-destruct."

"Are you crazy? We can still win this!"

"No. Even if we kill these guys, more will come. They're coming now." He showed Chase his phone, linked to the security monitors, showing more agents running up the trail. "We can't stop them now."

"How much time do we have to get out of here?"

"Five minutes."

"We'll never make it."

"You can go right now. I'll stay."

"You're not staying."

Machine gun fire erupted on the other side of the room. "See? They're going for the computers. They don't care about us. They just want the data."

"It's Wen. She's got them on the run."

"Go help her."

"Wen against two guys," Chase mused. "*They're* the ones who need help. Come on, can you walk?"

"I don't think so."

"All right. Luckily you're so puny and skinny. I'll have no trouble carrying you."

"You saw the agents coming. I'll just get you shot. Save yourself. Just get out of here."

"I came here to save *you*, and that's what I'm going to do." Chase picked Lindy up.

The scientist screamed in pain.

"Sorry, man."

"Promise me, if Wen gets killed, you'll still get the backup to the lighthouse. It *has* to go."

"I will, but what happens to it then?"

While carrying the great scientist out of the biosphere, Chase listened as Lindy explained the back-up system.

"One of us needs to survive this," Chase said quietly.

"That's a good idea, but it sure isn't looking good."

They reached the entrance. Chase looked back, trying to see Wen, but couldn't find her.

Lindy checked his phone. "Two minutes, three seconds, until detonation."

Chapter Forty-Five

Wen knew the end of the biosphere would be particularly wet since the snow had drifted highest there, and the soil consisted of a mix of clay and sand, meaning the agents were about to sink into a soupy, swampy muck. She made sure they could see her, so they would pursue. The first agent sank immediately above his knees while the second, seeing what happened to his comrade, stopped in time.

The stuck, and still sinking, agent fired at her, knowing he was a sitting duck. Wen, impressed by his bravery, put him out of his misery quickly. The other one had taken cover behind a fallen elephant cactus and a staircase-stone. Realizing she was penned in, Wen knew she would be unable to help Chase and Lindy if she couldn't figure out a way to overtake the agent. He had an excellent position, with the slotted staircase stones affording him concealment while also giving him the ability to shoot without having to expose himself. She worried about the other two agents, then she saw the answer.

Above him was a Quad. Lindy had explained on their

initial tour that the Quads were packed with bio sensors that monitored air, moisture, soil, and a host of other metrics. This one was linked to the air handling system, and due to the added weight, was mounted to a tall tree. Wen fired her MP7 submachine gun until the heavy piece broke free. The agent realized too late, and was crushed while trying to get out of the way. Wen, wanting to be sure, fired a few rounds into him as she headed back to find Chase, Lindy, and the other agents.

Wen sprinted to the other end of the biosphere. *Where are you Chase?* Knowing there were at least two remaining MSS agents, she moved carefully, trying to avoid the open areas, and dared not call out. *Lindy is probably dead.* She knew he'd been hit.

The large space felt eerily empty. Halfway across the desert, Wen heard a strange buzzing sound.

What is that?

The noise came from the corner where the main RF Antenna was located. She headed back to investigate further, but only made a few steps before the explosion threw her backward. Wen instinctively rolled to cover as soon as she hit the ground. Shrapnel flew all around, leaving the ground strewn with hot metal and burning debris. She crawled behind a small boulder and quickly inspected herself for injuries. The back of her left shoulder had a pretty good gash in it, and a chunk of metal remained lodged near her shoulder blade that she was unable to see or pull out. First aid would have to wait. She peered over the surface of the boulder and saw that the explosion had blown out the entire back corner of the biosphere, leaving a swiftly growing fire.

The explosion had served one good purpose—no other

agents had stirred. Wen, now confident she remained alone in the biosphere, looked toward the main entrance.

Time to make the dash.

The first half had enough shelter and topography to afford her some decent cover, but then she'd have to go through forty feet of open space. Taking one last look around, assessing her chances, Wen rushed to the next landscape feature. Another loud explosion, this time much closer, rocked the artificial world. Luckily, large rocks between her and the disturbance shielded her from further injury.

That was one of the laser tanks, she thought, pivoting, trying to locate the next group of tanks. They exploded, too. *Lindy must be setting off the detonations, or else it's a built-in self-destruct command sequence.*

Wen decided to use the explosions to her advantage. There were at least three more laser tanks that she knew about. She darted from one hiding spot to the next as another explosion occurred. While sprinting across the open area, two more explosions provided the perfect diversion. Stopping only when she reached the open doorway, unsure what she would face on the other side, Wen crept low and cautiously, for a moment beginning to believe no one was there. She wondered if maybe they had all gone into the adjoining northern pine forest sphere.

Then she spotted Lindy and Chase, both handcuffed to the hitching post next to the horses.

Chapter Forty-Six

Wen, still concealed, managed to make eye contact with Chase. He shook his head almost imperceptibly and opened his eyes wide as if to warn her the agents were close and waiting for her. Wen knew that they didn't care about her, except to the extent that she could stop their mission of capturing Lindy. No doubt they had also identified Chase and apparently decided to keep him as a nice bonus—otherwise he would've already been dead.

She could see that Lindy was in bad shape, but several wounds had been bandaged. Obviously they were trying to keep him alive.

That's a positive sign, and might give me an advantage in taking out the other two.

Chase, who had not been staring at Wen to avoid giving away her location, glanced in her direction as casually as he could. She held up two fingers. He assumed she was asking if there were two agents. He nodded slightly, but couldn't figure out how to warn her more were coming.

After Chase confirmed only two remained, Wen knew

that the inside of the biosphere was almost certainly empty, and the two MSS agents were waiting for her to come out of the main entrance. She pulled back inside, flames now ringing most of the walls, and ran across the desert, back up the cliffs, above the lake. Without slowing at the top, Wen flew off the cliff, knowing if she didn't make the jump, her body would hit the shallow water like it was concrete, but she was already in the air, clawing toward the outer wall.

Made it! The force of slamming into the aluminum skeleton knocked the wind out of her, and she bounced backward. At the last instant, Wen's right hand found something to grip that prevented her from plunging into the lake.

She kicked into the aluminum lattice, trying to get purchase, finally able to hook her left leg, then swinging her left arm up to grip the tubing. Pain from the earlier shrapnel wound sent an electrical jolt through her body, yet she clung to the wall, then climbed over to one of the panels that had been knocked out by a nearby explosion. Pulling herself through, she scaled the outside of the sphere as if she were a giant spider.

It had been less than forty-five seconds since she'd left the doorway, and now, at the curved peak of the top of the biosphere, she positioned herself to take out the two MSS agents.

The angle isn't right. . . I'll have to go down to the next tier and risk being seen.

The biosphere continued burning beneath her. Thick black smoke smothered the area. She knew there wasn't much time before the entire structure collapsed.

While climbing down the sloping surface, Wen slipped on the smooth glass, sliding quickly down, desperately trying to regain her grip.

They've probably spotted me now.

Still moving as she hit the lower level, Wen, a submachine gun in each hand, fired. She cut down one of the agents, but the spray of bullets from their guns and the weakening structure collapsed the glass panels. Wen tried to grab a twisted rod from the space frame, but couldn't reach it. She plummeted back into the biosphere.

Wen dropped into a stand of palm trees, clawing at the sweeping leaves with one hand, desperately trying to break her fall. Her other hand readied and aimed her gun at the entrance, anticipating the agent would be coming in to confirm her death or finish her off.

There he is!

The bullets demolished his head, but she lost her grip on the leaves. She flailed, still shooting while falling through the void. Just after the agent's bloodied body dropped to the ground two hundred feet away, Wen splashed into the ooze of mud, dirt, and sand not far from where she had trapped the other agent earlier. The three feet of muck broke her fall and saved her life, but left her with an aching back and head. It took almost two minutes before she could struggle free of the swamp.

Wen could no longer see the entrance or the last agent she'd taken out. The entire biosphere was engulfed in smoke and flames. With a wet, muddy bandanna tied around her nose and mouth, she crawled low to the ground. Racing against the dwindling air and the pending collapse of the structure. Flaming debris began falling around her.

Wait, am I going the right way? she wondered. Realizing her confusion might kill her, she yelled for Chase.

"Wen, it's clear! Are you okay?"

She followed the sound of his voice. "Keep yelling!"

As she finally reached the entrance, the back half of the structure collapsed, sending a surge of smoke and flames over her. The wet mud, coating her from head to toe, shielded her from the worst of it.

Chase desperately tried to free himself from his bonds in order to help, but it was no use. She pulled herself up and staggered over to them.

"Are you okay?" Chase asked.

"I'm alive. Beyond that, I have no idea." She looked at him and managed a smile, seeing he had escaped unscathed. "How's Lindy?"

"Slipping in and out of consciousness," Chase said. "Do you still have the drive?"

"Yes."

Suddenly, the entire biosphere collapsed into a heaping, melting, smoldering fire.

Chapter Forty-Seven

Wen removed the handcuffs from Chase's wrists, and the two of them began beating out the flames, trying to stop the entire jungle from burning. "We've got to leave the fire," Chase said. "More agents are coming up the trail."

"How many?"

"Six."

Wen started running toward the trail. "You stay here with Lindy and work on the fire. I'll be right back." She inserted a fresh magazine into each MP7 submachine gun and ran—two JH16-1 submachine guns, pulled off dead MSS officers, hung at her sides.

Chase looked at Lindy, then back at Wen as she disappeared around the burning frame. Powerful sprinklers rose from the ground and watered a thirty foot ring around the biosphere buildings. *Lindy thought of everything*, Chase thought. He checked that the scientist was still breathing before running after Wen.

He heard the gunfire before he made it through the black smoke. By the time he reached the trail head, Wen was jogging toward him, carrying an armload of machine guns.

"What happened?" he asked.

"They chose the wrong trail."

When they got back to Lindy, he was awake. "I guess we're still alive," he said, seeing them.

"For the moment," Chase replied.

"Take the data to the light house," Lindy said. "Please do it now."

"We have to get you to a doctor," Chase insisted.

"Forget me! Take the data!"

"I'll take it to the tower," Wen said.

"No, you get Lindy to the clinic," Chase argued. "I'll transmit the data."

"Why should you take it?"

"Because *you're* a certified field medic. I wouldn't know what to do if Lindy starts spitting up blood on the way to town."

"If he does, then he's probably not going to survive." She looked at Lindy. "Sorry to be so blunt."

Lindy waved a hand, as if it didn't matter.

"See, you just made my point. And you speak Spanish—I don't."

She nodded.

"And, I shouldn't even have to bring this up, but since MSS agents are probably in town, we both know you can handle them better than I can. Plus, I'm the tech guy. It's the one thing I can do better than you. The transmission *has* to get out. If there are any glitches, I'm an engineer, I fix things, I'll figure it out."

"No glitches," Lindy said.

Wen got Ash on the phone and told him what had happened.

"I'm sorry," he said, sounding distraught. "I should've stayed."

"I don't think you could have done anything."

"I'm not bad with a gun, but I would've gladly taken a bullet for Lindy. I guess that's what poor Garcia did. Man . . . I loved that guy."

"Tell me where the hospital is."

"We don't really have a hospital, but we have an okay clinic." He gave her brief directions. "But I'll meet you on the trail. And I'll let the doctor know we're bringing Lindy in with gunshot wounds. Lindy helped them out quite a bit."

"See you soon."

Chase looked back at the burning biosphere, then at his friend Lindy, bleeding, unconscious again, and possibly dying. The brilliant scientist's life's work contained on the tiny drive in the palm of Wen's hand. A mind like his came along every hundred years or so. The potential of his invention was at the heart of everything that Chase fought for on a daily basis. Aeolus could be used to end droughts, eradicate hunger, and, ultimately, poverty, and, even as Lindy had dreamt, to potentially reverse global warming . . .

Yet it could also be used to control and punish populations, for weather wars, and that could wind up destroying the entire ecosystem.

"It's up to you now," Wen said, handing him the drive, pulling his face to hers for a muddy kiss.

He knew what she meant. He could destroy the data, potentially preventing the weather wars and all the horrible consequences, or he could transmit it to Puerto Vallarta, thereby preserving it to be used for all the good things, even in ways they had not yet imagined.

"Is he going to make it?" Chase asked, checking Lindy for a pulse. They had both lifted him onto one of the horses, and then Chase had tied him and Wen together so that he couldn't fall off.

"Depends on how quickly I can get him to the clinic, and how good their doctor is," Wen said.

"You sure you know where you're going?"

"Back the way we came toward the river. Ash is going to meet me. I'll figure it out. The question is, how are *you* going to find the lighthouse?"

"I didn't really understand the directions that Ash gave, but it's up there on that ridge. I plan to just keep heading toward it. How hard can it be?"

She held out her hand and he squeezed it, staring into her eyes in lieu of another kiss.

"Stay safe," she said, taking her hand back and coaxing the horse to go.

"I'll meet you at the clinic," he said, watching her go for a moment before mounting his horse. "Giddy-up," he said, heading down a different trail that was supposed to lead to the ridge line, knowing all previous horse issues could no longer exist in his mind—not now, not this time.

The mare seemed to know her way, and Chase pushed her to go faster. He wanted to safely get the data transmitted to Puerto Vallarta, and then get back to Wen and Lindy. It was still quite warm, and he welcomed the parts of the trail that descended into the jungle, but much of it was open terrain. Soon he was at the river, although much farther up than where they'd lost the boat. Here, above the waterfalls, the river was shallow, but wide. He found a good spot to ford. His horse took the opportunity for a drink. Impatient, Chase urged her on, and she complied. The mare resumed her gait, and along a lengthy, flat section of trail, Chase got her back to a fast gallop.

Eventually, he and his horse went up steeper terrain, where the trail climbed a series of switchbacks. Just before reaching the ridge, Chase saw movement below, from down on the trail he'd been on a few minutes earlier. He might not have noticed it if not for the speed at which the pursuers were going.

Agents, he thought, *coming for me . . . and Lindy's data.*

Chapter Forty-Eight

Waxxman reached the smoldering biosphere within an hour of Chase and Wen's departure, having just missed them when Wen and Lindy took the lower fork into town.

"Who else is after this guy?" he asked one of the Wrestlers.

"Chinese," he answered, since they'd seen the MSS agents chasing them.

"I think this is bigger than that," Waxxman said. "Get me the sat-phone. The rest of you look around for any sign of . . . well, anything that could help us." Waxxman punched Weist's number into the satellite phone.

"Do you have him?" Weist answered.

"Who is this guy, really?" Waxxman asked. "Chinese agents tried to blow Chase Malone's boat out of the water, and then we finally reach Lindbergh's space station out here in the jungle, and the whole place has already been blown up."

"Is he alive?"

"I don't know, but what I *do* know is you need to tell me

a little more about why the Chinese are willing to wreak havoc in this rinky-dink Mexican village in order to get this guy."

"How should I know? He's messing with some serious stuff."

"What stuff?"

"Military tech."

"My price just doubled."

"You can't do that."

"I just did."

"*Fine*. But *finish* it."

Chase pulled out his phone, hoping for a signal, wanting to warn Wen that there were more Chinese agents, but he had no service. He couldn't actually tell for sure if the two riders were MSS, but he was certain they weren't friends of his, and knew there were probably more heading from town who could easily run into Wen and Lindy.

Chase told the horse, who he now called "Yegua," after remembering Wen using it on their ride up, "We have to go fast now. As fast as you can on these trails. And there may be shooting."

His muscled, hundred and seventy-five pound body hunkered down on the saddle as he kicked her sides. She sped up. At the same time, he got out his submachine gun and began looking for a place where he could wait to ambush them. For now he had the advantage of surprise and the high ground, but that would change as soon as the agents reached the top.

Chase considered stopping somewhere to hide the drive so they couldn't get its contents. *If they kill me*, he wondered, *who will ever find it?* He decided he would just have to stay alive.

As he crested the ridge, he caught a glimpse of the lighthouse, rising above the trees. It was still farther than he thought, maybe a twenty-five minute ride. Certainly he'd have to engage his pursuers long before then.

There's nothing but open trail and sparse trees ahead—not an ideal area for an attack. I might have to settle for a bend in the trail, but even that might be too far away. What would Wen do?

Yegua was at a full gallop. The tension in Chase's brain mimicked her pounding hoofbeats. He kept looking back, waiting for them to come up over the hill.

Once they see me, they'll know that I know they're after me. I've got to get farther ahead.

And then he saw it. The trail forked.

Chase took the thinner path as it went up to a small plateau. The path dead ended at what appeared to just be a viewpoint with remnants of an old campfire, and an empty, dusty clearing the size of a small swimming pool.

There might be time.

Chase tied Yegua to a sapling at the far end of the meadow where she'd be less visible. He ran back and concealed himself in the trees just above the original trail. The spot was located before the agents would be able to see the fork. His shooting skills were below average, and he was going to be facing two elite agents, who could shoot as well as Wen.

I'll have one chance.

Being this high in elevation, he quickly checked his phone, hoping to catch a signal, wanting to warn Wen, to explain he might be about to die, to tell her he loved her. Nothing.

The men—definitely Chinese—came riding fast, dust

trailing behind them, guns held out in front, ready to fire. His mouth went dry.

Hold your fire, he told himself. *They haven't seen you yet. Don't give it away. There's only going to be one shot.*

Then one of the agents looked up and saw him.

Chapter Forty-Nine

Hongbin's assistant interrupted him during a meeting with department heads and whispered that Li Dazhao, Minister of State Security, was waiting for him up in the Sky Forest. Hongbin excused himself. Li often arrived unannounced, but never when Hongbin was away from his office.

Li knows my movements, Hongbin thought as he waited for the elevator to take him to the upper floors of the Aznotech building.

Hongbin found him smoking under a large tree.

"We have enough agents flooding into the village to outnumber the locals," Li said.

Hongbin knew the Minister was exaggerating, but couldn't be sure by how much. "Aren't you risking war with Mexico? With the United States?"

"You, of all people, should know we've been at war with the United States for decades—and that we're winning."

"Of course, but that's been covert. This has now become an overt operation."

"You surprise me. Nothing is more important than

making certain that China dominates this technology. Nothing!"

Chase, still new to all the cloak and dagger aspects of his life, had learned one thing for sure: *hesitation kills.*

And so do machine guns, he thought, firing his Heckler & Koch MP7 submachine gun.

The lead rider's chest opened in a red gutting as he flew backwards off his horse, landing dead on the trail. The second agent fired toward Chase while turning his horse and charging through the trees up the hill.

Dirt, bark, and debris flew all around Chase, as strafing bullets tore apart the area. The slight rise and difference in elevation giving him a moment of cover, Chase bolted through the trees, unsure where to go or what to do. Finally, spotting a wide tree, he dove behind it and clawed his way up the vines and exposed roots to an opening in its trunk twelve feet off the ground.

Chase had barely gotten in position before the second agent came storming up on horseback. It was obvious the agent did not know where Chase was, but clearly his experience told him his quarry was hiding behind the big tree. Without slowing, the rider began firing at the tree even before he passed it. As he swung around in a wide sweeping turn, still firing at the back of the tree, Chase, concealed high above, returned fire with three bursts of the MP7.

The man rolled off the horse, riddled with bullet holes.

Wen would be proud, Chase thought. *Not that I like killing people, but it's a hell of a lot better idea than them killing me!* As she had taught, he quickly checked the body to be certain the agent was dead, took the weapons and ammunition, and, after finding nothing else useful, scrambled back down to his own horse. *I would have made an excellent cowboy.*

It would be getting dark soon. He needed to get to the lighthouse and back to town as quickly as possible. Finding Yegua right where he'd left her, Chase mounted and continued riding as fast as he could toward the tower, desperately hoping he would not encounter any more agents.

The lighthouse was on Cerro Plasta, a high point on the coast. Chase suddenly realized that while there, he would be visible to his enemies—not just the agents, but helicopters, drones, and satellites would be looking for him.

Inside Mission Control, Tess monitored more than ninety live feeds from all over the world, trying to sift through the false sightings of Chase.

"Ma'am we've got a location on Chase Malone," a technician told Tess.

"Where?"

"Yelapa, a small village in Cabo Corrientes, Jalisco, Mexico, located in a cove in Bahía de Banderas, about sixty miles south of Puerto Vallarta."

Good for Drina, Tess thought. *She was telling the truth about Puerto Vallarta.* "Do we have visuals?"

"Not current, but . . . " The technician showed her some grainy shots of the boat chase into the channel, then enhanced the images with AI, which clearly showed Chase was on the boat that had made it through the channel.

"Where'd he go?"

"The boat exploded, but he was already clear. He and two companions rode into the jungle on horseback. We're working on penetrations," the technician said. Tess knew that penetrations meant using highly advanced AI and other algorithms to see into the dense forest. She also knew it would take many hours to complete.

"Run all potential destinations now," she said.

"Ma'am," an analyst interrupted, "there are, at least, twenty-six MSS agents there."

"How close are we?" Tess asked. She had ordered two IT-Squads to Puerto Vallarta as soon as she left Drina's.

"Eighty-four minutes."

She looked at him as if he'd told her eighty-four days. "The world can *end* in eighty-four minutes."

Chapter Fifty

Chase continually looked over his shoulder as the trail grew steeper and narrower, as if not many people had come this way, and certainly few on horseback. The tower came back into view. He was close.

Something rustled in the thick vegetation behind him. Even Yegua seemed a little spooked. He aimed his gun toward the sound, debating whether he should fire sight unseen. He knew there was no time to decide. He had to act. The Chinese agents had certainly not been alone.

Shoot or they will!

What if it's kids playing?

He fired a shot into the air. A couple of raccoons scampered out of the bushes as if they were on fire. Chase rode on, relieved, feeling foolish. He patted Yegua.

A few minutes later, he rounded the final switchback and could see the trail straighten out ahead, leading right to the base of Navigational lighthouse #22. The gray metal tower stood close to fifty feet high. A covered crow's nest at the top was hung with several antennas and a small satellite dish. Solar panels covered the roof, a bank of batteries suspended below.

Chase jogged up and surveyed the area. Access would not be easy, as the only way up was a fixed ladder starting about fifteen feet off the ground. It took some doing to reach it by using the support girders and wedging himself into the corners, but he finally caught hold of the bottom rung. Once at the top, he couldn't resist a moment to take in the stunning views. In the distance, Puerto Vallarta's rows of tall beachfront hotels glimmered in the setting sun, a bit like an ancient fortress built along the ocean cliffs. The sweeping views temporarily soothed him.

To the north he could see Punta Mita, farther south Cabo Corrientes, and through his digital binoculars, out across the Pacific, to the northwest, he could faintly make out Cabo San Lucas on the tip of the Baja Peninsula. He was glad he'd listened to Ash's many descriptions and stories, making all these places more familiar.

Chase estimated that it would be at least twenty minutes until it was dark enough to attempt the transmission to Puerto Vallarta. He wondered who would be receiving it on the other end.

Is there really a person deserving of so much trust to be the sole depository of Lindy's life's work? It seemed like a huge gamble, as if he were rolling the dice with Earth's future at stake. *I have no choice. His last light transmission was done before the gamma test. I may well die here in Yelapa, and his life's work would be buried with me. So I'll roll the dice, and hope that whoever receives the light in Puerto Vallarta is worthy of Lindy's faith.*

He took one more look at the sunset. Endless miles of water, dancing a silvery orange with the sky, as if the weather gods were teasing him, tormenting his decision. Lindy had accomplished what humans had dreamt of since they'd wandered out of their caves—making the weather bend to their will. Chase understood nature's fury. The philosophical debate on whether man should possess such a power had been bouncing around his head ever since a manufactured blizzard inside of a dome, behind a ridge in a sleepy fishing village on the western coast of Mexico, had almost killed the love of his life.

What am I about to unleash with this transmission? A miracle breakthrough, decades ahead of its time, that puts Lindy on par with da Vinci, Nikola Tesla, Einstein . . . Or?

Chase shook his head. *The same powers chasing down Aeolus would kill just as quickly for his LightSpeed invention, and it was but a footnote in the day's events, unnoticed because they were too focused on the weather.* He couldn't help but laugh. *What if Tess knew?*

He did a three hundred sixty degree scan of the area, looking for Chinese or CISS agents. Nothing.

Chase found the old rusty green metal panel, pried it open, and flipped the lever underneath Lindy had told him about. At first he wasn't sure it was a lever because of its small size, and because nothing happened. He was about to switch it again or look for a different one, but then, as promised, a compartment opened, and a small section about the size of a circuit breaker appeared. There was a slot for the flash drive. Chase slid it in. Then he reached around and found a padlock with a ten digit combination, which Lindy had given him. Once the lock was off, he was able to swivel around a control unit and had access to the positioning and power settings for the lighthouse.

"This is it," Chase said out loud, checking again for any signs of trouble. He took out the slip of paper Lindy had given him so he would get the programming details right.

"If you punch the wrong digit," Lindy had told him, "all the data will be lost in the ethers."

Chase read the paper three times, concentrating, resisting the urge to look below even when he heard another rustle in the leaves. If there were agents down there, he was sure he'd hear them coming up the tower, and he would get the transmission off before the shooting started. Even as he read Lindy's handwriting, he wondered if the scientist was already dead.

Is Wen still alive? Did they make it to the clinic?

Concentrate.

He read the instructions a fourth time. There was a gusty breeze a thousand feet above the ocean. Chase clutched Lindy's note, afraid the wind would take it—the irony of that would be too much. Finally, he keyed in the codes and coordinates. There was a built-in photocell which would automatically determine when it was dark enough for the light to transmit. He could leave now, but was afraid to trust the auto-settings.

What if it doesn't work? What if I did something wrong?

Chapter Fifty-One

Wen spotted an approaching horse up ahead on the trail and slowed her mount, ready to fire.

"Wen, it's Ash." He waved and rode toward her. "How is he?"

"Still breathing," Wen said. "I can feel his breath. He actually woke up once and complained about the heat."

"That's a good sign."

"If we get him help soon, I think he'll make it."

"We don't have far to go. Do you want me to take him?"

"No, let's not waste time."

"Right." He turned his horse around. "The doctor is waiting for us at the clinic."

"Any sign of more agents?"

"No. Could you have gotten them all?"

"Never. There are always more coming."

They galloped onto a long, straight trail heading gently downhill. It was a welcome change from where she'd come, and easy riding. They rode right up to the gates of a fairly modern-looking clinic. The doctor and a nurse ran out to meet them and helped get Lindy down from the horse, which woke him up.

"Hey, I'm still alive?" Lindy smiled at Wen. "Was Chase successful?"

"We're waiting to find out."

"Let me know when you hear."

Wen had already tried calling him three times, but there was no signal.

Chase wondered how the mysterious person in Puerto Vallarta knew the transmission was coming, assuming the receiving site was somehow automated.

Will the data just sit somewhere, unprotected, until Lindy's person does something on that end?

The questions were making him crazy as he paced around the top of the tower, looking for agents. He had a clear view of the town of Yelapa. A few lights were starting to come on down there. He tried to pick out which building might be the clinic, but couldn't tell. The painted brick and concrete structures climbed the hills like a colorful picturesque scene out of a travel magazine. It was a beautiful place, but he hoped they would be leaving in the morning.

Chase pulled out a cell phone, planning to contact Wen, but instead grabbed the one he used for Tess. He'd removed the SIM card as soon as they'd left Ecuador. He took out his other phone—an untraceable burner, at least until the NSA voice ID them, but by then he'd have an entirely different burner phone. He and Wen went through them like an ex-smoker went through chewing gum.

He pushed the button to speed dial Wen and waited. Nothing.

Chase studied the town through his binoculars, trying to memorize its tiny streets and alleyways. What would be the quickest route to the clinic? He identified four structures he thought had the best chance of being the clinic, but they were just guesses. Still, it would give him a place to start, in case he couldn't find anybody to speak enough English to point him in that direction.

Suddenly, he heard a series of clicks. In a moment of panic, he feared an agent had somehow silently gotten to the top of the lighthouse and was about to shoot him. Then he realized it was the light, preparing to move into the coordinates he had programmed. Although an engineer, Chase still watched with amazement as the machinery took on a life of its own and did what it had been told to do. He used his binoculars to try to see where it was pointing to in Puerto Vallarta. Somewhere in the historical section was his best guess, there was no way to be sure. Then, with a big whooshing sound, the light flashed on. He celebrated silently while watching the beam from behind, wondering how Lindy had managed to compress all that data into those particles rocketing across the water. There was no other way to be sure it was working, and it was a long dark ride back to town.

Time to go. The future is in the light.

Chapter Fifty-Two

Chase arrived at the clinic, adrenaline pumping, knowing he would have to face the full wrath of whoever was there for Lindy. He and Wen had come to this quaint Mexican hamlet only trying to save his old friend and prevent his invention from being used for harm, and he felt guilty for having brought this kind of evil and destruction on the friendly village. The eight men guarding the biosphere and Garcia had been known by all the native inhabitants in the shattered, close-knit community.

Yet they still stood strong. Four large local men, standing guard at the gate of the clinic, refused to let Chase enter. In a broken Spanish/English conversation, he convinced one of them to go in and ask. Chase watched as the man crossed the small grounds and climbed the steps to the entrance, wondering why the clinic had such a fort-like set-up. He felt exposed standing on the narrow stone road.

Finally, after several minutes, he saw Wen come to the door with the guard. She looked at Chase and told the man in fluent Spanish that he was the one they'd been waiting for.

"How is he?" Chase asked once inside and after a brief, tight hug with Wen.

"Better than expected. The doctor wants to keep him overnight, but Lindy should be able to get out tomorrow as long as he doesn't travel."

Chase looked at Wen. "But he can't stay here tonight. He can't stay here a minute longer."

"I know. But I wasn't ready to argue with el Medico while he was saving Lindy's life."

"And he's going to have to travel. He needs to be on a boat in the next thirty minutes, heading back to PV."

"It's not like we've been sitting around playing checkers. Lindy has *just* stabilized. The doctor removed six bullets!"

"Everyone here is at risk if he stays. And if we go, only Lindy is at risk. Have you talked to Lindy about leaving?"

"I thought you could talk to him, and I'll talk to the doctor."

She led him back to the small room where Lindy was. Chase thought he looked worse than when he'd left him at the biosphere, and wondered if he'd be able to travel after all.

Lindy," Chase said, smiling at his friend. "You look great."

"Shut up," Lindy responded weakly. "I look like I've been run over by a truck and then eaten by a shark."

"No, you look great."

"And I feel just *wonderful*. Should we have a party?" he asked, trying for a smile that wouldn't appear.

"Good, because you know we can't stay."

"Did you get the transmission done?"

"It's away," Chase said, making a fluttering motion with his hand.

Lindy closed his eyes. The relief made an instant improvement in his pallor. "Thank you. Did you run into any more agents?"

Chase nodded, but said nothing. Lindy understood.

"I guess you saved my life again," Lindy said.

"Me? You did some fancy gun work back there. Where did you learn to shoot like that?"

"I grew up in West Texas."

"So? Is everyone in west Texas a great shot?"

"Pretty much. You should always assume so."

Wen joined them. "The doctor says he needs to stay, but he can't stop us from leaving."

"Did you explain that the men who did this to him will come here, and are probably on their way already? That when they get here, they'll do the same to anyone they find?"

"I did tell him something to that effect. He is a brave man. He said his patients are his patients, and he will not abandon them like a coward."

"A good man," Lindy said. "That's another reason we should leave this minute."

The doctor came in and told them he'd just had a phone call. "Fifteen or twenty Chinese men just arrived at the pier," he said. "They were asking if there was a hospital in town."

Chapter Fifty-Three

Lindy looked out the window, as if trying to see up into the mountains. "We were right to destroy the biosphere," he said sadly. "Too many agents. We'll be lucky to escape the village."

"You were right. They won't find anything left at the biosphere, but is the data safe in PV?" Chase asked.

"Yes."

"What if we don't survive?"

"It will still be safe."

"Are you up to leaving the clinic?"

"No." He winced, as he started to get up. "But let's go."

One of the guards came in. "My cousin just told me he saw a bunch of Chinese dudes heading this way," he said to Wen in Spanish.

"They know he's injured . . . we have get him out of here now," Wen said. "The MSS will be here any minute."

"We can't put him back up on a horse," Chase said.

"Stop talking about me like I'm not here," Lindy groused. "I can walk."

"Maybe, but you can't run."

"Did someone say they needed the day to be saved?" Ash asked, coming through the door.

"I seem to say that every day," Chase said. "Good to see you, man. Tell me you have a helicopter."

"Nope. I've got something better—an ATV. A pretty red one."

Chase shot Wen a look and groaned. "First horses and now ATVs? It's déjà vu."

"I hope so," Wen said. "Those horses back in Nevada saved us, and so did the ATVs."

"True enough, but this time Ash is driving, so it may not turn out the same."

"Hey, me and my boat did all right by you before. What we need to hope is that the ATV doesn't wind up demolished like my boat did after *you* drove."

"Can you children shut up long enough to help me get outta here?" Lindy said. "Or else we're all going to be demolished when those agents get here."

Chase and Ash helped support Lindy as he limped out to the ATV. They loaded Lindy onto the back; there wasn't enough room for anyone else. Wen handed him a gun. "Now that I know how good you are with this weapon, I might just let you keep it."

Ash ran back inside.

Chase kept looking up the street, waiting for the battle to begin. "Where is he? We've got to get outta here."

Ash came running back down the steps. "Catch," he yelled to Chase, tossing him a set of keys. "You can take that one." Ash pointed to another ATV parked in a tiny ally.

"Thanks!" Chase said as he and Wen jogged toward it. "It's a pretty red one, too."

"Yeah, just don't blow it up. I promised to have it back in the morning."

"Morning?"

"Daylight is our friend."

Chase looked at the controls and noticed a governor which would limit their speed. Taking out the multitool he always carried, he quickly opened the governor screw all the way out to maximize their speed, then ran over and did the same on Ash's.

They were on the ATVs and already driving north before Wen, riding in the back of the small vehicle, hit Chase's shoulder. "Company!"

Chase turned around and saw headlights. "I thought Ash said there weren't cars in this town?" Chase yelled.

"Those aren't cars."

Chase looked again and realized it was two ATVs, each with a pair of Chinese agents on them. "I'm glad we're heading out of town. We would've run into the MSS on those narrow streets with no room to pass, just a wall of bullets." He recalled the area from riding into the village from the lighthouse.

There are still a couple of hills to navigate—up and down—before we make the turn onto the wider road heading east toward the jungle.

Chase signaled Lindy, who had also seen the Chinese, to be ready to fire just as bullets from the MSS agents whizzed past.

Chapter Fifty-Four

Ash and Chase opened up wide leads on the pursuing Chinese agents thanks to the adjustments Chase had made on the speed governors. In the fading evening light, they blazed up the dusty road heading east out of town, passing burros and people walking home from work. The jungle began to encroach on the road as they progressed farther from the beach. The dwellings became more primitive and less frequent. Chase hoped it meant less chance of innocent locals getting caught in any crossfire.

"Look out!" Lindy yelled to Ash, warning him to avoid a train of four pack mules loaded with building materials. Ash swerved, taking the ATV up onto a slope.

"Hold on!" Ash said, fighting to keep control and avoid rolling the vehicle. Somehow, he managed to steadily steer it back onto level ground without losing time.

"How long until we run out of road?" Chase shouted back to Wen. "Sooner or later this is going to turn back into a trail, or climb up into the hills so steep we can't make it. Got any good plans?"

"Same plan as always—we're going to have to kill them."

Chase knew she was right. Based on his earlier rides to the biosphere and the lighthouse, he estimated that they didn't have more than a few minutes of road remaining. Even if they could head back to town, that meant facing even more enemy agents, getting stuck in dead ends and bottlenecks, and endangering all the innocent locals who were already in for a long night of terror.

"Look for a place," Wen yelled.

Chase recalled a similar predicament when they were on the horses in Nevada, being pursued by possibly the same men, when Wen wanted him to find an ambush point. However, he knew that this time he didn't expect any Native Americans to materialize.

"I think there's a bridge up ahead," Chase yelled.

"It's got barricades on either end to prevent ATVs from crossing it," Wen said. "I saw it earlier when we brought Lindy down. Pedestrians only."

"Okay."

"Actually, it might be a great spot if you can reach the bridge before they get any closer. Maybe we can get in position underneath the bridge in time. If it works, I can take them out."

"What about Ash and Lindy?"

"Get ahead of them."

That's not as easy as it sounds, Chase thought. *Ash is driving full speed, and so am I. How do I pass him?* The road was still barely wide enough for two ATVs, but it wouldn't be much longer.

Chase began flashing his lights, and was surprised to find a button that produced an overly loud truck-like horn blare.

Ash looked back to see Chase waving him over.

Seconds later, Chase was in front of Ash's ATV, just in time to veer off under the bridge. Ash followed. Wen leapt off before the ATV even stopped, rolling up to a crouching position with two Heckler & Koch MP7 submachine guns ready and aimed at the road behind them. She realized it would be too easy for the Chinese agents to avoid her ambush by simply stopping, since they would've seen Chase and Ash pull off. Without the element of surprise, Wen decided to improvise and try to create one.

Wen ran, charging at the road, concealed in the darkness until the headlights from the first ATV hit her. She fired both guns, standing firm as the vehicle raced toward her.

Chase, Ash, and Lindy, all now aiming guns at the approaching vehicles, watched in horror as the ATV barreled down on her.

The passenger in the second Chinese ATV fired at Chase and Ash.

"Wen!" Chase screamed, the first ATV only inches from her.

Chapter Fifty-Five

As the Chinese ATV careened right at Wen, she stood, unwavering, firing at the MSS agents onboard. At the final instant before impact, Wen jumped straight into the air, landing one foot onto the back of the slumped and now dead driver, then kicked her right foot into the face of the injured passenger, snapping his neck backward. She continued her momentum, flying off the back corner of the ATV moments before it smashed into a thick tree. Wen sprang into the air the instant she touched the ground to lessen the impact, and then came down again in a roll. By the time she swiveled around, ready to engage the second ATV, it was rolling down the bank toward the river, its two passengers discharged and dead. Chase, Lindy, and Ash had taken care of that one.

Chase ran over to her, at once furious for the risks she'd taken, and relieved she had survived. They shared a quick embrace before jogging back to their ATV.

"What's the plan?" Ash asked.

"We could camp out here for the night," Lindy suggested. "Of course, the mosquitos . . . "

"They'll just come and find us," Wen said. "Better we take the battle to them. Fight on our terms."

Chase nodded.

"All right then, tough girl," Ash said, getting into the driver's seat. "Let's go liberate Yelapa."

"I'm all for playing commando," Lindy said as he limped to the ATV. "But the real reason to head into town is that we need a boat. Half the nasties of the world are either in Yelapa, or on their way. It's far too small of a town for all of us."

"*This town ain't big enough for the two of us,*" Ash said in his best John Wayne voice.

"We need to get out of here," Lindy continued, ignoring him. "There are places we can hide back in the States, but we need to leave *tonight*, in the darkness."

Chase thought about the importance of protecting Lindy and his work, and knew CISS IT-Squads would be arriving anytime—along with more Chinese and whoever else had been after them. "He's right. We don't need to fight, we need to run."

"I doubt we'll be able to run away without fighting first," Wen said. She tried to hide a limp. A bullet had grazed her left shin, leaving her black pants soaked with blood. "But it's fine with me if I don't kill anybody else today."

Hoping to avoid more agents, they decided to cross the river and follow the road on the other side back to the beach. Finding a shallow section, they forded the river. Now heading toward town, they drove a little slower, in an effort to attract no attention. They planned on ditching the ATVs and walking the last quarter mile so they could steal a boat from the river where it met the beach. Chase thought about when they'd first arrived at Yelapa, and almost laughed that their escape might lead out the "channel."

It's not a channel!

Ten minutes into their return journey, they spotted three ATVs across the river heading into the jungle, back the way they'd been going. "Did they see us?" Chase asked, trying to see if they, too, had crossed the river.

"I can't tell if they were agents," Wen said, looking through the binoculars. "There are too many trees in the way. If they were MSS, then they will have seen us."

Chase knew Wen would be watching for a "place," somewhere to ambush the agents, if they pursued them. "We're close enough to the beach," Chase yelled over the noise of the engine as he pushed it faster. "Let's just get there."

"Do you want to fight on the open beach?" Wen shouted back.

"I don't want to fight at all!"

"They aren't going to give you a choice."

"What if I buy the beer?"

"MSS agents don't drink," she quipped, not feeling humorous. "Find a place."

"They might not turn around until they locate the crashed ATVs, and it's possible they weren't even agents. We've got a lead. I want to keep it."

"It's always better to decide where to fight then to let your enemy choose, or allow fate to make the choice. Fighting them on the beach is suicide."

"We'll be on a boat by the time they get to the beach."

"You don't think they'll follow us on a boat? How far do you think we'll get? We won't even escape the cove before they blast us out of the water."

"You think they brought those kinds of weapons?"

"This is a full MSS battalion, maybe more. They have engaged Americans on foreign soil without regard to the consequences. They are fighting a silent war, and the MSS knows they have to win. I won't be surprised if Chinese fighter jets fly overhead in a few minutes and start dropping bombs on this beautiful little village."

"So you want me to pull over?"

"Yes, honey, I want you to find a damned place for me to kill more people."

"As you wish."

Just ahead, the road, which on their side of the river was called "Calle Dorado," took a ninety degree turn to the right before making another ninety degree jog to the left in a span of about two hundred feet. The second turn occurred in a thick grove of trees. The place had other advantages—after the hard right turn and a short stretch of road, their adversaries could not be traveling very fast.

Chase turned the ATV into the trees. Ash pulled in behind.

"What's the plan?" Ash asked as they stopped.

"Chase and I can handle the agents," Wen said. "You two go ahead."

"Why don't we stay and help?" Ash said, looking at Lindy, who nodded his agreement.

"We need to save Lindy," Wen said impatiently, "and the best way to do that is to get a boat, and Ash, you're the best one to do that."

Everyone wanted to argue with her, but they all knew she was right.

"Are you sure?" Lindy asked.
"We're sure," Chase replied.
"Go!" Wen said, hearing approaching ATVs.

Chapter Fifty-Six

Tess stalked across the open area outside Secure, the area of Mission Control where she could take phone calls without being overheard by the analysts or technicians. The entire room was filled, as two operations of critical importance were ongoing simultaneously.

"Get me visuals!" Tess shouted. "Why can't I see Yelapa?"

"We're working on it," a technician responded.

A second later, murky green images appeared on one of the larger monitors. An IT-Squad was still in the process of landing.

"Why are they going in on the beach?" Tess asked, watching them land on the deserted strip of sand between the river and the ocean.

"The tight village doesn't offer many opportunities for a drop," the Team Leader replied. "And we are not certain of the whereabouts of all the hostiles."

"Chinese and Russians?"

"And another group we've still been unable to identify.

The village is hot," Team Leader said, meaning fighting was already occurring.

"Any sign of Lindbergh?"

"Not yet."

"Take me to his biosphere again," Tess said to one of the technicians, who quickly brought up the still smoldering shell of what had once been Lindy's incredible realm. A few small fires continued burning in the interior. The smaller spheres still stood, entirely intact. "Show me the remains."

The technician zoomed in on several bodies they had previously seen that were impossible to identify either because they were face down or too badly burned.

"We need to get a Squad in there," Tess said.

"I think keeping A and B in the village is the bigger priority right now," the team leader said, referring to the designation given to the first two IT-Squads on site. "We can drop Squad C at the spheres once they arrive. They're still fifty-seven minutes out."

"If Curtis Lindbergh is one of those dead bodies, we can pull all the Squads out now."

"What about Chase Malone?"

Tess shook her head.

"Okay," Team Leader said. "Tango-two, this is Team Leader, we need an extraction of four and re-deposit in strike-five."

Tango-two, the helicopter, was on its way back to the airfield, where a US Air Force Globemaster cargo plane had landed with the two IT-Squads and two helicopters. Normally, an operation such as this would not be elevated to a point of military assistance on foreign soil. However, with Chinese, Russian, and unknown forces engaging, the president had authorized Tess to utilize military assets so CISS could get there in time. Sixteen members of the Air

Force's 1st Special Operations Wing were on standby at the plane.

Tango-two circled back around toward Yelapa to pick up four IT-Squad agents and fly them up to the Spheres.

Another monitor lit up, showing a masked IT-Squad entering a remote weather station outside Ushuaia, Argentina.

No one was surprised to see Chinese personnel—that's why CISS was there. Two of the men were with Aznotech. The others were scientists from China state universities.

"Do. *Not*. Let. Them. Kill. *Any* of those people," Tess said. "We do not need things to get any worse with the Chinese right now."

Team Leader reiterated the command that the IT-Squad had previously been given.

"Roger that," one of them replied, using a sound code via a wrist-mounted communications device. The entire mission would be conducted in silence so that the Chinese could not verify they were Americans. The IT-Squad quickly took control of the station without incident. The personnel were blindfolded and led outside, where they were detained, while Squad members dissected the equipment, took what they needed, and sabotaged what was left.

Tess checked the time as she alternated between watching Argentina and Mexico. "Anything?" she asked the team leader in charge of Yelapa.

"We're still dark in the village," she said. "I don't know what happened, but the Squad is reporting power issues in the entire area. According to local information, the grid is often unreliable. However, this seems beyond that."

Tess watched as the four Squad members from the beach dropped down from the copter next to what was left of the biosphere. Even before they could check the bodies, they had to secure the two smaller, still standing spheres.

"Team leader, this is whiskey twelve. Dome one is clear."

"Dome two is clear," a female member of the Squad confirmed.

Seconds later, close up images of the victim's faces began appearing on the screen. A couple of minutes was all it took.

"Team Leader, this is Whiskey-twelve."

"Go ahead."

"We have determined that all but three of the bodies are Chinese. The remaining are Mexicans, believed to be locals."

Tess sighed. "Lindbergh is still alive," she said to the Team Leader. "Find him."

Chapter Fifty-Seven

Chase, peering around the trees as Ash and Lindy sped away toward the beach, almost choked himself on a clothesline running back to a house. He checked the distance to the ATVs and made a fast decision. Pulling out his multi-tool, he cut the line, then hurried to the other end and did the same.

"Wen," he yelled. As soon appeared, he tossed her one end of the rope and pointed to the other side of the road. "Is there time?"

"Let's find out," Wen replied. She jogged over and tied the rope almost four feet above the ground while Chase secured his end. They hid about ten feet away from the line and waited. Chase worried that they might catch locals or some other innocents.

Too late to turn back now.

The roaring motors of approaching ATVs vibrated through the air, feeling almost as if they were in his throat. The headlights pierced the darkness, blinding their ability to count the vehicles. Chase knew if there were three, it almost certainly meant the Chinese had turned around and crossed the river.

The line can't catch all three vehicles.

The ATVs were cruising fast. "I don't think the villagers would drive so recklessly this close to houses." Chase aimed his submachine gun, took a deep breath, and stole a glance across the road, trying to see where Wen was.

"Ready?" Wen yelled, as if she'd seen him looking for her.

"Ready!"

The first two ATVs were driving side-by-side and hit the line perfectly. The stinging impact ripped the two drivers from their seats, slamming them violently into their passengers and sending all four people onto the dirt road. The third ATV, swerving to avoid the first two, ran over two of the men before crashing into the two stalled ATVs. There might've been three survivors of the disaster if Chase and Wen hadn't each fired more than a hundred rounds in less than ten seconds. There was nothing left.

They rushed to their own ATV and headed to the beach, hoping to catch up to Lindy and Ash.

As they reached the mouth of the river, a horrible site greeted them. More than a dozen boats were burning in the tiny inlet that served as the town's natural marina.

"You were right," Chase said. "The MSS is at war." He felt horrible that the livelihoods of all those fishermen and tour boat operators had just been torched in an effort to prevent Lindy from escaping.

"We've got to find Ash and Lindy."

"And then what?"

"Then we kill every. Single. Agent. In. Yelapa."

Chase nodded. There were no boats left.

"Don't shoot!" they heard Ash yell.

Chase scanned the area, his eyes temporarily night blinded by the flames reflecting off the river.

"Over here," Ash yelled again.

"There they are," Wen said, pointing to the other side of the river.

Chase and Wen waded across the same channel they'd taken Ash's boat through the day before while being pursued by the Chinese. The tide was coming in, and the water, now waist deep, would've made getting a boat through much easier. Chase noticed blood staining the water near Wen's leg. They looked at each other, but said nothing out loud.

Once they joined Ash and Lindy, they all retreated from the wide open beach into the shadows of the buildings.

"There are more boats in the center of town at the pier," Ash said.

"Do you think they're still there?" Wen asked.

"Maybe, maybe not. But we have to try," Ash said.

"How you doing, Lindy?" Chase asked as his friend limped across the sand.

"In the mood for a cold beer. How about you?"

They found a narrow staircase against the cliff that rose six stories from the sand.

"Are you going to be able to make all those steps?" Chase asked, looking up the steep staircase.

"No, can you carry me?" Lindy said in a sad, sarcastic tone.

"I will," Chase replied.

"No, I'll make it."

About two-thirds to the top, Chase ended up giving Lindy a ride on his back the rest of the way.

"Thanks, man," Lindy said at the top. "I kind of miss that ATV."

"Let's see if we can find another one," Ash said.

"On second thought, I'd prefer a boat."

They emerged onto one of the little streets in town, far above the beach.

"Now, about that beer," Lindy said.

Wen, leading the group with two guns aimed ahead of her, told them to be quiet. "MSS could be anywhere, waiting."

A military-type helicopter suddenly swept in over Yelapa bay, and they all realized stealing a little fishing boat was not going to save them.

Chapter Fifty-Eight

Dr. Skyenor, at his office, inside the ultra-protected DARPA headquarters, ended an upsetting call and considered checking in with Tess. *Perhaps she has better news.* Instead, he punched a thirty-seven digit code into a keypad behind his desk. A quadruple cobalt and titanium reinforced door opened. He reached inside the small space and placed his hand on a sixty-eight thousand point biosensor, which verified his identity, as well as the fact that his hand was still attached to a live body. A keyboard and small monitor slid out. Screen prompts required him to answer a long string of random questions, and then enter a fifty-six digit code. Finally, he had access to one of the most secure files in the world: the HAARP command overrides.

If they didn't get Lindbergh soon, he would have to implement an unthinkable protocol and shut down the highly classified program so that the rogue scientist would not be able to use them to perform a Delta-level test. Although Skyenor would love to see the results, he had a good idea that the tests would be successful, and he couldn't risk that kind of data being available to the Chinese or any other interested nation.

The black helicopter made a circle above Yelapa Bay and appeared to be heading toward the beach.

"It's definitely military," Wen said as they watched it approaching.

"American?" Chase asked, peering around the rebar and bricks of a wall along the high road.

Wen, staring into her digital binoculars, mumbled.

"What?"

"I think it's Russian."

"*Russian?*" Ash exclaimed.

"So we have Chinese *and* Russians in town?" Chase said. "Is World War III really going to start in Yelapa, Mexico?"

"Once the Americans get here," Lindy muttered.

"World War III started a long time ago, it's just that nobody's noticed yet," Wen said. "This is simply another battle."

"I thought this was the weather wars."

"The weather wars are coming. Once somebody gets hold of Lindy's Aeolus, that's the real World War III, because the weather wars can do something the world hasn't been able to do for more than seventy-five years—the super powers can go at each other."

"They think they can use and weaponize climate control because it's safer than nuclear," Lindy said. "But it's not. It's even more dangerous because they think it won't kill us all, but it will, just a little more slowly."

"Look!" Chase heard the explosion before his eyes refocused.

The Russian helicopter partially exploded, as if hit by a missile. It spun down toward the water, hitting with a large, fiery splash, the wreckage slipping beneath the kilometer-deep water in less than twenty seconds.

"Who the hell did that?" Chase asked.

"My guess is it was our 'friends' from the IT-Squad," Wen replied, handing Chase the binoculars. Using the night vision setting, and relying on her training, she'd quickly found the source of the attack.

"Apparently someone didn't tell them this isn't World War III yet," Chase said, seeing people who were clearly IT-Squad. He even recognized one of them from a prior operation. Wen gave Ash and Lindy a quick rundown on what IT-Squads were and CISS.

"That's going to be a tricky international incident to avoid—Americans shooting down a Russian military helicopter in Mexican airspace."

"I'm pretty sure the Mexican government didn't invite either one of them to this party," Lindy said.

"If IT-Squads are here," Wen said, "we'd better get moving."

"Because they're here to kill me," Lindy said.

"This is going to be a long night," Wen whispered as they moved deeper into the village through eerily quiet streets—like a ghost town. "At least three groups are after us. We need a place to hide . . . a place we can defend."

A few minutes later, they came across a half-finished concrete building with good visibility in three directions. It wasn't the best place, but it would allow them to get their bearings and make a plan. Wen was also worried about pushing Lindy too hard. He hadn't said anything, but she could tell he was fading.

Wen patrolled the open air windows, looking for the enemy, then changed Lindy's dressings with fresh bandages and medicine they'd brought from the Clinic. While the others checked their weapons and took defensive cover, Wen secretly tended to her wounded leg.

One of Chase's phones vibrated. He saw it was Drina. "It's your ex-girlfriend," he said to Lindy.

"Not a good time to talk, I'm afraid," Lindy said.

"She's a smart and beautiful woman, why didn't you two stay together?"

"Drina is definitely both those things, and a lot more. I've never known a woman so compatible. We share a deep interest in climate science, she was instrumental in the early development of Aeolus, but she thought I was taking it too far. And she definitely didn't agree with my plan to share it with so many countries."

"Couldn't you just agree to disagree?"

"You haven't spent enough time with her to know that she can be pretty intense. Drina had a tough childhood. Her mother was a little crazy."

"What was in the letter?" Chase asked.

Lindy handed it to him. Chase read it in the dim light coming from some homes above them.

Dear Lindy,
Please change your mind.
Don't end up like my father.
Love forever,
Drina

"What happened to her father?"

"He was a renowned nuclear scientist in Iceland. He went to Chernobyl, after the nuclear reactor disaster, and was contaminated. Died a long, painful death, which apparently destroyed her mother."

"Too bad."

"She's always been afraid that my science would cause a similar destruction to my life if I pushed too far."

"Does she mean change your mind about getting back together, or . . . ?"

"No, she means change my mind about releasing Aeolus."

"But doesn't she understand what your invention can do to bring *positive* change?"

"She thinks weather control is the same as nuclear."

"Huh?"

"Nuclear weapons are horrible, but nuclear energy—"

"Also horrible."

"Some people think it's good. The point is, Drina is afraid that even the good that can come from Aeolus can destroy everything."

"A large force of Chinese is heading this way," Wen suddenly said.

"Another group is coming from the beach," Ash added. "We can't stay here. We'll be caught in the middle. Let's go now."

"Where?" Wen said.

"See the taller building in the center of town? If we can get there without being seen, these two groups might end up in a fight without us," Ash said.

They began descending toward the tall building they could no longer see, other buildings keeping it out of sight.

Then the entire village went dark.

Chapter Fifty-Nine

Waxxman spotted the group moving silently down a long, steep curve. He and twelve Wrestlers took up a position at the bottom of the street. The plan was to stay hidden until the four people were close enough so that Lindbergh could be identified and killed.

Wen, walking briskly in the lead while staring into her night vision binoculars, spotted a "trained" movement down below that she believed was someone with military experience. "Over the wall," she hissed.

No one argued. On the way down the steep embankment, Lindy slipped on the loose rubble and slid. Ash caught him before he fell into a near vertical twenty-foot drop. They forced their way through a locked gate and pushed in an unlocked door of a two-level home.

"Empty," Chase said after checking upstairs.

"Where are they?" Ash asked.

"Everyone in this town knows everything that is going on," Lindy said, breathing heavily. "They're hiding in the hills or in houses upriver."

Wen, watching from the windows, told them it was time to go again. It had only been seven minutes.

"Where?" Chase asked.

"Two buildings down. It's more open, single story. Less surprises."

They snuck out a side window and moved down an alley.

A minute later, they were in another unfinished building, taking fire.

"Who the hell are those guys?" Chase asked, ducking behind an adobe wall.

"There's no doubt they're Americans," Wen said. "That's part of MSS training 101—be able to spot an American in any situation."

"So those guys shooting at us are from Tess?"

"I don't think she sent them," Wen said. "That's not an IT-Squad."

"So a different part of the CIA?" Ash asked, having only just learned about CISS and IT-Squads.

"If they're not from CISS, but they're Americans," Lindy said, "who are they, and why the hell are they shooting at us?"

"I don't *know*," Wen said, shooting out of an opening and killing her target.

"Do you have any other enemies you want to tell us about?" Chase asked Lindy.

"I'm afraid it's a long list." He looked sad for a moment. "When you're trying to change the world, there are an awful lot of people who prefer the status quo—and even more who want to control that change."

"I guess anybody in the world could have hired American mercenaries to come after you," Chase said.

"Maybe they're a supplemental force to the MSS," Ash suggested.

"No," Wen said. "The MSS doesn't use Americans."

"What about the Russians?"

"The Russians are already at the bottom of the ocean."

"Then who?"

"What does it matter?" Lindy asked. "They're shooting at us. All we need to know is how many there are, and how long will it take us to kill them."

"Man don't mess around," Ash said.

"I'd prefer to live through this ordeal," Lindy said. "And I'm not particularly fond of, nor do I *care* about, people who are trying to *kill* me. Self-preservation and all—"

Suddenly, Lindy started choking. Wen dropped her gun and applied the Heimlich on him, then turned his head and dug something out of his mouth.

"What the hell, Lindy, that was a piece of gravel!"

"When I fell earlier, crossing the river, my mouth hit the sand. I thought I got most of it out . . . "

Wen made him drink water. Ash gave him some meds from the doctor.

Wen returned to her perch, then stealthily climbed up on a rebar and concrete column that towered over the west side of the structure, as if one day there would be more floors. She waited. Counted. Four Wrestlers died before they knew of her presence. She was back inside the building before the Wrestlers repositioned.

The Wrestlers, reeling from the barrage, scrambled.

"We've covered our exposure," one of the men said to Waxxman. "I think we have them pretty well pinned now."

"This town has too many alleys and passageways, hundreds of open-air-windows, balconies, and ledges, for us to think we've ever got them pinned," Waxxman said. "And that little Chinese chick has me afraid to count on anything after she took out four of our guys. *Four!* Five minutes ago, we were about to take them. Now, I've got *four* dead bodies!"

"What do you want to do?"

"You and Norm see if you can get behind them. I'll engage from here and keep them busy so they won't try to slip out the back or notice you coming in."

"Roger that."

Two Wrestlers dropped down outside of the building and disappeared into the darkness.

Waxxman wondered what he'd gotten involved in. For the first time, since starting his 'freelance' firm, he wondered if he'd live through the assignment.

"Team leader, this is whiskey six, we have a location on believed target."

"What percentage of likelihood that's a positive ID?" the team leader asked.

"I've got two sides exchanging fire. A small guerrilla force consisting of fourteen Caucasians, most believed to be Americans. The other group is three Caucasian males and an Asian female."

"That sounds like them," Tess said as she paced mission control. "Can't you get me a damn visual?"

"It appears the Chinese are using some sort of electromagnetic pulse down there, keeping us blind," a technician explained to Tess.

"I swear, Li is *asking* for open warfare," Tess said.

"What do you want us to do?" Team Leader asked Tess. "The Squad is waiting for instructions."

"Stand by," Tess said.

The team leader repeated her command to the Squad in Yelapa.

"Team Leader, we have four dead guerrillas. Ten remaining, two are on the move to the other group."

I need to see, Tess thought. *A little light, anything . . . I don't like having to make a decision in total darkness.* She had no doubt that her people on the ground could kill Lindy, but she wasn't sure it would be the right course of action. *If they take out Lindy, what do I do about Chase? I'd like to have Lindy, Chase, and even Wen on my team, but they'll never go along with it.*

Never say never.

"Engage that guerrilla force," she said.

The team leader looked at her questioningly.

"*Do it*," Tess snapped.

"I need to be clear," the team leader said. "By 'engage,' you mean . . ."

"Take. Them. Out."

"We don't even know who *they* are."

Tess realized that the guerrilla force could be working for any number of corporations, most likely an American company. They could even be freelancers for another US government agency, and it was a risk to initiate an attack against a group she could not identify, but she was not afraid of any of that. She didn't care about making mistakes, losing a battle, Tess just wanted to keep some sort of peace and win the war.

"I don't give a damn who they are, they're shooting at my damn assets!"

Chapter Sixty

The two Wrestlers, covertly jogging around to the backside of the structure where Wen, Chase, Lindy, and Ash were hiding, were simultaneously killed before even getting halfway to their destination. IT-Squad snipers had hit their targets, each with a single shot. At the same moment, IT-Squad operatives engaged Waxxman and the Wrestlers with a massive onslaught.

"Coming heavy!" one of the Wrestlers yelled, unable to return fire as the concrete and wood around him chipped and splintered against hundreds of incoming rounds.

Waxxman realized what he had been fearing for the past couple of days. Something was very wrong. He'd stumbled into a hell *way* out of his league.

Four more Wrestlers died before he, and the last surviving three, could escape.

Successfully removing the bulk of the guerrilla threat had been easy. That maneuver and its aftermath were still being assessed when a technician reported accounts of forty-eight Chinese MSS agents moving through the streets toward the action.

Tess jogged across CISS Mission Control to get a better look at the screen. They received the first grainy images from Yelapa since the lights went out.

"I still can't *see* anything!" she snapped.

"We're working on enhancing it," the technician said. "Better?"

"No."

"Give me a minute."

"We've got two IT-Squads down there with hostiles and we're *blind*."

"Ma'am, we have confirmed it was an EMP weapon," another technician said.

"Of course it was," Tess barked. "What else wipes out everything like this?" She fanned her arm up at the black monitors. "Damn Chinese, next thing they'll be nuking Puerto Vallarta!"

"We don't believe they have that capability," the tech said.

She shot him an exasperated look.

"How about this?" the tech, who'd been trying to improve the visual feeds, asked.

"The shapes are nice," she said, "but I've seen shadow puppet shows in Thailand with twice that detail. Do we have any assets even *close*?" Tess had asked the same question twice already, and knew the answer hadn't changed.

"No ma'am."

IT-Squads are the best, they don't die, she thought. *But this is the worst situation they've ever been in. This is a mission better suited for Green Berets or Navy Seals, not computer guys with guns.*

Tess could feel the mission slipping away, and not just Yelapa. It was possible the Chinese were about to win the weather wars before they really even got underway.

From their vantage point, they saw the boats that had been moored near the pier were all burning.

"There goes our last chance of escaping," Chase said.

"I'm sure some of the locals got their boats out to sea once they saw what was happening," Ash said. "And maybe others are hidden along the shore."

In a rapid series of decisions, Ash took advantage of the sudden break in action to flee into the coal-shaft-like dark streets in search of locals who could help them find a boat.

Wen, Chase, and Lindy made a dash for the shallow river and picked their way through the rocky shores. Sporadic gunfire and echoing sounds of running changed Wen's strategy. She led them out of the wide gully and into another abandoned building. A few minutes later, Chase and Wen crouched in the unfinished upper level of a four-story structure and opened the pack to see if there was any chance they could get the Antimatter Machine going.

"Nothing," Wen said.

They'd been hoping to contact Tess to see if she'd be willing to extract them without a CISS of Death for Lindy, but the phones had all gone dead when the lights went out across the whole area.

"It must've been an electromagnetic pulse," she said. "Otherwise the machine would still have power. The Astronaut uses special batteries."

"Scary," Chase said.

"It must be my government," Wen said, putting the Antimatter Machine back. "That kind of technology is only held by a few."

"I didn't even know it had been made portable," Chase said. "But it could be the Russians, or even the IT-Squads."

"It would help if we knew which one it was," Lindy said, leaning out over the edge of the building and peering down into the alleyway. "And whoever they are, they'll be using night vision, which puts *us* at a huge disadvantage."

"I've got night-vision mode on the binoculars," Wen said. "Not the same, though."

"Maybe Ash will find a boat," Lindy said. "Even so, he's got to find us again."

"We're meeting him in thirty-eight minutes," Chase said, checking his watch. "Assuming . . . "

"He's alive and we're alive," Lindy said matter-of-factly. Their rendezvous spot was a closed restaurant near the pier.

Wen surveyed the village with the night-vision binoculars and saw the Chinese spreading through the streets like ants. *Thirty-eight minutes is an eternity.*

Chapter Sixty-One

Just outside the city of Mohe, in Heilongjiang province in northern China, several scientists prepared to conduct the first test of its kind in the world.

"It's referred to as a Delta level test," Hongbin told Li, "because it is the fourth test in the string, but it's really the first meaningful one."

The area, nicknamed China's "Arctic Town," due to it being the northernmost Chinese settlement, was cold and remote, but both powerful men had personally shown up to watch the triumph.

"Initiate sequence," the senior member of the team said.

Everyone was extra nervous, knowing that the leader of the Peoples Republic of China was watching live from Beijing.

The technicians had conducted multiple successful Alpha and Beta level tests, and a Gamma level test had been completed in the Harbin Wanda Indoor Ski and Winter Sports Resort two days before. Although it had not actually manufactured a storm, conditions were changed. The failure had been blamed on design flaws in the facility, which had not been specifically constructed for the purpose of testing their StormStarter.

"Sequence initiated," a technician announced.

The hope was that they had secured enough data from covert raids on several prominent climate research centers and weather stations in recent days to bypass the need for Lindbergh's process.

"This better work," Li said to Hongbin, not giving eye contact, but keeping his gaze determinedly straight ahead.

"It will. Both simulations were perfect."

Each of the two powerful men had come from a long past of hard-earned leadership through discipline and use of force, and it showed on their wrinkle-free, yet stressed and emotionless faces.

"That was inside computers," Li said.

"Exactly. Everything was measured precisely, and the sequence elevated the storms in every natural order."

"You trust computers much more than I do," Li said.

"Of course. Computers are my life. They are more trustworthy than people. Because they are very predictable."

The storm would take place thirty-eight-hundred miles from Mohe, in southern India

"If this works, we are technically committing an act of war," Li said quietly.

"It will work, and the Indian government will never know the cause."

First strike in the weather wars, Li thought. *The President will be pleased.*

A large screen displayed the live feed of the area. Another screen showed what was going on inside the computer. None of the dignitaries present could understand the numbers code or series of commands whisking across the screen, but they could see the clear blue sky from the live feed and waited in anticipation for a change, for something dramatic to happen. It wouldn't just be a normal storm. If they could make the winds change, the temperature drop, and precipitation from nothing, then this storm would do more than change the weather—it would change the *future*.

A future which China would lead.

"Once we have successful results," Li began, "then we must make sure Lindbergh is dead."

Hongbin nodded. Both of them understood that if they controlled the wind unchallenged, no one would catch them.

"The President has ordered us to use the full resources of the MSS to be certain that no other entity obtains this power," Li said.

Hongbin nodded again, knowing that tens of thousands of MSS agents around the world would soon have an order to kill any scientist close to breaking the secret.

In Bangalore, India, there was a breeze of less than one mph, a relative humidity of less than thirty-four percent, and clear skies. The temperature was mild and stable.

"Sequence is synching," the technician declared.

"This is it," Hongbin said.

All eyes remained fixed on the screens, going back and forth between the live feed from India and the other one filled with digital data. The data monitor had all the action, at least at this point; colorful rows of digits, graphs, oscillating bars, and patterns that seemed straight out of Fantasia.

Hongbin knew from an earlier orientation session that the storm conditions should begin forming within twenty minutes from the sequence initiation. It had been fifteen, and now that the program was fully synced, the event should begin happening much faster. He set a timer on his smartwatch—4:59, 4:58, 4:57 . . .

"Where is Lindbergh now?" Hongbin asked Li quietly as the two men stared at the screens from a back corner of the room.

"Still in Yelapa. It's nighttime there, and we've got forty men on the ground—although I'm not entirely sure how many remain alive."

"Have we lost some?"

"A quarter of that, maybe more. The Russians, the Americans, and at least one other unknown force are also in theater."

"Sounds like a diplomatic disaster. How are we going to clean that mess up?"

"If this test is successful, it won't matter. And even so, the only one that's going to want to make any noise about it will be the Mexicans, and that's an easy fix."

Hongbin knew all they needed to do was to transfer funds to the right account and the Mexico problem would go away. The sequence display had sped up, with the seemingly endless stream of digital hieroglyphics streaming across the screen. He checked the timer—2:12, 2:11, 2:10 . .

There was a murmur in the room as the live feed showed winds increasing in India.

Li read the monitor. "Five mile-per-hour winds, but still not much more than a breeze."

But soon the winds were up to six, and then seven mph.

The timer counted down— :14, :13, :12 . . . :03, :02, :01, :00.

"Winds are slowing," Li said bitterly. "Back down below

four miles-per-hour. Did we even have anything to do with it?"

A moment later the winds were only reading two miles-per-hour. Li shook his head.

China's leader, in Beijing, had already signed off without a word.

"How did it fail?" Hongbin asked, mostly himself, as the experts in the room were all scrambling, knowing more than the experiment was in jeopardy.

"Let's get out of here," Li said. He and Hongbin walked in silence to a waiting helicopter which would take them to a plane standing-by to fly them back to Beijing.

Li made a call on the way.

"Do not fail," he told the officer in charge of the Yelapa operation. "We must have Lindbergh at any cost."

Chapter Sixty-Two

Chase tapped Wen on the shoulder. "We're going to get surrounded down here," he said. "Between the Chinese, Tess's people, and whoever the hell that other group is, somebody is going to find us, corner us, shoot us, or all of the above."

"But we need to be close to the meeting place with Ash."

"We can go to Gringolandia," Lindy said. "It's only ten minutes until Ash is supposed to be there. We can meet him on the way."

"What or where is Gringolandia?" Chase asked.

"That's around the South end of town. A trail leads out to a point. The locals call it that because mostly gringos live out there. A lot of nice homes spread out, cut into the jungle—good places to hide. And almost all of them are where we have lots of warning if someone comes."

"Oh, someone *will* come," Chase said.

"How do we get there?" Wen asked.

Chasing Wind

"There's one street that heads out of town onto a rocky trail which hugs the water."

"Let's go."

Although their eyes had adjusted to the darkness, in that section it was so black, they couldn't see without the aid of their flashlights, which they didn't dare risk in the open. Instead, they stumbled along, only able to see a few feet in front of them. Wen insisted they go even slower than necessary so she could listen. The locals had all vanished, locked in their homes, afraid of the battles that had erupted in their traditionally safe little village.

As they passed a long, narrow alley that couldn't have been more than two feet wide, a spotlight nearly blinded them. Without hesitation, Wen sent a burst of machine gun fire between the two buildings, not stopping until the light hit the ground. She quickly moved into the alley, scooping up the light and aiming it at the other end, where the beam crossed another man trying to escape. Before he could round the corner, Wen took him down.

A few seconds later, she ran out of the alley. "Now it's time to move faster."

"Who were they?" Chase asked.

"Americans. Mercenaries. Nothing to tie them to any organization."

"Could they be Tess's people?"

"I don't think so. Ex-military for sure, but I don't think CIA."

"You fired before you knew they were the enemy," Lindy said. "How did you know that they weren't locals or tourists?"

"An instant before the light went on, I heard him insert a fresh magazine into his weapon. That told me all I needed to know. Anyone pointing a gun at me is my enemy."

Waxxman, and the only other surviving Wrestler in Yelapa, signaled another Wrestler on a boat offshore. A few minutes later, he picked them up on an isolated section of beach.

"Where are the others?" the man piloting the boat asked as they climbed in from the surf.

"Dead."

Stunned, the man said nothing.

"We're going to PV," Waxxman instructed.

"And then back to the States?"

"Not until I know this scientist is dead," Waxxman said as the boat moved into open water. "We'll wait at the pier in PV."

"For how long?"

"As long as it takes!"

Skyenor called Tess. "I have indications that the Chinese attempted a Delta level test in India," he said when she picked up from CISS Mission Control.

"India? Why didn't they do it in China?"

"Because it's a weapon. They want the test to be a weapons test."

"Was it successful?"

"No. But they're close."

"You want me to send a team, don't you?"

"I want to blow every single weather station they have off the face of the earth."

"We can't do that."

"There will be a time, not too many years from now, when you'll look back at this day and recall having the chance to stop the Chinese from taking over the world's weather, and you'll think, '*If only I could go back to that day and make a different decision.*'" Skyenor's voice was cool, collected, and loud. "But you won't be able to. It'll be *too late*, and then the world will *end*, and it will be *your damned fault*!"

Chapter Sixty-Three

Chase, Wen, and Lindy came around the corner just past a small bakery. It was as if they'd walked into the center of the sun. A blazing fire lit the street, burning in the front yard of a building that appeared to be a residential house.

"They must be using it as security," Wen said.

"Or so they can see who's coming and going," Chase said. "There's been a lot less action on this side of town."

"I don't like it," Wen whispered. "There's no way around, and if we go on, we'll be completely visible."

"Let's just run through," Lindy said.

They all knew he had been limping more and more. Running would not be easy for him.

"It will only be less than a minute," Chase said.

Wen held the group back with her arm. "An MSS agent can kill the three of us in less than a second," she said in a hushed but forceful tone.

"We need to get out of town," Lindy insisted. "We've already seen less trouble over here. Just past these houses, the street curves around, and then after thirty or forty more feet, we'll pick up the trail straight into Gringolandia."

"There's nowhere else to go," Chase said.

"Okay, but everyone keep your guns ready," Wen relented. "Shoot anything that moves."

Wen knew that even though Lindy had proven he could handle his weapon more than competently, he was in a lot of pain, and the walking had already fatigued him. There was also no doubt that he was the main target of all those who were pursuing them. Once again, Wen longed for proper night vision goggles—or even basic reconnaissance, another agent, or simply a decent map of the area—but nothing was available.

"Walk briskly, but as quietly as you can. Keep your eyes wide open and weapons ready," Wen repeated again, stressing her extra concern in this area. "If in doubt, pull your trigger."

They stepped silently, like deer in the woods. Wen estimated they would be in the glow of the firelight for as long as sixty feet. *To walk that distance will probably take fourteen to sixteen seconds—forever when being hunted.*

Wen stepped forward into the light, her steps silent, somehow almost invisible due to her years of MSS training, very aware that their adversaries possessed the same skills. She counted down. *Fifteen . . . fourteen . . .* Lindy limped behind her as quietly as he could, which to Wen sounded like an elephant marching on a path covered with potato chips. *Twelve . . . eleven . . .* Chase went last, with the difficult task of looking behind them as well as ahead and everywhere else. *Ten . . . nine . . .* Wen cursed the fire as it dilated her pupils, meaning as soon as they reached the darkness again, she would essentially be blind for two minutes or more. *Eight . . . Seven . . .*

"Lindy!"

The loud whisper came from somewhere in the blackness surrounding their bubble of orange fire glow.

"Run!" Wen said, abandoning all efforts at stealth and sprinting forward into the dark. As she crossed the invisible line separating the visible from the hidden, she rolled into a crouch behind an unidentified object. Lindy tripped past her, crashing to the ground with a noisy groan. Chase somehow avoided tumbling on top of Lindy while, at the same time, he lifted him back to his feet, in spite of the scientist's protests.

"Damn it, Lindy," the voice was loud and clear now, "it's *Ash*."

"Sounds like him," Chase whispered as he and Lindy found Wen.

"Step into the light," Wen demanded.

"And get myself killed?" he responded "No thanks."

"That's Ash," Lindy said.

"He's going to get us *all* killed if he doesn't shut up," Wen hissed.

"I'll be right there, just don't shoot me," Ash said.

A few moments later, he dropped in from the wall above the street just ahead of them. Wen heard his feet hit the cobblestone and pounced.

"Damn it, Lindy, don't you recognize my voice?" he asked, panting. "Get off me, Wen!"

"I do believe it's him," Lindy said.

Wen, taking no chances, shined a light into his face for only an instant, confirmed his identity, and then got off of him. "Sorry," she said.

"What are you doing sneaking around out here?" Chase asked.

"Trying not to get killed, same as you," Ash said,

dusting himself off. "But I might've been better off alone and taking my chances with the Chinese agents after this greeting."

"Glad you're with us," Lindy said.

"Everyone stop talking, let's go!" Wen whispered loudly.

"Where?" Ash asked.

"Gringolandia," Lindy said softly.

"Good idea," Ash whispered.

"Shhh!" Wen, out of patience, was ready to forcibly gag them.

Machine gun fire erupted behind them.

Chapter Sixty-Four

Wen resisted the urge to return fire, instead silently tapping Ash, Chase, and Lindy on the back, and motioning them to keep moving south, out of the village. Once they were a reasonable distance away, she told them why they weren't followed. "It's an old MSS trick to draw fire from people who are otherwise safely hidden."

"But how did you know?"

"Based on the sound of the gunfire—angle, distance, intervals between bursts—the bullets were not aimed at us."

"They obviously don't know they're chasing a former MSS agent," Chase said, smiling.

"Still, that was a close call, and a sobering reminder of our predicament," Lindy said. "Particularly since we now know the MSS is close."

"We also have no idea where the IT-Squad is, or what's left of those mercenaries," Chase added as they walked briskly through the winding streets. "Either way, the shooting from the MSS is going to bring the other two groups closer to us."

"Shhh," Wen admonished. "No more talking." She used hand signals to guide and quiet them the rest of the way.

The next time they heard machine-gun fire, it was an exchange between two of the groups. Wen wondered if more Russians had arrived. She believed it might be the IT-Squad trying to take out the Chinese, since neither side wanted the other to get away with Lindy's secrets, but it was impossible to verify. Their main concern was how close the battle was getting to them.

They moved faster until Chase told Wen they needed to stop. Although only jogging for about five minutes, and not as fast as Wen wanted to, it was way too much for Lindy.

"Should we stop and take a stand?" Chase asked Wen as they huddled behind a cluster of trees. "Lindy can't go on much more."

"Not until we have to," she replied. "There could be twenty or thirty MSS agents back there, and who knows how many CISS IT-Squads are here. Better to keep moving. Carry him."

"I'll stay here," Lindy said. "Leave me a gun. You go on without me."

"No way," Chase said.

"Gringolandia is only a few more minutes," Ash said. "None of the locals I talked to could help. They're pretty scared, but everyone agreed—if there's a boat to be had, it would be around the point, which is at the end of this trail."

Chase carried Lindy on his back as they resumed their jog. They kept up their pace until they suddenly rounded a corner and found themselves on a narrow trail by the water. It hugged the edge of the steep land, high rocks or walls on their left, the bay on the right.

"This is a dangerous place to get caught," Wen said. "We have nowhere to go."

"Then we better not get caught," Chase replied, setting Lindy down because he'd insisted he could walk again.

"I'm going to go take up the rear," Lindy said.

"You stay up in front. There's less likely to be trouble this way," Wen said, moving to the back.

A movement in front of them forced Wen to click on her light for an instant, ready to shoot.

"It's just a damned cat!" Wen said, glad she hadn't risked the noise of shooting and hoping the light had not been seen.

They started walking again, as fast as the trail and their pace-setter, Lindy, would allow.

"Gringolandia would be a great idea," Ash said quietly as soon as Wen got back to where he was, "if they didn't know we were going this way. But it feels like they keep getting closer to us."

"What's your point?"

"There's no other way out of Gringolandia. The trail winds around to the point, and along the way it gets thinner and thinner until there's almost no trail at all."

"So we'll be trapped?"

"Afraid so," he said as the trail climbed over a jutting boulder. "But there are some places where we might be able to get the high ground that would make it almost impossible for them to sneak up on us."

"I'm listening."

"There's a rustic vacation rental called Casa Coco. It's not too far—maybe another ten minutes to the gate, fifteen to the house, up about a hundred steps from the trail."

"Can you see the house from the trail?"

"No."

"Then that's where were going."

"Once we get situated up there, I'll sneak back down and hunt for a boat," Ash said.

Even as they continued along the trail, the sound of sporadic gunfire seemed to follow them, growing louder every minute.

"Whatever war is taking place back there isn't letting up," Ash said.

"Are there going to be people at Casa Coca?" Wen asked.

"It's usually booked this time of year. Mostly with gringos or Canadians."

"Well, I hope they can shoot."

Chapter Sixty-Five

Wen, Chase, Ash, and Lindy continued to stumble along the rocky coastal trail. Their eyes, fully accustomed to the darkness, gave them little help. The only light came from the stars and the ocean, which reflected the subtle glow of the world. Although it had been several minutes since the sound of gunfire had shattered the calm, they didn't dare use flashlights. Wen was now convinced at least one group was searching in their direction.

Lindy slowed as the trail sloped up and then back down, twisting and curving around wet rocks. At one point, splashing waves in the high tide soaked their pants. Twice Lindy had fallen. Wen finally found a spot she liked where the trail opened up around the corner of a fancy resort and the trail behind them bottlenecked. She told everyone to rest while she listened. She heard the sound of the lapping waves on the rocks, the shush of the breeze through the trees, the scurrying of raccoons and other critters in the jungle, but no footsteps, and no gunfire.

"It's not far now," Ash whispered, breaking her meditative concentration. "Let's go."

"Where are we going?" Chase asked.

Since the trail was wider now, going away from the water, they were finally able to walk together in a group again. Wen explained the plan to Chase and Lindy.

"Somewhere along here there *has* to be a boat," Chase said. "Let's find it and get the hell away."

"The only boats that will be around here," Ash began, "will be smaller rowboats, or ones with tiny outboard motors. Neither will ever make it to PV, but I'll go look once we get the house secure."

"The MSS and CIA are most likely out there in boats waiting for us," Wen said.

"All we have to do is go around the other side of this point," Lindy said. "Just hug the shore. At least we get through the night."

"And then what happens in the morning?" Wen asked.

"In the morning, the people of this town are going to rise up and kick these gringo invaders the hell out of here."

"Let's hope," Wen said.

"I think he's right," Ash said. "I believe that will happen in the morning. The locals are planning right now."

"I don't want to fight with four of us sitting ducks in a rocking rowboat," Wen said. "I like the high ground."

"You're the expert," Chase said.

They were at the gate to Casa Coco. It was closed, but unlocked, which didn't matter anyway. The gate was just a gate, with no wall connected to it, so they walked around it. There were a hundred long, winding steps leading to the house. Lindy nearly collapsed halfway up.

At the top, Wen was disappointed that she couldn't see the town, but happy the house wasn't visible from the trail.

"Normally, if you could see anything, it's really beautiful . . . acres of lush tropical garden and wild vegetation with hundreds of bougainvilleas, hibiscus, palm trees, tropical fruit trees . . . " Ash said. "Friends stayed here once, and I ate so many mangoes, grapefruit, lemons, bananas—"

"Is anyone here?" Wen interrupted. "That's a palmed roof, isn't it?" She didn't like defending a place with nothing but grass above as protection.

Wen and Ash went to look around while Chase got Lindy comfortable on a chaise and rested for a moment himself, exhausted after carrying Lindy up the last fifty steps. Chase looked out across the miles of open water to a stretch of lights like a mirage of a futuristic city. "Puerto Vallarta," he said, pointing. "They still have electricity."

Lindy grunted.

My plane is there, Chase thought. *Civilization. Survival.* "Wait . . . where's Wen?" he asked, realizing she was gone.

"I don't know, I thought she was right here," Lindy mumbled from the chaise.

Chapter Sixty-Six

Chase jogged into the house with his gun ready. There weren't really any walls, most of the space left open to the jungle. He bumped into Ash.

"Two doors," Ash whispered. "They're the only rooms closed off from the outside. I tried one off the kitchen and it was unlocked. Nothing."

They went to the other door.

"Locked . . . from the inside," Chase gestured.

Ash pointed. They went out the back entrance of the building—a wide open arch with no door. Ash motioned his gun toward two wooden louvered window coverings. "Easy enough to break through or shoot through," he whispered.

"Probably tourists scared and hiding inside," Chase whispered.

Ash tapped Chase, indicating they should move away. They stood near a stone wall about twenty feet from the window and continued their deliberations in hushed tones. "I'd say hundred percent they're not armed. These are vacationers."

"I'll tell them through the windows that they should come out, and that we won't hurt them. Explain that there are people coming who will kill them."

Suddenly a door opened, and Chase and Ash ran back into the house.

Wen led four people out of the room. "There's a patio entrance on the other side. I caught them trying to escape."

Chase began his speech. "We're not here to hurt you. There are people after us. The people who did this to the town knocked out the power. I'm an engineer, the man outside is a scientist . . ."

The two couples turned out to be from Oregon, and, although still clearly nervous, appeared to believe Chase's story. No one knew it at the time, but their two sons were hiding under the beds of the room they'd just come out of.

"Tell us about the property," Wen said. "We may not have much time before the men come."

"There's a palapa—it's like a little meditation gazebo structure—down a little ways from the house, in the jungle."

"That would make a great defensive position," Wen said.

"The upstairs of the building has balconies facing the trail and two more on the sides of the house. There's also a trail leading up to another house where locals live."

"We need to get ready. You can go hide in the jungle, but not toward the trail."

The two couples then admitted their children were still hiding.

"Get them and go!" Wen told them. "Run as far as you can from the house so no stray bullets hit you."

The families left immediately.

"I hope we don't regret letting them go," Wen said,

bending down and rubbing her shin, which had stopped bleeding, but remained swollen.

Wen, Chase, and Ash quickly, and as quietly as possible, ripped wooden blinds out of the windows, then rounded up blankets and cushions—anything that could burn. They made two piles—one at the switchback, another farther down the hill in a clear patch of dirt between the tropical plants. Like a medieval battle plan, the piles would be lit at the first sign of invaders.

Lindy, having a difficult time moving, yet with his excellent shooting ability, was selected to go down to the palapa. Wen quickly cleared a sight path in the foliage from his position to the steps so he could see anyone approaching. Then she hid in the dense vegetation a little higher along the steps at the last switchback, giving her a good view of Lindy and anyone coming up. From there, Wen could also see the house. Ash and Chase took up positions behind the concrete pony walls that separated the inner living space to the open air patios.

Then they waited for what they all knew would come.

Chapter Sixty-Seven

Two MSS agents slowly came up the hill, clearly scouting the area. Wen, waiting next to the steps, invisible in the darkness behind a thin shrub filled with hundreds of white flowers, sprang silently. They were dead before they heard her. She never stopped moving. A second later, the first bonfire was lit. Its erupting glow revealed two more agents. Lindy shot fast and accurately from behind the concrete wall of the palapa. They both dropped onto the steps. By then, Wen had lit the second pile.

Night vision, she thought as she found another hiding place.

Lindy took out one more before other agents spread out into the trees and tall plants.

With the spreading fire light stealing Wen's cover, she quickly retreated back to the house and found Chase.

"There are too many of them," she said, panting hard from running up the hill.

"We've got the high ground."

"I don't think it'll be enough. They'll sweep around

through the jungle where we can't see and come from the sides and behind. We need more people."

"Is Lindy going to be okay down there?"

"I'm afraid they'll overrun him," Wen said, firing over the wall. "They know where he is."

"But they don't know it's Lindy."

"They will when they kill him."

"We have to get him out of there!" Chase said.

"I'll go," Ash said. "Cover me." He flashed a smile. "I've always wanted to say that."

"Let's all go," Chase said. "After we get Lindy, we'll cut into the jungle from there and make our way back to the water."

"And then what?" Wen asked, firing over the wall again.

"We stay alive 'til morning," Ash said. "Daylight is our friend."

"There could be forty agents down there. They'll swarm us in the jungle," Wen argued. "We'll never even make it to the trail. And what about those two families huddled in the trees somewhere? Do you really want to take the battle to them?"

"What about the men you talked to, Ash?" Chase asked. "Do you think there's any chance they'll come and help?"

"Not with forty agents on the trail. What are they going to do against that?"

Chase looked down and saw three men heading toward the palapa. "Lindy's got trouble. They're coming in his blind spot. I'm going."

Before Wen could stop him, Chase was already on the patio, dropping into the foliage. Wen moved out onto the patio behind the column and laid down a wall of machine gun cover fire. Ash darted to the other end of the house, closest to Lindy's position, shot into the trees, and then, in the darkness, sprinted back to the far end, firing down toward the steps. Knowing the fires would burn out the MSS agents' night vision, Wen did the same as Ash, continually shifting her location and firing positions. By pressing their advantage of the high ground and the absolute darkness, they had a chance to look like more people than they were.

"How long is this going to work?" Ash yelled.

"Hopefully until he gets Lindy back up here," Wen said, rolling to another column. She could see the top of the palapa, barely able to make out the faint silhouettes of two men. Wen aimed her gun, still unsure if she was looking at agents, or Lindy and Chase. Her finger flicked across the trigger, deciding whether or not to shoot, knowing the decision would mean either saving Chase and Lindy, or killing them.

I can't risk it, she thought.

Instead, Wen dove into the vegetation as if it were water. The coarse leaves and thorns cut into her arms and legs, but she didn't notice as she rolled to her feet and forced her way through the tangle of plants toward the palapa. Once close enough to see the silhouettes in more detail, Wen opened fire. Almost simultaneously, Lindy and Chase emerged from behind the trunk of a thick tree where they'd been pinned down.

"We're surrounded!" Chase yelled.

Wen stepped up into some kind of short palm bush and watched agents closing in on the palapa. They were also coming at Chase and Lindy's tree from all sides. She picked the closest one and fired, revealing her location, but opening up a path back to the palapa. It was their best chance— ringed in a four-inch concrete wall, and with the commanding position except for the hill up to the house. She'd have to assume Ash could cover that.

"Come on," she yelled, pointing to the palapa.

If she could've seen Chase's expression, Wen would have seen a look that questioned her sanity. He had just fought to rescue Lindy and then himself *from* the palapa, and now she wanted them to go *back*? However, Chase had learned long ago to never question her tactics during combat.

As soon as they reached the palapa, Wen was already there, shooting. Lindy and Chase each took a direction to defend, counting on Ash to handle the back.

"There was too much exposed ground between us and the house," Wen yelled. "At least here we have a chance."

"Is that what you call it?" Chase asked. "I have no idea how we're going to get out of this. And this isn't my idea of a great vacation rental!"

Chapter Sixty-Eight

It was an ugly firefight—three against too many. The MSS agents, all trained, elite killers, fought with an urgency and an efficiency that would have been impressive if it wasn't bearing down on them like an evil, poisonous fog.

"They're like machines," Chase shouted above the machine-gun fire.

"That's how the MSS trains them," Wen replied, recalling the oppressive, never ending militant training sessions during her time with the organization. The most intelligent agents earned a reprieve, which only meant practically living in classrooms, simulators, and computer control centers. That had been her path, and it had saved her, because it showed her a way out of China. Ironically, MSS training had drilled that idea into all their agents—*there is always a way out.*

But kneeling behind that chipped concrete wall in the palapa with Chase and Lindy, on that moonless Mexican night, outnumbered and out trained, more than she could ever recall, Wen wondered if, like so many of the communist China lies, "There is always a way out," was just more propaganda.

Ash, doing his best to keep agents from getting around to the back of the palapa, had to also deal with the MSS agents closing in on the main house. His trick of being in two places at once had become both exhausting and increasingly ineffective. He believed there were only a few minutes left before the house was overrun.

Their fires had begun to dwindle. Although it was the dry season, and normally that would've meant they could spread, because the caretakers kept the area regularly watered, there was no danger of that tonight. As soon as the fires died out, they would be in complete darkness again, while the Chinese agents maintained their advantage with night vision goggles.

"I've got to do something, now," Ash whispered to himself.

It felt like a clock ticking in his head, but the sound reverberating inside him was the constant machine gun fire. Ash didn't know how he'd wound up in this situation. Sure, he was a bit of a hustler, but deep down Ash was really just a happy-go-lucky beach bum. Definitely the worst shot among the four, he didn't understand how *he* had been left to defend the house and the three of them.

Maybe a rescue's coming. Maybe Wen will fight her way out and steal a grenade. I shouldn't even be here. I was supposed to meet my girlfriend in PV hours ago. He fired another burst at an agent near the corner of the house. *That was the closest one yet.* And probably the fourth person he'd killed in his whole life—all of them at Casa Coco.

Ash moved back over to the open kitchen. It was the nearest point he could get to see the palapa and still be protected by the concrete walls separating the house's inside living area from the patios. As the light faded from the fires, it was harder to even make out the difference between the palapa's palm roof and the plants around it, but he could see agents crawling around the area down there, closer and closer to his friends.

"They aren't going to make it," he muttered to himself. "Maybe I should sneak out the back right now, before the agents get up here . . . I might be able to get away, possibly hide with those families in the jungle. The Chinese don't give a damn about me, anyway. If I could make a difference . . . somehow save Lindy, I would stay, but there's nothing I can do anymore. I have to go now or I'm a dead man."

Ash stepped away from the kitchen, carefully looking around before dropping to the ground and crawling through to the open back entrance, a wide breezeway. He took one last look just as he was going to dash to a little outbuilding. From there it would be an easy sprint into the jungle. But, in that moment, he saw a huge, bright orange glow, as if the fires had reignited. Ash turned back to see what had happened.

"Oh, God!"

The roof of the palapa was burning in raging flames.

Chapter Sixty-Nine

Ash ran back toward the patio without even thinking. The MSS had the palapa completely surrounded. The burning roof was an instant from falling in on them. From his vantage point above, and with the brightness of the fire, he could see them clearly. Their choice was to either burn to death as soon as the roof collapsed, or run into a Chinese ring of machine gun fire. It all flashed through his mind in those split seconds as he ran down through the vegetation toward the palapa.

Ash waited to start shooting until he could see Chinese faces, and then, pretending he was an action movie hero, opened fire, squeezing the trigger again and again, fanning out a hail of bullets that more than doubled his previous death count in a matter of seconds.

Wen, who had been firing from one of the sides and the back of the circular wall, was the first to witness his heroics. Seeing the opportunity as their last, Wen cried out, "Get to the house!" She wasn't even sure if Lindy could make the climb, but knew if she and Chase were killed, Lindy would be dead anyway. The fire rained down on them as they climbed out of the palapa. Chase pushed Lindy over the wall, and as the last one still within the Palapa, he caught the worst of the burns as a section of flaming palms crashed onto his back. He dove out, landing on an exotic pink and yellow leafed bush, before rolling into the dirt to extinguish his scorching back. When Chase came up firing, Wen and Lindy were already twenty feet ahead of him.

How many damned agents are there? he wondered as he tripped over a body and shot another. Instead of following directly behind Wen, he veered off to the edge of the jungle where it was darker, and crawled commando-style up the hill.

Wen found Ash bleeding and gasping just below the patio. "Help me!" she yelled to Lindy, grabbing one of Ash's arms with her left hand while still shooting with her right.

Lindy stumbled along and took Ash's other arm. Together, they dragged him onto the patio and leaned him behind one of the columns.

"Are you okay?" Lindy asked him. Wen continued shooting, searching desperately for Chase.

"Did . . . every one . . . make . . . it?" he asked in a raspy voice.

"Yeah. Yeah, thanks to you, we got out of there."

Ash coughed up some blood. "I don't . . . think . . . I made it."

"No, you're fine," Lindy said. "As soon as Wen finishes off these evil bastards, we'll get you to the clinic. You can have my doctor. He'll fix you right up."

"No." Ash shook his head. "Do me . . . a favor . . . don't let it . . . rain on . . . my funeral."

"Come on, we're not going to need to *have* a funeral."

"I need you shooting!" Wen yelled.

"I'll be right back," Lindy said, but Ash didn't hear him.

Chase had come around the back of the house and appeared next to Wen. "Miss me?" he asked, joining her chorus of bullets.

"Just your gun."

"I bet you did." Chase looked over at Lindy, firing from the corner column. "Where's Ash?"

She shook her head. "Didn't make it."

"No!" Chase stopped shooting.

"Hey," Wen yelled. "We're only here because he sacrificed himself. Now don't let him down. Keep shooting. We are going to get out of this!"

Chase picked out the closest agent and lit into him.

"Where are they all coming from?" Lindy yelled.

Chase couldn't believe it. He knew they must have already killed twenty of them, but there were still at least that many. He couldn't see how they were going to survive. He only had two magazines left. Wen might not even have two. Lindy only had three to start with.

"We need to run," Chase yelled to Wen.

"You take Lindy and go. I'll keep them busy for a minute, and then I'm right behind you."

"No way!"

"If all three of us run, they'll follow us, and we'll all be dead with bullets in our backs."

"We're going to run out of ammo."

Suddenly the roof of the house burst into flames. The dried palms might as well have been gasoline. The wooden upper floor of Casa Coco ignited in seconds, and the roof—much bigger and thicker than the palapa's—dropped chunks of flaming debris.

"Still want to stay?" Chase yelled.

"Lindy!" Wen shouted, pointing to the back. As soon as they were behind the house, they made a new plan. "Forget the jungle," Wen said. "They'll know that's where we'll go. Follow me back to the house."

"The house?" Chase yelled. "It's on fire!"

Chapter Seventy

Wen led them to the side of the house. "I saw it earlier, just before I discovered the families staying here." She kicked a grate vent into a crawl space piled with maintenance equipment. "It goes under the house."

"The house is *on fire*," Chase repeated.

"Exactly why they won't look here. Hurry."

Once they were all inside, she replaced the grate. "The floor above is concrete. We won't burn."

"But they've got night vision," Lindy said. "It won't take them long to find out we're not in the jungle, and then they'll be back."

"I know this is different than your line of work," Wen said, "but this is *my* line of work. And the first thing you learn is there is nothing more precious than time. All we are doing is buying a little time. And in that time, we will figure out how to stay alive a little longer, and maybe even find a way to escape."

"Then how do we do that?" Lindy asked.

"I'm working on it."

Everyone stayed quiet for a while, listening to Casa Coco burning, to the shouts of the MSS agents, and to their own inner agony at the loss of Ash and the prospect that they would die next. No one said anything, but they were all feeling it. Ash had given them this chance, and they would mourn him once they were free.

The agents had left an unknown number of men patrolling around the house while others went into the jungle. With their night vision goggles, the MSS could easily spot the few trails leading away from the house. The vegetation was too dense for anyone to have gone into the jungle any other way. Lindy had been right; it would not take the agents long to discover that they had not escaped into the jungle.

Concealed under the master bedroom patio balcony, from behind the grate, Wen tried to detect a pattern as she watched the agents passing by on patrol. There wasn't one.

An agent stared at the side of the house, as if looking for hiding places. It appeared he had not yet seen the grate, but a couple of minutes later, he returned with two of his comrades. Wen tensed and tried to withdraw farther back into the shadows, at the same time pointing her Heckler & Koch MP7 submachine gun at them between the slats.

"Do they see us?" Chase whispered.

"I don't think so, but they're going to come check this out."

"What's going to happen?" Lindy asked.

"The three of them are going to die, and then we need to get the hell out of here before any more come."

"To buy more time," Lindy said.

"Exactly."

Wen took a deep breath, trying to remain calm as the three men, their guns aimed at the grate, moved toward their hiding place. She considered shooting as soon as they were fifteen feet away, believing she could hit them all, but waited, hoping somebody would call them away, knowing if she dropped those three, a dozen more would be there in seconds.

Twelve feet.

Lindy and Chase also had their guns pointed, but waited, following Wen's lead.

Ten feet.

Wen's finger flicked lightly across the trigger, her mind racing, working out a hundred possible scenarios.

Eight feet.

The only way out is through them, she thought.

Six feet.

It was no longer a certainty that she could hit all three.

Four feet.

Bullets seemed to come from everywhere. A violent eruption of gunfire shattered the tension and took Wen's breath. The three agents, bullet tracks of blood across their bodies, fell dead. Wen hadn't fired a shot.

Chapter Seventy-One

The Mexican Navy had arrived from Puerto Vallarta. Four gunmetal grey boats floated in Yelapa bay. More than two hundred men disembarked on military rafts equipped with outboard motors. Two Mexican Air Force jets flew overhead. Troops filled the streets, rounding up stragglers and injured Chinese agents. The IT-Squads had pulled out twelve minutes before the Navy made landfall.

"You cannot get caught there," Tess had ordered.

No one was quite sure what had happened to Lindy, Chase, and Wen. Facial recognition had not picked up any sign of the three targets. The Mexican officials would search Yelapa for their bodies, but Tess suspected they had slipped out in the night. Once again, she couldn't help but be impressed with Chase and Wen's resourcefulness. She could, at least, also celebrate the fact that the MSS hadn't gotten Lindy.

Tess left strict instructions to call if any major developments occurred, then retired to her private office for some quick sleep. As she lay there, contemplating her next move, she whispered into the darkness.

"I'll find you, Chase."

Li and Hongbin were still together when they got word that the MSS had suffered thirty-four casualties, and that eight agents were being held by the Mexican military. The Minister's limousine rolled along a nearly empty service road outside Beijing.

"The test failed, and we have lost Lindbergh," Li said in a death-sentence tone. "Drastic action is needed."

"But the Americans don't have him either," Hongbin countered.

"Lindbergh may be dead," Li admitted. "One of the final reports said he had been badly injured. Our people forced him to flee from the local hospital."

"What about Malone and the woman?"

Li shook his head.

Chase, Wen, and Lindy limped into a tiny local restaurant in Puerto Vallarta, and ordered some desperately needed food. They'd been constantly on the move for almost twenty-four hours. The last three had been spent coursing through the jungle from Yelapa.

Moments after the Mexican soldiers killed the MSS agents outside their hiding place under Casa Coco, Chase, Wen, and Lindy had fled up the trail to a neighboring house. After pleading with the local man, and paying him $2,000 US, he took them to his two motorcycles. Chase drove one with Lindy holding on behind him, and the man drove the other with Wen. It had taken them nearly three hours to navigate the primitive trails and roads that cut through the jungle. They had not seen another vehicle until they picked up Calle Mexico Route along the coast just south of PV. The man had dropped them at the restaurant, where he said they could get a decent breakfast, and had a nice restroom where they could clean up. Still, they looked so jungle-worn they elicited stares from other customers.

After traditional huevos rancheros with extra guacamole, they made their way through the quaint, cobbled streets of old town Puerto Vallarta, feeling unconnected to the strange new reality without bullets flying from all directions. Wen continued to insist they stop often so she could survey the area and Lindy could rest—although he kept insisting it wasn't necessary.

"The biosphere is gone," Chase said to Lindy as they stepped into the shadows of an old building. "A lot of people died last night. What now?"

"I have to finish it."

"What?"

"The tests." They passed an early morning fruit and vegetable market.

"You did the Gamma test at the biosphere. It *worked*. Aeolus *works*."

"There are still two more levels to be completed before I know everything is right. It's the only way I can be sure all the bugs are worked out."

"What do we need to do?"

"Delta and Epsilon level tests have to be completed."

"Where?" Chase asked as a motorcycle sped past.

"I have sites selected in Sonora Mexico, and one in Texas."

"Will they be able to find those sites?"

"You mean the CIA? Or the Chinese?"

"Or those other mercenaries after you, or anyone who means you harm."

"I don't believe they could backtrack from any of the data at the sites they've raided to find out where I'm going to do the last two tests. But I have to do them there. Everything is preprogrammed for those sites. It would mean days, maybe weeks of work to change it. I don't need to tell you that we don't have that kind of time."

"Obviously not," Chase said, looking at Wen. "Then we'll get your backup data and fly on to Sonora."

Wen nodded. "And then what? I mean after the Delta and Epsilon tests."

"Then I have to deliver Aeolus to the list of countries." They'd argued several times about Lindy's insistence to share his invention with China, Russia, America, New Zealand, Australia, France, and several other smaller countries.

"Still want to give it to China?" Chase asked, stepping aside as two Mexican men burst out of a small shop.

"They have more than twenty percent of the world's population," Lindy said.

"We still don't agree," Chase said, "but it's your decision." He let out deep breath. Chase and Lindy stared at each other for a long moment.

"You still meditate?" Lindy asked his longtime friend.

"Not like I used to." Lindy squinted at him. "All these months on the run has taught me one thing . . . Stillness is the way to see the secrets of the universe."

Lindy held Chase's gaze again and nodded.

"You'll have to somehow get Aeolus to all those countries without getting yourself killed in the process," Chase said.

"Right. Are you two willing to help me with that part?"

Chase and Wen exchanged a thoughtful glance. Like soldiers in combat, they'd learned to speak entire conversations in a quick look.

"Yes," Wen said. "We'll stay with you."

"Thank you. We might just save the world."

Chapter Seventy-Two

As they neared their destination, Wen looked at each person as if they were assassins, assessing their weaknesses and vulnerabilities, every vehicle a threat, all windows and doors potential escapes.

"See anyone suspicious?" Lindy asked.

"Everyone," Wen said, scanning an alley they passed.

"It seems strange now to not be running and hiding."

"We're still running and hiding. A lot of our adversaries died last night, but there are a lot more out there, looking for us, planning us harm."

"I know." Lindy stopped and looked up at an incredible building. "La Iglesia de Nuestra Senora de Guadalupe," Lindy said in Spanish, then in English, "The Church of Our Lady of Guadalupe."

"Strange time to pray," Chase said jokingly.

"I'm not a religious man," Lindy replied, "but even so, I think this is an excellent time to pray. Meditation, prayers, affirmations . . . It's really all the same thing, don't you think?"

"It all depends on where you are and whether the idea is connection, surrender, or—"

"Is that where we're meeting your contact?" Wen interrupted.

"My contact?"

"The person who downloads the backups from the lighthouse transmissions," Chase said.

"There is no person."

"Then how—?"

"It's all automated," Lindy explained.

"I wondered how you could trust somebody with that kind of data."

"I trusted *you*," Lindy told Chase.

"You didn't really have a choice."

"We always have a choice. And even so, I trusted you completely. I trust you with my life. You saved it a few times."

Chase nodded, staring his old friend in the eye. "You'd do the same."

"Without a doubt, but not necessarily as ably as you and Wen." They walked around to the front of the building. "It's too early for the throngs of tourists who normally crawl all over this beautiful building like ants," Lindy said, gazing up at the church tower. "As soon as the cruise ships disembark, the masses will descend with their smart phone cameras and loud voices."

A few souvenir vendors were already set up, a handful of early risers milling about the steps leading up to the entrance.

"Say what you want about religion, but they do put up some gorgeous structures," Wen said, marveling at the iconic church with its triple bell towers, the ones on the sides topped with basilica style yellow domes and large crosses, the center one, extending at least fifty more feet toward the heavens, culminated in an ornate wrought-iron crown hoisted by eight angels.

"Magnificent," Chase agreed, seeing Wen lingering for a moment at one of the tables. Chase went over, picked up the pendant, and asked how much it was. He bought it, curled it into her hand, and winked at her, because he knew what that look meant. *I know*, he said with his eyes, *I paid too much*.

"How did you automate it?" Chase asked, turning back to Lindy.

"If you look up at the top of the large central tower, there is a crown which is capped with a sphere and cross. At night, those light up. There is direct line of sight to the navigational tower above Yelapa."

Wen stared intently at two men approaching the steps where they were standing.

"Incredible," Chase said, not noticing. "But then what happens?"

"The data is transmitted via hardwire inside the same conduit that powers the light on top of the church."

Wen readied the Glock concealed inside her light jacket.

"From there," Lindy continued, "it follows the lines into the nave and comes up under one of the pews."

Chase finally noticed Wen watching the men and immediately slipped his hand inside his coat, gripping the handle of his Beretta.

"How did you get the church to agree to all this?" Chase asked, steering Lindy to the corner of the building, feeling it would be better suited for a gun battle.

"I made a nice donation, told them the truth, that it was for weather research, and, you know, I have pretty respectable credentials, which they could easily check.

Because we used existing wiring and conduit channels, it was not invasive. I paid for the work, of course, and—"

"Hold on," Chase said.

"Tourist," Wen said. She sighed. "And I was about to shoot them."

"Let's get in, get the drive, and get out of here," Chase said. "Where is it?"

"That's just what I was telling you. There's a secret compartment under the last pew on the far right row. It's easily accessed while sitting and listening to a sermon without being noticed. Especially if you each sit on either side of me."

"But there's no sermon right now."

"It doesn't matter. We can still sit there and absorb the peace of the building."

"God knows we need some peace," Chase said.

"Then you've come to the right place," Lindy replied, smiling.

A few moments later, the three of them sat together on the last pew of the far right row. Lindy, sitting between the two of them, casually reached down between his legs, where a tiny biometric sensor had been recessed into the wood. Once his finger was placed on it, an almost imperceptible clicking sound could be heard, and a compartment tilted open at a thirty-degree angle, allowing Lindy to eject a slim computer drive.

"Got it," he said, pushing the compartment closed. "Let's get out of here and go play weather god."

Chapter Seventy-Three

In the quiet light of the morning, the Church of Our Lady of Guadalupe appeared to be a sacred place even to nonbelievers. The massive intersecting arches and grand columns, accented in gold leaf, visually lead any visitor to the giant, throne-like gold alter, made even more stunning that morning as it was bathed in natural light from the soaring dome above. Lindy stared at it for a moment, as if contemplating what he was about to do—a duel between nature and himself.

Chase and Wen rose, ready to leave. At that same moment, Waxxman entered the church, prepared—*Of all places*, he thought to himself—to shoot Lindy. The impact of the holy grandeur within the church caused him to instinctively hesitate.

Wen, Lindy, and Chase exited the pew into the central aisle and headed to the main entrance. Its big, heavy, wooden double doors swung wide open as a group of forty or fifty tourists entered in a swarm. Waxxman's easy target dissolved into the crowd, and he no longer had a clear shot.

The push of people swelled around him, forcing him into the church as his quarry slipped out onto the sidewalk. By the time he shoved enough "idiots" out of his way and made it to the street, Lindy, Chase, and Wen were nowhere to be found. He dashed up the roads in four different directions, but discovered nothing except "more damned tourists."

In the taxi, unaware that Waxxman had been in the church, Wen described another man she had seen on the street who seemed suspicious. "He was ex-military, but I don't believe he saw us, since we were surrounded by all those people from the tour bus." Two buses had arrived at the same time, probably from the same cruise ship.

"If it wasn't for all those tourists," Chase said, "we might not have gotten out of there."

"Somehow they followed us from Yelapa," Lindy said, gripping the backup drive in his pocket.

"Impossible," Chase said. "They found us another way."

"I don't think they were CIA," Wen said. "And clearly not Chinese."

"Then who?" Chase asked.

"Same question we've been asking for two days: Who else would be after you?" Wen asked Lindy.

"Russians, Israelis, Germans?"

Wen shook her head. "I heard him speak English. He's American, ex-military, same as we saw last night."

"Hopefully we lost them and we won't have any more trouble," Chase said. "Once we're in the air to Sonora, maybe we can finally relax a little." Although he had a feeling his words weren't true, Chase, exhausted, needed to believe them.

"Maybe," Wen said. However, Chase could see the doubt in her eyes.

Waxxman and his associate were still scouring the area around the church when his phone rang. Even before he looked at the number, he knew it would be Wiest, because that's how his day was going. He didn't want to answer, but he'd already ignored two calls last night, and Wiest *was* his client.

"Waxxman here."

"What the hell's going on?" Wiest demanded.

"Lindbergh is still in Mexico. A reliable source just spotted him in Puerto Vallarta."

"Great, and where are you?"

"Puerto Vallarta. A few minutes behind him."

"That's fantastic news! So you'll have them soon?"

"That's the plan, as long as I can get off the phone."

"Absolutely. I'll be waiting to hear from you."

"Talk soon." Waxxman ended the call and called his associate who was half a block up, wading through tourists. "They got away. Let's bail on the church and head to the airport."

"Why the airport?"

"Because I don't think Lindbergh and his buddies are going to hang around this crowded know-nothing city where they don't even speak English any longer."

Tess, back in Mission Control, continued watching the data streams and live feeds from Mexico. "He can't just *vanish*," she said. They'd already identified the plane he flew in on, and had it under surveillance.

"Still zip on the plane," a tech told her.

"Skyenor on two," an assistant told her.

Tess shook her head. She didn't need that conversation to make her headache worse.

"Mexican military reports only one American body found other than the mercenaries already ID'd," an analyst announced. "Stewart Ashton, ex-pat. Apparently he did work for Lindbergh."

"Have they completed their search?"

"They believe they have located all wounded and dead."

"Where is he?"

"Could still be there, hiding."

"No. They got out. And the MSS aren't going to stop just because they lost a few dozen people," Tess said. "We *have* to find Lindbergh."

"The IT-Squads are all over PV."

"Skyenor again," the assistant said.

"Okay," Tess relented, taking the call. "We believe Lindbergh is in Puerto Vallarta hiding out. And we have people searching."

"No way," Skyenor said. "If Lindbergh is still alive, he's going to do a Delta test. And there are only a handful of places in Mexico where he could do that. I just emailed you the list. Now get the bastard!"

Chapter Seventy-Four

A four-seater plane that the Astronaut had arranged landed just after eleven AM at a private airstrip in Sonora, Mexico. Chase and Wen stepped out onto the dusty field and immediately searched for any sign of agents. The man that met them had four new burner phones and two still-factory-sealed laptops. He'd already set up a small tent.

Lindy went to work immediately. Even Chase had slept on the flight, against his usual pattern, and all were feeling somewhat recharged. Lindy, however, appeared frail. His excitement for the experiment masked it well, but Chase could see his old friend was hurting.

"Isn't it risky to tap into your network?" Chase asked.

Lindy didn't answer, but shook his head as his fingers raced across the keyboards. The Astronaut had also, remotely, managed to get the Antimatter Machine running again—apparently it had a failsafe override for EMP and other high-tech attacks.

Lindy was using that while waiting for the other

powerful laptops to boot up through their initializing sequence.

"What's going to happen?" Wen asked. "How are you going to change the weather without all your laser banks and all the other stuff you had at the spheres?"

"This is a Delta level test. First we'll see a drop in temperature, increasing wind speed, hopefully hail, some rain."

"No snow?" Chase asked, looking at Wen.

"No. Well . . . at least I don't expect any. I've never done this before. Anything is possible. But not likely."

"Sounds like every weather forecaster I've ever heard," Chase said.

"You still didn't answer my question," Wen said. "How is all this possible with only two laptops and the Antimatter Machine?"

"I use these to access my equipment. I've got trillion watt lasers firing into the sky that will rip apart the electrons and create ions. That gets rain and lightning. And, most important, by changing the air temperatures in just the right way, we can make the wind and move the jet stream."

"Catastrophic," Chase said.

"Not necessarily," Lindy responded. "I've initiated a sequence utilizing the Antimatter Machine and the two laptops."

"Please don't snow," Wen said.

"Not today, but given enough prep time, it would be possible to at least generate flurries under these conditions," Lindy said. "But for now, I'll be happy with just a good old-fashioned rainstorm."

"That will also be pretty impressive, since there's not a cloud in the sky." Wen looked up and then back to the screen of the Antimatter Machine. "I understand cloud seeding, since they've been doing that for decades and China has really mastered it in recent years, but cloud seeding requires clouds, and we don't have any here today, so *how* can you do this?"

"Remember all the snow in the biosphere?" He smiled, since he knew that she would never forget what had almost killed her.

"Yes, but that was inside. You had complete control over the conditions."

"It only looked like I did, but actually, even though the biosphere allows for perfect climate conditions, we still have to change the same parameters in there that we need to do out here."

"But how do you *make* clouds?"

"I don't actually manufacture them from scratch, I move them. Like I said, it's all about the wind. The upper level winds. I move the jet stream and bring clouds from wherever they are." Lindy continued typing and using the touch screens at a blindingly fast pace. "Right now there's a typical cold trough over the Rockies, but an unusual high-pressure ridge over the Southeast United States for this time of year. That's sending warm, moist air into the central states. I'm just making a few adjustments to bring that here. The jet stream is the key. It's like a super factory, constantly manufacturing weather events, but until now, nature has been in charge of it. Today, Lindy is taking over the factory."

Wen didn't like that they were so exposed, and continued staring down at the horizon and up into the heavens, not for an approaching weather storm, but a storm of a different kind brought by the CIA or MSS. She knew it would happen, she just didn't know when.

After almost forty minutes, the sky changed. "You see

those cumulus clouds?" Lindy asked. "The big, puffy, cotton-like ones you normally see in the summer time? They can only be there because the humid air mass is rising on the updrafts."

"An abundance of water vapor swimming on currents of air," Wen said, recalling her MSS cloud seeding training.

"Nice translation," Lindy said, smiling. "Those clouds will continue to rise through the atmosphere."

"Expanding as they cool," Wen said.

Chase took Wen's hand while they watched Lindy and the scene before them.

"Right again. Then the water vapor condenses into liquid water, which in turn releases heat into the surrounding air."

The clouds were growing bigger. Lindy's hands never stopped moving on the keys, even while he continued to explain. "That latent heat then causes the air mass to rise faster. That upward movement of air is what we want. It'll reach speeds of more than fifty miles-per-hour."

The winds were picking up. Wen used her digital binoculars to scan for any approaching vehicles, and also to watch the clouds literally forming before her eyes.

"The process continues, updraft, and more condensing moisture, more heat, and all those liquid water droplets are suspended to form large clouds like those." He pointed at a massive formation rising seven or eight miles into the sky.

"Here we go!" Lindy yelled as rain began to fall. "Look at it! Look at it!" He took his hands off the computers for a moment and walked, still limping, out of the tent, throwing his arms up and spinning around like a child. "Feel the rain? I just made this!"

A lightning bolt struck at that moment, as if on cue.

"That lightning is more than forty thousand degrees!" Lindy yelled. "Hundreds of millions of volts of raw electricity! And *I* conjured it! Me! A mere mortal!"

Chapter Seventy-Five

As the rain soaked the parched ground in Sonora, Wen grew nervous that somehow the display would telegraph their location to the adversaries who, at that very moment, were utilizing every manner of advanced technology to search the globe for Lindy.

"It's a stunning display," Chase said loudly, trying to be heard above the storm noise, as the now heavy rain pelted the tent. Winds continued to increase and thunder rumbled. "No wonder the Chinese and American governments are willing to kill for it."

"It's too dangerous to give away," Wen said.

"They'll get there anyway," Lindy said, returning to the tent. "By sharing it with all the superpowers, as well as a group of smaller, environmentally conscious countries, we have the best chance that this will not be misused."

"It's hard to imagine this tool *not* being misused," Chase said. "I think we've just witnessed the first shot fired in the weather wars."

Lindy shook his head, working the computers once

again. "Think of all the *good*. *Fire* can be misused. It's misused every day somewhere, but imagine life without it."

The storm began to break apart, as if all its energy and force had been sucked away.

"What's happening?" Wen asked.

"I had programmed only a tiny window of time to move the jet stream. It's now returning to its prior course."

"That's almost as impressive as creating the storm itself," Chase said.

"That's my point," Lindy said. "Don't you see? Aeolus can be used to break up dangerous storms, end droughts, prevent and extinguish damaging wildfires, alter climates, save crops—even enable food to be grown in areas it's never been able to before! This, like fire, is a *good* thing. And by sharing it, we're ensuring that no one country can dominate."

"Certain countries will always find a way to dominate."

"That's why they *all* have to have the same capabilities," Lindy said. "Mutually Assured Destruction. It works."

"So Delta is done," Chase said. "Can we start Epsilon?"

"Not here. We have to go to Texas."

"Why?"

"The conditions have to be different. My satellite—"

"Wait, you have a damn *satellite*?"

"Six of them, actually."

"And trillion-watt lasers, a network of worldwide weather stations, and whatever else . . . who funded all of this?"

"The CIA, the Chinese, DARPA, HAARP, the Russians."

"You mean they've already paid you?"

"Deposits, expenses, that sort of thing."

"And do they all know the others are involved?"

"It's complicated."

"I'm sure it is."

Lindy shrugged. "They all think they're dealing with different people. Although, I guess the US and Chinese governments have put the pieces together."

"Insane."

"There was no other way to pull this off without all the subterfuge."

They packed up and boarded the plane. Chase saw blood staining Lindy's shirt.

"Why Texas?" Wen asked as they went airborne.

"It's close, and Drina can be there."

"Drina?"

"I need her help." He put his hand to his side, feeling the wet blood.

"With what?" Chase asked, shooting Lindy a sly smile.

"She helped with the early designs for Aeolus, remember? This next test—Epsilon Level—is far beyond anything we've seen yet. This is the one that will change everything."

Wen changed Lindy's bandages on the plane. "I think this one is infected."

Chase argued that they should get him to a hospital, but Lindy refused. "I'll be fine after some more rest."

Still depleted by the prior day from hell, all three napped again during the short flight. When the plane touched down around 2:30 PM on another tiny airstrip, in the dusty flatlands of southwest Texas, they were ready for the final test. The pilot had to refuel at a nearby airport, and promised to be back in an hour.

Drina and her boyfriend, Tab, were waiting under a

large tent, and had brought tables, chairs, and extra meteorological monitoring equipment.

"Thanks for coming," Lindy said to Drina and Tab. "You were both with me at the beginning. I wanted you here for the big one. And I need your help."

"You really did Gamma and Delta?" Drina asked.

"It was incredible," Lindy said. "Wait until you see."

Suddenly excusing himself, Lindy went behind the tent and threw up.

After introducing Tab to Chase and Wen, then hugging all of them, Drina went out to see Lindy. They exchanged loud whispers, mostly Lindy insisting he was fine.

"Is this going to be bigger than the Delta Level test?" Wen asked when they made their way back, looking at the blue skies and wondering how much he could do to top Sonora.

"Remember in Sonora, when we had the cold trough and the high-pressure ridge over the Southeast?" Lindy asked.

"Yes."

"That pattern is still in place, only now we're keeping the warm, moist air here, moving it enough so that we set up a battleground where the two air masses collide. That will produce a strong wind shear at the boundary. If I can get the action big enough, severe thunderstorms will form, and then, if we keep it cranked up and wobble the jet stream, you'll see the perfect conditions to spawn tornadoes."

"You really did it," Drina repeated, a quizzical look on her face.

"We're creating a super cell," Lindy said.

"Will you explain this one as you did the last?" Wen asked.

"First we have to get winds to increase in strength, and, at their height, change direction," Drina answered for Lindy. "The warm updraft rotates against a cool downdraft. That is the simple explanation."

"Then what happens?"

"It turns at the higher levels and, if the descending air causes rotation, we'll actually get a tornado. But it doesn't happen in every case."

"Why not?"

"The temperature of the air has to be just right."

"Are we going to get a tornado today?"

"I hope so," Lindy said.

Drina shook her head.

"But not to worry, nothing big," Lindy said. "If we're lucky, we'll see an EF0."

"EF0 is the weakest tornado on the Enhanced Fujita scale," Drina explained while Tab set up the monitoring equipment. "Which is how we determine the strength of a storm. An EF0 has winds between sixty-five and eighty-five miles-per-hour and only does minor damage, where as an EF4 will produce winds between a hundred and sixty-six and two hundred miles-per-hour and cause devastating damage. Entire frame houses will be leveled or even swept away, cars and other objects thrown about like toys."

"Is EF4 the worst?"

"No. An EF5 has winds that exceed two hundred miles per hour and will cause incredible damage to well-built, steel-reinforced structures. I'm talking demolished off their foundations and swept away, critically damaged. Tall buildings will collapse. Cars, trucks, and even trains, can be thrown approximately a mile."

"Yikes," Chase said. "Lindy, I hope you know what you're doing."

"I think I'd rather go back to the blizzard than face an EF5," Wen said.

"Don't worry, EF5s are rare," Drina said. "And certainly can't be generated from scratch."

Forty minutes later, the blue skies began to close in. The darkening came faster than Lindy had said it would.

"Is something wrong?" Chase asked, looking up at the billowing clouds.

Chapter Seventy-Six

Dr. Skyenor called Tess. "We should have been in Sonora," he said. "We've picked up a weather anomaly a couple of hours ago."

"What's that mean?"

"It was Lindy. He manufactured a rainstorm out of a clear blue sky!"

"We didn't have the manpower close enough to cover the whole list," Tess said, pulling up feeds from the site. "At least the MSS weren't there either." She looked at the loops. "There's a plane. My people will identify it and we'll find out where he's going next." Tess had already backtracked Chase to the Church in Puerto Vallarta, and had a team headed there to find out why they'd stopped at a church while running for their lives.

"He's going to one of those sites on the list," Skyenor said. "And this time he's going to rip open the sky!"

As the equipment alarms began to beep, Chase suddenly had the feeling of being in the intensive care unit of a hospital with a patient going into cardiac arrest.

"Are you in control?" Chase yelled at Lindy.

"Everything is different in the real world, that's why a Gamma Level test isn't enough," Lindy said, peering into the equipment while placing his hand on his side.

"But the Delta test in Sonora developed much slower. Aren't you doing this one with the same parameters?"

"It can never be the exact same parameters," Drina answered. "We're at a different latitude and longitude, the stations aren't lined up in the same configuration from here. The base temperature, humidity, pressure, and other atmospheric variables are all different. Wind speed, time of day, the presence of any clouds at all—a thousand things affect it."

"But don't the programs take that into account and make the adjustments?" Chase asked, referring to the AI component sensitive to the details, since it was his specialty.

The winds whispered louder. The air felt electric. The first crack of lightning split through the ashen cumulonimbus clouds.

"I'm trying to make adjustments," Lindy said, not bothering to look up, then running behind the tent again. This time he noticed blood in his vomit.

"Is this dangerous?" Wen asked.

Drina, appearing terribly worried, looked back for Lindy, but she answered calmly, "In the long run, yes. But today I think we'll all just get a little wet and windblown."

"Weather control will benefit humanity," Lindy said, coming back, wiping his mouth and immediately tapping on the keys. "I'm going to make sure of it."

Growls of thunder erupted out of the now towering clouds, shattering the calming hum of the winds.

"Can I help?" Chase asked.

"Yeah, get on that other screen and tell me all the laser readings starting with T-hook and right through the entire sequence."

"Seventeen-point-two, fifteen-point-five, twenty-four-eight."

"K-port is at twenty-four-eight? Are you sure?"

"That's what it says."

"Too high. What's J-loft at?"

"Twenty-nine-point-three."

"Are you still in control?" Tab asked.

"Damn it!" Lindy said, ignoring Tab.

"What?" Chase asked as Wen and Drina exchanged glances of concern.

"*That's* the problem," Lindy barked. "The lasers are too concentrated."

"I thought there wasn't a problem," Wen said, eyeing the sky suspiciously.

"How big a problem?" Drina asked.

"I don't know yet. Keep those readings coming."

Lightning grew violent. Fierce winds swirled dust. A palpable energy of a storm out of control built as Lindy grew more frantic.

Chase steadily read more of the readings, and every third or fourth one caused Lindy to cuss or moan.

He went over to Lindy and put his hands on his shoulders, looking intently at him. A moment of silence between them, then fat raindrops started hitting. The tent, set up next to the rented SUV, shook in the stronger air.

"What's going on, Lindy?" Drina asked. "It's looking pretty ominous."

Tab shook his head, and muttered, "It's out of control."

Daylight seemed to be fading as darkness descended with a thick blanket of clouds. A furious display of lightning lit the sky, now appearing to be cracking apart.

"I can reverse it," Lindy announced in a not too confident tone.

A dark sedan with red and blue flashing lights on the dashboard approached from the west.

"Looks like somebody wants to know what we're up to," Wen said.

"I want to know, too," Chase said.

"Drina, tell him it's a university research project," Lindy said. "Get rid of them."

The sedan pulled into the scrub brush and stopped not more than ten feet from them. Two men, appearing to be police officers, got out and approached the group. One of them, surveying the situation, glanced over at Lindy working on the computer. Drina headed toward them to try and explain.

Suddenly, the man drew his gun and shot Lindy.

Chapter Seventy-Seven

Before the man could fire again, Wen leapt at the shooter and snapped his neck. As he fell dead in the dirt, she fired her Glock at the remaining man, who turned out to be Waxxman, and had clearly not been expecting armed resistance.

"Weist, what the hell!?" Waxxman yelled to Tab, firing several more shots from around the car. "Call off your dog!"

Chase had rushed to Lindy's aid, and the two were taking cover under the table.

"Where are you hit?" Chase asked.

"Why do you always ask me that?" Lindy said, clutching his abdomen.

"Because you're always getting shot."

Wen tried to find a clear line of sight to shoot Waxxman.

"This one's not good," Lindy said, revealing the wound.

"Hold on," Chase said.

"I can't. The storm." He coughed blood.

Waxxman fired again. Wen moved around, looking for a shot.

Chase looked up, and amidst the gunfire he saw something even more terrifying. A funnel cloud forming in the east.

"Looks like a tornado," Chase yelled, panic in his voice.

Lindy had blood smeared across his cheeks. "How big? Hand me the Antimatter Machine."

Chase reached up and pulled the machine down. "Narrow, but long." He handed it to Lindy.

Wen flattened to the ground and made herself almost invisible as she crawled toward Waxxman.

"Narrow is okay, we can deal with that." Lindy's bent-over body began to shake uncontrollably.

Chase nodded, as if he understood, but in spite of all he had learned in the past two days, and everything Lindy had demonstrated in the biosphere and at Sonora, watching the sky go from clear blue to a dangerous storm swirling above them left him in awe. How it had happened in such a short period was seemingly impossible to fathom.

"Weist, I'm here to finish the job for you! Tell her!" Waxxman yelled, staring directly at Tab.

"You know him?" Wen screamed at Tab.

"He hired me," Waxxman shouted. "Put down your weapon!"

"Tab, tell him to stop!" Drina yelled.

"Not while Lindy is still alive," Tab shouted back above the now howling wind.

"Someone better start explaining," Wen yelled, crawling to her bag.

Chase pulled out his Beretta and yanked the table down on its side to give Lindy and himself cover.

Tab had moved toward Waxxman.

"Where is she going, Wiest?" Waxxman yelled at Tab, firing toward Wen.

Wen reached her bag and retrieved a Heckler & Koch MP7 submachine gun and returned fire, cutting down Tab/Weist. By shooting his leg, he would still be alive enough to question, something she wanted to do, since it was obvious he'd set up this ambush.

"How are you doing?" Chase asked Lindy.

"Good enough for the moment." But clearly not good at all.

"Is this a supercell?" Chase asked.

"Yeah, do you like it?"

"Depends on if it's done getting worse."

"How's the funnel cloud doing?"

"Getting thicker. Can you stop it?"

"I'm not sure yet."

"How can you *not* be sure?"

"I never simulated a stop because the idea was to see if the storm would play out in a natural way. That's not the problem. In this case, a glitch caused the storm to get too big."

Wiest was on the ground holding his bleeding, splintered legs, and screaming.

"You're not leaving here alive," Wen yelled to Waxxman, "unless you give up your weapon."

"Same goes for you!" Waxxman shot at her.

Chase fired, rapidly releasing four bullets. Waxxman hadn't been expecting it, and surprisingly, two connected.

Drina, who'd been inching her way over to Chase and

Chasing Wind

Lindy, stopped as Waxxman, now with two bullet holes in his arm, started firing back at Chase.

"Drina, you'd better tell us why Tab knows this guy!" Wen yelled, blood spilling down her arm.

"I don't know!"

"Wiest, who you're calling Tab, hired me to kill Lindbergh," Waxxman repeated, furious that he'd been hit. "None of that matters, because now we're in *this*."

Drina resumed her crawl toward Chase and Lindy. "Winds are clocking at a hundred twenty-nine miles-per-hour in the funnel," she yelled. "You've got to stop it!"

Waxxman continued shooting wildly at both Chase and Wen.

Chase looked up and saw the tornado heading toward them. "Lindy, how soon will that get here?"

He checked his model on the computer screen. "If it doesn't get any bigger, we've got ten minutes, maybe more." Lindy's hand was trembling. He coughed more blood, now feeling light-headed.

"What if does get bigger?" Chase didn't know what to worry about more—the weather, Lindy, Wen, a man shooting at him . . .

"Let me work!"

Waxxman ran around the back of his car to get a better angle. Wen shot at his feet from underneath the vehicle. He went down moaning. As he tried to crawl behind the tire, she'd already jumped on the hood and unloaded the rest of her magazine into him. She dropped down, grabbed the gun from his dead hands, and ran to Tab.

"Winds are at one-sixty-two!" Drina yelled as she got closer. "That's an EF3!"

A second later, the tent blew away.

"Want to go to the hospital?" Wen asked Tab.

"Yes, pleeeease," he begged, his voice in desperate agony as his legs bled uncontrollably.

"Then tell me why you hired that guy to kill Lindy. Tell me everything, or I will put a bullet in your head right now."

He said something, but the freight train roar of the wind made it impossible to hear.

Drina, seeing that Waxxman was dead, ran over to Lindy. "Let me help," she shouted. "We have to turn off the storm!" She looked at the monitor and screamed, "We're at EF4! Winds are two-hundred-nineteen miles-per-hour!"

"How much time do we have?" Chase yelled.

"Two minutes," Lindy said, but nobody heard him.

Chapter Seventy-Eight

Wen leaned close to Tab as he confessed, her face filling with horror while she strained to hear his words. Suddenly, Wen stood and dashed toward Chase, Lindy, and Drina.

"Why, Drina?" Wen screamed, pointing her submachine gun at the other woman. "Why did you send those men to kill Lindy?"

"We don't have time for this now!" Drina yelled. "We're approaching an EF5."

"I don't care," Wen shouted. "Talk!"

"We are about to die, and so are a lot of other people if we don't stop this storm now!"

"Lindy, stop this damned storm!" Wen shouted louder.

"I think he's gone," Chase said, thinking he, too, was yelling.

"What?" Wen had not heard him.

Drina looked at Lindy and began to sob.

"He's dead," Chase said. Only the wind could hear him.

"I couldn't let him give Aeolus to all those countries," Drina said hysterically. "What if you were alive in the early

1940s, and you could've stopped the invention of nuclear weapons by sacrificing one person? You would save millions, maybe billions, the planet, all of humanity. Wouldn't you do it?"

Chase stared at her as if she were some kind of a monster. "Who made *you* God?"

"Look at that storm!" Drina screamed. "This is the first test, and it's already out of control. Doesn't that show you the kind of power Lindy wanted to unleash on the world? Can't you imagine what people would do with this? The military, terrorists—once it's out, the genie never goes back in the bottle. Earth's ecosystem will be a disaster after a few years of this kind of manipulation."

"Didn't you love him?" Wen shouted, wind whipping her hair.

"Of course I loved him! That's why I had to do this. It was so hard," she yelled, sobbing between words.

Drina's van blew over.

"Help me!" Tab/Weist yelled.

"The storm!" Chase shouted or whispered, no one could tell, pointing as the massive funnel cloud that was barreling right toward them.

"See?" Drina screamed. "You can't screw around with mother nature."

"Can you stop it?" Chase begged at the top of his lungs.

"No one can stop it! Run!" Drina took off toward the last remaining rays of sunlight, as the sky transformed into a kaleidoscope—golden glow, ebony black, cyan blue, and a hundred shades of gray, punctuated with cracking, searing lightning and winds reshaping the patterns every moment.

Wen scooped up the Antimatter Machine. "Chase, we have to go!" She grabbed his hand

He looked at Lindy one last time, then back to the storm. "This way!"

The sky moved and contorted like a monster about to attack.

"Hey!" Tab howled. "Heeey!"

A metal windmill flew past them as they ran toward the highway. "Maybe there's a ditch by the road we can get in."

Seconds later, the black sedan soared through the air. Chase looked back and saw that Drina's van was also airborne. Drina had known better than to get in a vehicle. She was already a hundred yards ahead of them, but veering in the opposite direction.

"We're going to get sucked up in that thing!" Chase yelled, feeling the vortex pulling at him.

"Keep running! We are *not* going to die!"

Debris pelted them. Chase felt as if they were running through a food processor. The funnel cloud was now over the test site. Chase had a fleeting thought that there was a kind of poetic irony to the fact that Lindy had been taken into the storm, his body a part of his creation, the sky his funeral.

The ground under them turned hard. Chase looked down and saw the pavement of the highway. They crossed the double yellow line and into the adjacent field, which sloped down off the narrow gravel shoulder.

Just as they dove into the small ravine, the tornado ripped up the road. They huddled tight against the ground. Unable to resist the urge to watch the hellish creation pass as it consumed everything in its path, they saw the final irony as the funnel cloud steam-rolled over Drina, swallowing her like a giant snake taking a mouse.

"Tough way to go," Chase said, as the storm moved away.

"It was good enough for Lindy," Wen said.

"Lindy was already dead. Drina got eaten alive."

Wen nodded. Tears rolled down her cheeks. "He was so kind and caring, and wanting to do only good . . . It's hard to think that he could actually exist in today's world, or any world. I will never forget him."

"He was too good," Chase said, nodding. "Can you believe he made that thing?" He pointed to the storm, still raging across the plain. "It's good his secrets died with him. Drina was right about one thing, men can't be trusted with that kind of power."

"His secrets didn't die," Wen said.

"What do you mean?"

"His back-up data drive is still in the Antimatter Machine."

"So what do we do?" Chase asked.

"What do you think?"

"You saw what happened. Delta, Gamma, Epsilon, each one kept getting increasingly more horrific. Lindy told me that Zeta level is a whole new world where weather modification is used, potentially, every day."

"We have the power to stop that, at least for now. Do you think the world is ready for Aeolus?"

"No," Chase said, staring into the sky as if looking for the next storm, or trying to see Lindy somewhere in the heavens. "We tell Tess it died with Lindy."

"Will she believe you?"

"Depends on where, and how well, we hide it."

"Another reason for people to be chasing us."

Epilogue

Minister Li stood in front of his wall of monitors. The fallout from the failure would be significant. Mexico had been protesting loudly and threatened to go to the United Nations, but they would go away with the right financial assistance—China had plenty of money to make problems disappear. The bigger issue was that with Curtis Lindbergh dead and his data lost, China was once again relying on Aznotech to develop the technology to control the weather. Although impatient with Hongbin, Li would allow him another year to succeed, but no more.

Three days later, after laying low and recovering in an off-grid cabin in Silver City, New Mexico, Chase and Wen boarded a plane to parts unknown. Once at cruising altitude, Chase placed a final untraceable and encrypted call to Tess via the Astronaut.

"Nice to finally hear your voice. Thought you might have perished along with poor old Lindy," Tess said. "Where are you?"

"Nowhere."

She laughed irritably. "You go there a lot."

"It's lovely this time of year. I'll send you a post card some time."

"That was some storm," she said. "More than eighty injured and five dead. The damage estimates exceed one hundred million dollars. Fortunately your friend chose a remote area of Texas, or the toll would have been much higher."

"Lindy lost control of it. The technology was too dangerous."

"We recovered his body . . . eight miles from the test site," she said. "But no data."

"It was destroyed in the storm. Maybe if you can find the equipment and computers, you can somehow retrieve the data."

"We're looking," she said in an annoyed tone, "but debris is scattered over more than one hundred miles."

"Good luck. Any sign of Drina's body?"

"Not yet, but we found a mangled mess, or most of a former person, in some trees a couple of miles away. Identified as Jeff Wiest." Tess was silent for a moment, looking at a screen in Mission Control. "After Yelapa, you stopped at a church in Puerto Vallarta," she said. "Why?

"Lindy wanted to pray," Chase said.

"Oh, come on."

"A man of faith."

"Faith in physics, but not in God."

"Same thing to him."

"I don't believe you."

"Then why were we there?"

"I don't know, but I'll find out."

"Well, remember to say a little prayer . . . to the weather gods."

Next in the Chase Malone Thriller series

vinci-books.com/chasing-dirt

A cure that could save the world. A race that could end it.

When billionaire fugitive Chase Malone and disavowed spy Wen Zhou stumble upon a miraculous cure that could wipe out deadly diseases, end hunger, and eradicate poverty, they uncover humanity's greatest secret—and its most dangerous threat.

Turn the page for a free preview…

Chasing Dirt: Chapter One

September in Paris. Sunlight filtered into the apartment through high, slender windows. It was one of those long, narrow, century-old Paris flats that would've been called cramped and dingy anywhere else, but in the City of Light, even the ordinary was often romanticized.

Chase Malone, once a celebrated tech billionaire, stood in the stale air of the closed space, wishing he were someplace else. As was his habit, he'd taken a mental inventory of objects that could be used as weapons and, more important, all the avenues of egress available. This place had few exits.

He had recently become part of an underground movement known as "The Cause," or to those who understood its mission more intimately, "WOLF."

In a back room off the kitchen, Chase watched as a man he'd just recently met counted cash—a stack of Euros totaling more than one hundred thousand dollars. The money Chase had delivered would be used to fund controversial operations of the group, including protecting and supporting whistleblowers and bribing officials for critical information.

"Mind if I open the window?" Chase asked. "A bit stuffy in here."

The man nodded without slowing his counting.

He had reluctantly joined WOLF at the urging of his girlfriend, Wen Sung, a former spy for MSS—the Chinese intelligence service. Chase wished she could have come with him, but she was elsewhere in the city, assisting in a WOLF operation. They were to meet in Lac Inférieur, Bois de Boulogne park, very soon.

It had taken him longer to find the apartment than he'd expected, so he was anxious to go. *I might be late to Wen,* he thought, checking the time on an antique wall clock. *However, there should still be plenty of time to make our train to Amsterdam.*

A violent crash shattered his thoughts. Chase, who had been on the run for nearly a year, didn't wait to find out who had kicked in the front door before he was squeezing out the window and dropping onto an ancient, rusted fire escape.

Can I make it down two stories before whoever busted in gets to this window? he wondered, looking for anywhere else to hide. Turns out the answer was no. Before he was halfway down, bullets ricocheted off the metal steps.

Without looking up, Chase leapt off the rickety platform, landing on the roof of a city bus that was cruising up the busy street. As his pursuers continued down the fire escape, one of their team, who'd been covering the sidewalk in front of the building, followed him on foot. Chase, now lying flat on top of the moving bus, watched as the man jumped onto the hood of a parked Mercedes, ran up the windshield to its roof, and then onto the top of a delivery van that was driving near the back left side of the bus.

Jumping from the van to the bus, the man pulled out a pistol, but before he could fire, Chase lunged at him. The two of them wrestled and struggled as the bus picked up speed. Chase jammed his elbow into the man's face—a trick he learned from Wen, an expert black belt fighter, that always produced a profusely bloody nose. However, the man continued fighting, seemingly oblivious to the injury. After dealing several hard blows to Chase's rib cage, he freed himself, and was able to aim his weapon again. Chase used the momentum of the bus turning to slide back toward the attacker and hooked his foot between the man's legs, causing him to fall backward. Blaring horns added another distortion to the minutes and actions that Chase felt couldn't be real.

I've got to get the gun, he thought, grimacing at a weapon he never liked and rarely carried, while throwing himself across the man's body before he could recover, thrusting his knee into the man's solar plexus and grabbing for the gun with both hands. The bus bounced over a pothole, allowing the man to pistol whip Chase's forehead.

Chase kicked his leg desperately, and miraculously his foot connected into the man's shoulder. The momentum left the two separated. An instant later, both were on their feet. The bus, now on a busy four lane boulevard, momentarily slowed as a changing traffic signal allowed more vehicles to enter the flow. The man now had an easy shot.

Like a scene in an action movie he would not want to see, the unpretentious billionaire dove onto another bus driving in the opposite direction. Barely getting a grasp, he dug for his beloved multitool, flipped the pliers open, and pinched its teeth onto the half-inch ridge of metal running along the edge of the bus' top. Before the man could react and adjust his aim, Chase was too far away.

Panting and shaking, Chase watched as the frustrated man jumped down off his bus. *He'll never catch me*, he thought, pocketing his multitool and turning to see if there was anything ahead that would stop his bus. Instantaneously, he threw himself flat against the roof a split second before it entered an overpass that would have knocked him off the bus into traffic.

Six minutes later, no longer hearing a cacophony of urgent horns, Chase jumped off the roof at a bus stop and walked the final three blocks to the park. Their routine had always been to meet at parks, or other easily accessible public places, before heading to their true destination. Chase sat on a tree-shaded bench, pretending to read a small book, while watching for Wen—or anyone else who might have followed.

They had talked about the possibility of having a small boat ride if neither of them were delayed. A lake in a Chinese park had been their special place when they'd first met and promised themselves to each other forever. They had been to Bois de Boulogne park separately, and were excited about sharing the experience. Wen had spoken enthusiastically about the Musee Marmottan Monet. She'd loved the impressionist's paintings since first seeing them as a child in her Chinese art classes. Chase had hoped that after the boat ride through the Parisian forest, they could sneak a visit to Le Chalet des Iles restaurant on the island in the middle of the lake, where he'd secretly made reservations as a surprise for Wen.

However, that was all before the man on the bus. Now, they would have to do what they always did—run.

"You got here early," Wen said, finding him twenty

minutes later. "Any trouble?" She eyed his bleeding forehead.

"We had visitors at the drop," Chase said.

"They found us again." She scanned the area. "We better go."

He nodded, frustrated that, more often than not, they didn't always know who was after them.

Chasing Dirt: Chapter Two

Chase and Wen exited Lac Inférieur, Bois de Boulogne park, just as a bus was approaching. "This one's going to the train station," Wen said. "We should take it."

"I've had enough buses for one day," Chase said. "Let's get a cab instead."

"So the meet up was compromised, and the funds did not make it," Wen asked rhetorically, once they were in the taxi. "How could they have known?"

Chase shook his head. He'd been asking himself the same question since getting off the bus.

"I'll have to call Margot."

Chase knew she meant as soon as the short ride was over. Margot Ariesen was the leader and founding member of The Cause. A decade earlier, her husband had been jailed after disclosing corruption among Europe's largest defense contractors and the French and British governments. There were no whistle blower laws to protect him, and three months into his prison sentence, he'd been killed in a suspicious accident. In their grief and outrage, a group of his friends began what later grew into WOLF. Margot was a fierce advocate of people's rights.

"You tore your coat," Wen said.

"I'll get a new one, and I'm not the one who tore it. At least it wasn't my fault."

Wen smiled. "But I gave you that one." Chase had a habit of getting his clothes torn, cut, blood stained, and even punctured by the occasional bullet.

He smiled, squeezing her hand. "Get me another one?"

Chase paid the driver as they pulled into the taxi rank at Gare du Nord. The massive station, the busiest in Europe, had first opened in 1846.

"Lots of police," Wen said, automatically surveying the huge space as they entered the main concourse. "The French are always concerned about terrorists."

"For good reason. They get hit often," Chase said, checking the time on his phone. "Are you going to call Margot now?"

"I was going to wait until we're on the train," Wen said. "We're taking Thayls, high-speed to Amsterdam, platform seven."

The crowds swirled in many patterns. Wen pulled out her phone to call the leader of WOLF.

"I can't wait to hear her theory on how they found the safe house," Chase said. He'd always been apprehensive about The Cause, believing they were too radical, too revolutionary—too dangerous. However, Wen was committed to the group, who had helped her escape China and the MSS.

"The breach may have nothing to do with WOLF,"

Wen said. "Whoever it was could have been after us. *We* may have compromised The Cause."

Just as Margot answered the call, Wen disconnected. "Trouble two o'clock," Wen said to Chase as she slid the phone into her pocket. "Not a good place for a gun battle."

"Split up?" Chase asked, knowing the protocol.

"Good luck. See you at platform seven." Wen casually walked toward the lavatories.

Chase reached into his messenger bag, as if looking for tickets, but instead brought out a gun, careful to keep it concealed in the sleeve of his coat.

In positioning the gun, Chase had let his guard down only for an instant, but it had been enough. An attractive woman bumped into him at the same moment a man grabbed his gun hand and relieved him of the weapon. Before Chase could protest, the three of them, with him sandwiched in between, headed for an exit. Each of his "new friends" had a gun stuck in his side. He scanned the area for Wen, hoping she had not suffered the same fate.

I can't let them take me out of this building, Chase thought. He glanced at them, to be sure he had not seen them before, and to look for weaknesses.

"Your cooperation is appreciated, Mr. Malone," the man said in a French accent. "No harm will come, I assure you."

"Of course not," Chase replied. "Why don't you let me buy you lunch at The Etoile du Nord? Chef Thierry Marx is wonderful. It's inside the station, near platform nineteen."

"It's only open in the evenings," the woman responded with laughter, as if he'd made a joke. "Perhaps another time."

"The restaurant *upstairs* is not open now. However, the brasserie downstairs is actually open all day. My treat."

"Amusing, Mr. Malone," the man said. "But we'll pick up something on the way."

"The way?" Chase asked. "Where are we going?"

"No more talking," the woman said sternly, jabbing her gun harder into his side.

A couple of minutes later, they exited the main terminal. Chase knew it was now or never.

Chasing Dirt: Chapter Three

About thirty yards ahead, Chase spotted two men waiting next to a large black SUV. They were obviously his destination. He looked around, desperately wanting an idea, a plan, some way out, that didn't include two bullets in his gut. The area was busy. He considered screaming for help, but decided that was likely to get some innocent bystanders shot as well as himself killed.

They were about twelve yards from the SUV. Chase, knowing he was going to die anyway if they got him inside the vehicle, decided this was the moment. He would fake tripping, which would get him to the ground, and—assuming they didn't shoot him in the process—as they were getting him back to his feet, he could use the leverage to bring them down, where he would at least have a chance to get one of their guns.

Just then, Chase's phone rang with an obscure ringtone, *Persecution of the Masses* by Shiro Sagisu, from the *Shin Godzilla* soundtrack, that he recognized as a signal from

Wen. It meant she could see him, she was coming, be ready to act.

"What's that?" the man asked, alarmed.

"It's my phone. Mind if I get it?"

"Don't even think about it."

"I'm pretty sure it's my parole officer. If I don't answer, I could get in real trouble."

"Forget it, funnyman."

The phone stopped ringing.

"It's okay, he'll probably send the FBI looking for me. My ankle bracelet will tell them exactly where we are. Don't worry about it. I'll give him a call later."

The man looked down at Chase's feet, as if looking for the electronic ankle bracelet, but kept moving.

Chase abandoned his tripping plan, instead putting himself in a Zen zone, trying to anticipate what his partner would do, listening to every sound as if they were clues.

They were about ten feet from the SUV when Chase heard approaching vehicles, even before he saw the flashing lights. A second later, his entourage noticed. People all around them were stopping, curious, not wanting to miss what might be happening.

"See?" Chase said. "They really get crazy when I violate parole."

"Shut up!" the woman snapped as the man pushed them all faster toward the SUV. The men waiting at the vehicle had also noticed and jumped in the front seat, leaving the back door open, obviously planning a quick getaway.

Multiple police vehicles appeared. Behind them, Chase saw two fire trucks. Five feet from the SUV, he began to wonder if Wen was going to make it in time. The man gave Chase a shove toward the vehicle.

Wen flew in from the other side of a burgundy van parked behind the SUV. In one motion she nearly picked up the woman, sending her sailing into the open back door, and kneecapped the man. Chase kicked his former captor in the face as the man went down.

Wen pulled Chase away. "Come on!"

They slipped past a shuttle bus and crouched behind a row of parked commuter cars. Police surrounded the SUV, guns drawn, screaming at the occupants in French to surrender their weapons and come out with their hands on their heads.

"What's going on?" Chase asked, wanting to hug her, but knowing it would have to wait.

"I called in a bomb threat as soon as we split up."

"You didn't even know they were going to grab me."

"I knew we'd need a diversion, one way or another. We were running into a hornets nest."

"How'd you know about the car?" he asked as they ran through the vehicles toward the terminal, careful to keep below the roof lines.

"As soon as I saw them take you out of the building, I looked for their getaway car. It was easy to spot. I called the police again and told them the bomb was in the black SUV. Even gave them the plate number."

Chase was used to being impressed by Wen, but this was a story he looked forward to telling his mother, brother Boone, and very close friends. Most of their stories could never be shared. "Where to now?"

"Platform seven," Wen said. "We can still make the train to Amsterdam."

"What if there are more?"

"There are always more," Wen said, kissing him quickly

on the lips. "However, today, all the ones that were here at Gare du Nord are in police custody."

Wen dumped her gun before they reached the baggage X-ray, metal detector, and passport check at the entrance to the platform.

"I've already gotten rid of mine," Chase said. "Earlier, a nice couple assisted me with the process."

"Do you miss them? Were you flirting with the woman?"

"We were going to have lunch at The Etoile du Nord."

"Ah, chef Thierry Marx," Wen said. "They declined?"

"Apparently they don't know his work, and in any case, they were late for an appointment with Préfecture de police de Paris," Chase said in his best French accent, which wasn't very good. Both knew that humor was their reality check.

Chase and Wen found the first class section and sat facing each other in the single seats. "Let's see if we can make it to Amsterdam without you getting into any more trouble," Wen said, watching a man carefully as he passed.

Chase looked at her, wondering if the passenger was another problem.

She shook her head. He leaned closer to her and held her hands.

For the remaining three hours before reaching Amsterdam, they were content and grateful to speak with only their eyes . . . creating a time filled with silent laughter and immeasurable love. And yet, in between those moments, Wen ran through every conceivable scenario for who could be on the train, or waiting at the final stop.

When and from where will the next attack come?

Grab your copy…
vinci-books.com/chasing-dirt

About the Author

USA TODAY Bestselling Author Brandt Legg uses his unusual real life experiences to create page-turning novels. He's traveled with CIA agents, dined with senators and congressmen, mingled with astronauts, chatted with governors and presidential candidates, had a private conversation with a Secretary of Defense he still doesn't like to talk about, hung out with Oscar and Grammy winners, had drinks at the State Department, been pursued by tabloid reporters, and spent a birthday at the White House by invitation from the President of the United States.

At age eight, Legg's father died suddenly, plunging his family into poverty. Two years later, while suffering from crippling migraines, he started in business, and turned a hobby into a multi-million-dollar empire. National media dubbed him the "Teen Tycoon," and by the mid-eighties, Legg was one of the top young entrepreneurs in America, appearing as high as number twenty-four on the list (when Steve Jobs was #1, Bill Gates #4, and Michael Dell #6). Legg still jokes that he should have gone into computers.

By his twenties, after years of buying and selling businesses, leveraging, and risk-taking, the high-flying Legg became ensnarled in the financial whirlwind of the junk bond eighties. The stock market crashed and a firestorm of trouble came down. The Teen Tycoon racked up more than a million dollars in legal fees, was betrayed by those closest to him, lost his entire fortune, and ended up serving time for financial improprieties.

After a year, Legg emerged from federal prison, chastened and wiser, and began anew. More than twenty-five years later, he's now using all that hard-earned firsthand knowledge of conspiracies, corruption and high finance to weave his tales. Legg's books pulse with authenticity.

His series have excited nearly a million readers around the world. Although he refused an offer to make a television movie about his life as a teenage millionaire, his autobiography is in the works. There has also been interest from Hollywood to turn his thrillers into films. With any luck, one day you'll see your favorite characters on screen.

He lives in the Pacific Northwest, with his wife and son, writing full time, in several genres, containing the common themes of adventure, conspiracy, and thrillers. Of all his pursuits, being an author and crafting plots for novels is his favorite.

Acknowledgments

Chasing Wind was so much fun to write. A big reason for that is certainly because I started writing it in Yelapa, Mexico, which is an important location in the book. Speaking of that special place, thank you Marc, Germaine, and Bez for discovering and exploring Yelapa with us, and to Marc for inspiring a character. Great friendships are the heart of these stories, and Teakki and Bez truly have a magical friendship, as do their parents. Let's go scout more locations—meet you there!

To my wife, Ro, where were we driving to when much of this plot unfolded? The roads sometimes blur, but as long as we're together, it doesn't matter. Thank you for writing our story with me every day.

There's always so much to thank my mother, Barbara Blair, for. She reads the manuscripts more times than anyone. If she wasn't a professional editor at the start, she sure is now.

Thanks again to Jack Llartin, my copy editor, for finding all those things the rest of us miss.

And, finally, to Teakki, who patiently waited to do math until I finished writing each day. That's actually not true, I just wanted to see if he actually reads these acknowledgements. He doesn't love math as much as I did (I'm not sure he even *likes* it), but at least there's history . . . and Star Wars.

Most important, thank you, and every reader who has

read one of my books. You make it possible for me to support my family with my writing. That's a big deal, and I can't express enough gratitude for being able to do what I love. I know there are endless choices for how you can spend your time and money—thanks for choosing me. I look forward to going on many, many more adventures with you.